BED BUGS

"A crackerjack read. . . . Witty and satisfying and smart. . . . McCafferty's plot is clearly clever, but her writing is what clicks with the reader. From her first sentence the pace picks up, charged like a battery in a classic coupe."

—*Lexington* (KY) *Herald-Leader*

"Her down-home delivery will make Southerners smile."

—*The Southern Pines* (NC) *Pilot*

"A solid example of soft-boiled P.I. writing. . . . Characterization and setting are good. . . . A novel of small-town manners that succeeds because of its use of humor."

—*Mystery News*

THIN SKINS

"A wonderful series."

—*Mystery Lovers Bookshop News*

"A hilariously good read. . . . McCafferty finds mirth in murder as she recounts the adventures of a small-town private eye."

—*Louisville* magazine

"A good read as are all of McCafferty's mysteries."
—*The Southern Pines* (NC) *Pilot*

Books by Taylor McCafferty

Pet Peeves
Ruffled Feathers
Bed Bugs
Thin Skins
Hanky Panky

Published by POCKET BOOKS

A HASKELL BLEVINS MYSTERY

HANKY PANKY

Taylor McCafferty

POCKET BOOKS
New York   London   Toronto   Sydney   Tokyo   Singapore

This book is a work of fiction. Names, characters, places and incidents are products of the author's imagination or are used fictitiously. Any resemblance to actual events or locales or persons, living or dead, is entirely coincidental.

An *Original* Publication of POCKET BOOKS

POCKET BOOKS, a division of Simon & Schuster Inc.
1230 Avenue of the Americas, New York, NY 10020

ISBN: 0-671-51049-5

First Pocket Books printing November 1995

10 9 8 7 6 5 4 3 2 1

POCKET and colophon are registered trademarks of Simon & Schuster Inc.

Cover art by John Zielinski

Printed in the U.S.A.

To my sister-in-law,
Judy Taylor

ACKNOWLEDGMENTS

I'd like to thank my agent, Richard Parks, for his help. And, as always, I'd like to thank my twin sister, Beverly Taylor Herald, for serving as my first reader.

HANKY
PANKY

CHAPTER 1

Money talks. I'd like to believe it isn't so, but I know it's true. It's even more true in a town the size of Pigeon Fork, Kentucky. Because in a place like this, with a population of only 1,511 people, it takes no time at all to spot the ones with more than a few nickels to rub together.

Around these parts, money doesn't just talk, it *yells*.

If I needed any proof of that, I got it on that cold Monday afternoon in November when the new silver Corvette pulled up in front of my brother Elmo's drugstore. At the time I, of course, was doing what I always seem to be doing these days.

I was mopping Elmo's floor.

Elmo, generous soul that he is, had made me a proposition some eighteen months before, when I'd first started up my private detective business here in town. Elmo had told me—with a straight face, mind you—that, being as how I was his baby brother and all, he was going to give me office space over his drugstore rent free. All Elmo asked in return was that I help out downstairs by running the soda fountain and mopping the floor. Not all the time, just during my slow times. As I recall, Elmo had said those particular words more than once. *Just during my slow times.*

Back then I hadn't even minded Elmo calling me his baby brother, even though I was thirty-four, for God's sake. I'd actually thought that Elmo was making me a downright kind offer. One, in fact, that I couldn't accept fast enough.

My only excuse is that I'd just spent the previous eight years working homicide up in Louisville. I reckon, having lived for so long someplace else, I'd plumb forgot just how many slow times a person could have in Pigeon Fork.

Fact is, in the year and a half I've been back—other than a very few notable exceptions—slow is the only sort of times I've had. This past April I was tempted to scratch out "Private Detective" on my 1040 and put down "Professional Mopper" instead.

I also don't mind telling you, that during these last eighteen months I've found myself wondering more than once exactly what kind of deal Elmo would offer a total stranger. The thought is a tad scary.

Still, true to my word, that November afternoon I was standing in the men's toiletries aisle in Elmo's Drugs, mopping to beat the band, when money started yelling its head off out front. It was money in the form of—as I mentioned before—a brand-new, shiny silver Corvette.

Outside the drugstore, I could see five different people on the street. Two old geezers sitting on a bench in front of the Crayton County Courthouse across the street, watching folks go by. A young woman, holding the hand of a little boy who looked to be about six, making a beeline for the Crayton County Federal Bank located next door to the courthouse. And Leroy Putnam who owns the Pigeon Fork Dry Goods Store right next door to Elmo's. Leroy was just coming out of the bank, and he was tucking folding money into his wallet.

All these folks were a tad occupied, but every single one of them stopped smack dab in the middle of what they were doing, and outright gawked at the Corvette.

Even the six-year-old kid.

Inside Elmo's Drugs, there were four people besides me—Elmo and Melba Hawley, the secretary Elmo and I share, and two customers. One customer I recognized—Sister Tallman, the wife of Brother Tallman, the minister over at the Church of the Holy Scriptures about five miles outside of town. The other customer, a tall, lanky guy in baggy overalls, looked faintly familiar, but I couldn't quite place him.

Would you believe, when that Corvette pulled up, every single one of these folks immediately rushed toward the front of the store? Where they all stood, jammed together in front of the two windows, staring holes through the Corvette.

Somebody—it might've been Melba—gave a low whistle.

I wish I could say that I myself did not join in the gawking frenzy, but I'd be lying if I said it. I would, however, like to point out that I was *already* at the front of the store. I only had to take a couple steps forward in order to get right up to the window and assure myself of a good view. I certainly didn't have to walk any distance.

Unlike Melba and Elmo, who had both come running all the way from the back, where the drugstore's office is located. Melba is not exactly a lightweight, either. At close to 250 pounds, Melba actually made shelves rattle as she thundered by, one aisle over. For a moment there, I was sure a few men's toiletries were going to bite the dust.

When Elmo and Melba reached the front, I couldn't help gawking a tad at the two of *them*. How in the world could they spot a Corvette from all the way in the rear of the store?

Of course, sometimes I suspect that Melba can smell money.

Her nose was all but quivering as she stared out the drugstore window.

"Well, now, would you look at that?" Melba said, patting at her brown beehive excitedly. "That one cost a pretty penny. Oh yeah, it sure as damtootin' did!"

Melba's comment was seconded, in a manner of speaking, by the lanky guy in the overalls standing on her left. "Ooooo-eeeee!" Lanky said. Once Lanky said this, I had a pretty good idea why he'd looked familiar to me before. Matter of fact, I was almost positive this was the guy who had won the hog-calling contest at the Crayton County Fair last year. Now I could certainly understand why. The man had talent.

"Lord have mercy, look at that pretty thing!" Elmo said.

As he was saying this, the door on the driver's side of the Corvette was opening, and a shapely leg was coming into view. I believe, however, Elmo was referring to the Corvette.

Although I wouldn't swear to it.

The shapely leg turned out to belong to an equally shapely blond. Ordinarily, in the kind of weather Kentucky serves up in November, females around these parts are wearing so many layers, you can't tell whether or not one of them is shapely or not. In this case, though, when the blond got out of the Corvette, she wasn't even wearing a coat. That Corvette must've had one helluva heater, because the blond was just wearing a black, scoop-necked top, skintight leopard-print pants, and black spike heels.

Oh yeah, I'd say she was plenty shapely, all right.

Elmo was two people away from me, and I could hear his hoarse intake of breath. He sounded like somebody was standing on his air hose.

As we all watched, the blond bent over and pulled a long golden-brown winter coat out of the back of the Corvette. I don't know much about women's coats, but this one sure didn't look like something you could get off the rack at Kmart.

Apparently, Melba agreed. She was now sounding like somebody was standing on her air hose, too. "Why, I think that there coat is genuine cashmere, oh yeah, I really do. Lordy, *that* cost a pretty penny, too!"

"Oooooo-eeeee!" Lanky said. Which, I believe, was Lanky's way of saying, "I think you're right."

Standing to the right of Melba was Sister Tallman. "A sinful waste of money," Sister Tallman pronounced. She was a tiny woman in her late forties whose most noticeable feature seemed to be exceedingly thin lips. Her lips got even thinner when she added, "Sinful! That's what it is. Sinful!"

I couldn't help recalling that the Church of the Holy Scriptures had just replaced all its plain windows with stained glass ones, at the cost of thousands of dollars apiece. I decided, however, that this was probably not the best time to discuss personal interpretations of the phrase *sinful waste of money*.

The blond outside had finished putting on her cashmere coat, and had reached back into her car to pull out a shoulder purse. Now she was stooping over again to get something else out of the Corvette. This time when she straightened up, it was hard to tell for a second what it was she'd picked up. Whatever it was seemed to practically disappear against the golden surface of her coat.

Then the thing moved, and I realized it was a dog. With golden fur the exact shade of the coat it was being held against, the animal looked to be a cross between a toy poodle, a Pekingese, and a dust mop.

I myself have never quite understood the sense in having a dog like this. Too small to be a decent guard dog, too nervous to be a decent companion, dogs like this have always seemed to me to be a shameless waste of good dog food. Apparently, however, there's a slew of folks who think differently.

Take this blond, for example. She was petting her little mop poodle, actually giving it little kisses, as she turned toward our building. That was when, for the first time, we all got a good look at her face.

While the Poodle Lady continued to stand out there on the sidewalk, loving on her dog and looking up and down the street—as if she wasn't exactly sure what her next move should be—Melba and Elmo and all the rest of us in the drugstore were leaning forward, trying to get a better look.

"Do you know who she is?"

"Does she look familiar to anybody?"

"Anybody ever seen her before?"

Everybody was talking at once, and everybody was

pretty much asking the same thing. I reckon we all sounded the way the rest of the folks must've sounded at the ball once Cinderella showed up.

Unlike Cinderella, however, the blond holding the mop poodle was not particularly pretty. Her eyes were a size too small, her nose was a size too big, and her chin was a tad too much like Jay Leno's. Nobody was going to run screaming at the sight of her or anything, but to my way of thinking, she wasn't even a Pigeon Fork eight.

What I mean to say—and I realize there are those who'd call me a male chauvinist pig for putting into words what, believe me, is common knowledge around Pigeon Fork—is that around these parts, we menfolk have gotten used to grading on the curve. Here a lot of the women are still wearing their hair in beehives, and some have arms quite a bit larger than country hams. So what might be a seven or an eight anywhere else in these United States would rate a solid ten here in Pigeon Fork.

Bearing all this in mind, Poodle Lady here was at best a Pigeon Fork seven. That's why I was so surprised to hear what everybody else in the drugstore was saying. To hear them talk, you'd have thought Poodle Lady was Julia Roberts herself.

"Ain't that the way? Not only does she have a great car and a great coat, she's gorgeous, too." This was from Melba, who sounded more than a little disgruntled.

"Oooooo-eeeeee!" Lanky once again agreed at the top of his lungs.

"Yep." This last was from Elmo. Coming from him, this single word amounted to outright drooling. Mainly because ever since the day he said "I do," Elmo has been convinced that his wife, Glenda, has supernatural

powers. He's absolutely sure that if he ever says anything the slightest bit enthusiastic about another woman,
Glenda would immediately know. And begin to exact
a horrible retribution.

"Beauty is just skin-deep," Sister Tallman intoned.

I actually took another look at Poodle Lady, just in
case the others were seeing something I'd missed. But,
no, the too-big nose, the too-tiny eyes, and the too-
Leno chin were still there. The woman did have herself a nice enough figure, and real pretty blond, shoulder-
length hair. I'd give her that. However, once you got
to her face—let's be honest here—the show was over.

And yet everybody around me was acting as if Poodle Lady was a sight for sore eyes. This is what I mean
by money talking. In this instance, it was saying, loud
and clear, *I'm stunning.*

What's more, everybody standing near me in Elmo's
Drugs seemed to be listening.

Glancing in both directions up and down the street,
then turning to look up again at this very building,
Poodle Lady clutched her mop dog a little closer, ad-
justed her cashmere coat a tad, and then, of all things,
headed directly for the stairs leading up to *my* very
own office.

"Oooooo-eeeeeee!" This time, would you believe, it
was not Lanky who made this sound. It was Melba.

"Haskell?" Melba stepped back from the window
to get an unobstructed view of my face. "Haskell, for
God's sake, get a move on! It looks like you might've
landed a live one this time!"

I believe I've mentioned how many people were
standing right there all around us. Melba, Lord love
her, said this loud enough to echo off mountains in
the distance.

I, of course, was torn. While a part of me wanted to run after Poodle Lady just as fast as my legs could carry me, another part didn't particularly want to give Melba—and everybody else standing there—the satisfaction of knowing just how all-fired eager I was to get myself an honest-to-God client. I took a deep breath. "Melba," I said, "we don't refer to clients as 'live ones.' "

Melba didn't even blink. Giving her beehive another quick patting down, she said, "Look, Mr. Uppity Britches, I don't care what you call her, you better get a move on, or she's going to get away!"

Melba made it sound as if clients were something I had to trap.

On the other hand, she had a point. Deciding to hire yourself a private detective is often an impulsive kind of thing, and if I didn't show up real soon after Poodle Lady got to my office, the impulse just might pass.

Oddly enough, I immediately decided that I'd waited long enough not to look desperate. Indicating my mop bucket with a nod of my head, I asked Melba, "Would you mind putting that away?"

Melba's response was predictable, being as how the woman spends the greater part of her day looking out the window—and she considers *that* to be real hard work. "Well, of *course,* I mind putting that away," Melba said, glaring at me. "But if *you* take the time to do it, you'll probably lose her, so I reckon *I* don't have no choice, even though I . . ."

I'm not real sure what Melba said after this. To tell you the truth, I'd stopped listening and had gone to the back to get my coat, which was hanging on a rack in the drugstore office. Once I had my coat on, I retraced my steps, heading back toward the front of the drugstore, as slowly as I could manage—considering that what I really wanted to do was run.

By the time I cleared the front door, I felt like I'd pretty much salvaged my dignity—not to mention, the reputation of my detective agency. Until Melba shouted after me, "I hope she's a *live* one, Haskell, because business sure has been *dead* for far, far too long!"

I tried not to break stride, but I'm afraid I froze for a split second. Thank you so much, Melba, for that unsolicited testimonial. Why don't you just put a notice in the *Pigeon Fork Gazette* and tell everybody in town just how poorly I'm doing? Maybe you could get Sister Tallman and the Church of the Holy Scriptures to collect canned goods on my behalf.

Knowing that folks inside the drugstore and across the street were still watching, I tried to climb my stairs real nonchalant-like. I couldn't keep it up, though. I could see Poodle Lady up there on the landing ahead of me, tapping her foot kind of impatiently as she peered through the glass of my office door. By the time I reached her side, I was taking the steps two at a time.

When Poodle Lady heard me coming, she turned to face me. Indicating the glass door leading into my office with a tilt of her blond head, she said, "Is that right?"

I'm not ashamed to admit that I wasn't real sure what she was talking about. I'm not ashamed to admit it because I don't believe any other private detective in the same situation would've known, either.

I looked from Poodle Lady to the glass of my office

door, trying not to let my bewilderment show in my face. Since most clients hire private eyes to solve problems for them, I think it's bad form to look baffled right off the bat.

I found myself staring at the fancy lettering I'd had painted right on the glass of my office door. These letters are real big, and they're done in this highfalutin typeface the sign painter called Times Italic. The letters say, *Haskell Blevins, Private Investigations, Inc.*

Poodle Lady seemed to be looking straight at this lettering, too. So the question was, exactly which part of this lettering was Poodle Lady asking about? Did she think that my name might not be Haskell Blevins? Or that this wasn't a detective agency?

If it turned out she meant the latter, I was pretty sure I was going to have my feelings hurt.

I decided she must've meant the former. "I'm Haskell Blevins," I said, "at your service. What can I do for you?"

I thought I sounded downright professional, but Poodle Lady actually looked a tad annoyed. "Oh, I already know who you are. I've seen you around town, and you don't have the kind of face a person would forget any too easy."

I didn't say anything for a moment. There have been rumors around town that I bear a striking resemblance to a famous television personality. That, of course, is the good news. The bad news is, the TV personality, unfortunately, is Howdy Doody. While I sincerely hope that these rumors were started by folks just being cruel, I have to admit that Howdy and I do have some things in common. Red hair, for one. And freckles, for, oh, say, the next million. I've always

11

thought it was a good thing freckles don't weigh anything, or else I wouldn't be able to move.

I stretched my mouth into a smile, and said with forced enthusiasm, "Well, I am real glad to meet you. And you are—?"

I started toward my office door, intending to open it for her, but Poodle Lady took a step backward, clutching her mop dog a little tighter. "Just a sec, before we go any farther, I still want to know: Is that sign on your door absolutely correct?" She gestured toward the lettering on the glass by pointing her poodle's nose at it.

The poodle had been dozing, but when it began to be used as a pointer—no pun intended—the motion must've woke it up. It opened beady black eyes and yawned. I looked in the direction of the poodle's nose. If you want to get technical, I do have to admit that the lettering on my door is not absolutely, totally correct. That is to say, I'm not really incorporated. The guy I hired to paint the sign on my door added that on his own. He told me he was trying to make me sound like some big company. Like, maybe, GE or AT&T or IBM. After he went to all that trouble, I didn't have the heart to make him wipe it off. I reckon having a lie painted right on my office door had been bothering me more than I thought, because at this point I had no doubt whatsoever what Poodle Lady was talking about.

I was actually a little shamefaced as I said, "Well, now that you mention it, it isn't *completely* right. I'm not incorporated. The guy who painted—"

Poodle Lady interrupted me. "I don't care about *that.*" She emphasized what she was saying by waving her poodle in the air. The animal's little black beady eyes blinked excitedly. "What I want to know is: Are your investigations *really* private?"

This time, instead of the poodle, it was me who blinked. "Well, of course, they're private," I said. What did she think? That I put out a newsletter?

Poodle Lady gave her dog several quick pats on the head. You might've thought the dog had been the one who'd answered her question. "Are you sure? Because I need me a real *private* detective," she went on, "on account of my having a real *private* problem."

She didn't have to say anything more. I immediately started trying to look discreet. "Ma'am," I said, in a voice that—in my opinion—rang with sincerity, "I pride myself on my confidentiality."

Poodle Lady cocked her head to one side. The way her dog might if it didn't quite understand what you'd just said. I decided to rephrase. "You can't get any more private than me." Poodle Lady cocked her head to the other side.

"I mean it," I added. "I don't talk to anybody."

Lord. Was there no limit to what I'd say in order to get a client? In another minute, I'd be telling her that I was so private, I didn't even talk to *myself*. Poodle Lady studied me for a long moment. So, in fact, did her dog. Of the two of them, the dog looked the most friendly. And it was doing a low growl under its breath.

"Well, you sure don't have the sort of face anybody would want to gossip with," Poodle Lady finally said. *"That's* for sure."

I tried to look as if I thought that was a compliment, but I knew it wasn't. Once again I started toward my door. *"Nobody* ever gossips with me," I said.

Give me another second or two, and I'd be telling

her that somebody who looked like me couldn't possibly have *friends*. So you certainly didn't have to worry about me telling anybody anything. Before I totally embarrassed myself, I got my office door open and was waving her through it.

Poodle Lady hesitated for just a second, and then she said as she sailed into my office, "OK, but you'd *better* be private, you hear? Because I sure don't want what I'm about to tell you spread all over Pigeon Fork. If that should happen, I'd have your nuts in a paper sack."

I'd been smiling at her, but my smile immediately froze. What a sweet and delicate thing to say. Being fairly fond of the body parts she'd just mentioned, I began to wonder if I really wanted this woman for a client, after all.

From the way she was now smiling at *me*, though, you could almost believe she hadn't just threatened the removal and subsequent packaging of a couple of my favorite body parts. "I'm Maedean Puckett," she said, "and this here is Poopsie." She stuck out her right hand to shake mine, and with her left hand extended the poodle toward me.

I wasn't sure what I was supposed to do to the poodle, but I started to shake Maedean's hand. That's all I succeeded in doing, though—*starting*. When my hand got within a foot of his head, Poopsie growled, baring a mouthful of sharp, tiny teeth. I snatched my hand back.

Maedean smiled. "Have you ever seen anything so cute?"

Actually, I was pretty sure I'd seen a couple piranha that were a whole lot cuter, but I nodded anyway.

Maedean gave Poopsie a quick kiss on top of his

head. "Good baby," she said. Looking back up at me, she added, "He's so protective."

As Maedean was saying this, she was taking a few steps into my office. She only took a very few, though. Then she just stood there, looking suddenly as if she thought she might need the aforementioned protection.

So, OK, I admit it, my office *is* a tad messy. Melba, in fact, calls my office the Bermuda Rectangle. She says it looks as if some mysterious force has sucked every magazine, newspaper, and scrap of trash from within a five-mile radius and deposited it on the floor of my office. Melba is exaggerating.

She really is, but you wouldn't have believed it, looking at Maedean's face. "Oh my," Maedean said, clutching Poopsie a little closer.

I brushed a stack of magazines off the chair in front of my desk, letting them fall onto the floor, and I waved Maedean into the chair. It took her a couple of seconds to decide it was OK, but she did finally take a seat, draping her cashmere coat across the back of the chair. Right after that I got a little demonstration of just how appropriately her dog was named. Maedean put her shoulder purse on the floor, put Poopsie down on the floor next to her purse, and took a pack of cigarettes and a lighter out of a side pocket of her dress. The dog immediately headed for the nearest stack of magazines. There he squatted. And poopsied.

This kind of activity indoors must not have been all that rare an occasion in Poopsie's life, because Maedean didn't act surprised. She'd been lighting her cigarette, and she didn't even pause as she said, "Oh, that Poopsie. You've just gotta love him, don't you?"

Actually, the only thing I felt truly compelled to do

to the dog was to drop-kick him into the middle of next week.

Maedean made no move to clean up Poopsie's mess. Taking a long drag off her cigarette, she said, "You know, if you didn't have all those papers scattered around, Poopsie would've never thought of doing that."

Looking over at Poopsie, I had the feeling it would've crossed his mind, regardless.

Maedean was now clearing her throat. "Now, you *did* say you were private, didn't you?"

I just looked at her. With Poopsie as my new interior decorator, the possibilities of anybody coming up here to *chat* were looking dim. "Oh yeah, I'm private, all right," I said. I got up and headed across the office to the poopsied magazines.

Poopsie must've thought my intentions were not totally of the cleaning persuasion, because he ran in a golden blur to sit at Maedean's feet.

Maedean was taking another long drag. "OK, then." Giving her blond hair a toss, she said in a sudden rush of words, "My husband, Dwight, and I have been having problems. You know, *merry-tull* problems."

I was right in the middle of picking up—very carefully—the magazines Poopsie had decorated, but I turned to glance over at Maedean. *Merry-tull?* What the hell was merry-tull?

Maedean was exhaling loudly. "I know, of course, in your line of work, you've heard this kind of thing before, and that anything I tell you won't be the least bit shocking ..."

I certainly wasn't shocked. I was too busy trying to figure out what the hell she was talking about. I was also busy picking up Poopsie's magazines, taking them over to the trash can next to my desk, and dropping them in.

Maedean was now reddening a little. Not, however, because she was at all embarrassed by Poopsie's lack of etiquette. "Dwight and I have been married seven years, and, well, I might as well say it, there's always been the suspicion of—of—infidelity."

I just barely managed to keep from slapping myself on the forehead. Marital! That's what she was saying. Not merry-tull. *Marital* problems. I resumed my seat behind my desk, and tried my best to look professional. It took some doing, being as how what was now going through my mind was, of course, *Hey, this could be getting good.*

Maedean now seemed to be directing her conversation at Poopsie. When I'd sat down, the dog had moved even closer to his mistress. It was now sitting on top of her right foot. "I know that this sort of work is what private detectives do all the time, and—well—I though that—well—if I could just have some pictures made, well—"

Maedean was looking more and more uncomfortable, so I held up my hand. Where she was headed with this seemed pretty obvious. I leaned forward, and now tried to look sympathetic. It was hard to do considering that the trash can I'd put Poopsie's mess into was far, far too close to my nose. I hoped, however, that Maedean would interpret my squinched eyes and pinched mouth as an expression of real concern.

"I think I understand what you want me to do." I cleared my throat. There didn't seem to be any delicate way to ask what I had to ask, so I just plunged right in. "Exactly how long have you suspected that your husband was unfaithful?"

I hated to embarrass her, but I had to know. There's a tried-and-true rule in the private eye business that goes like this: *If you don't get incriminating pictures of the philandering spouse in the first three months of the affair, you'll never get them.* That's because after the first three months, the new girlfriend—or the new boyfriend, in the case of philandering wives—begins to press for a commitment. After that, all you ever see is the spouse and the lover sitting in restaurants, arguing.

I'd known I was going to get a strong reaction, but Maedean's mouth actually dropped open. "What?" she choked out.

I hated to repeat it, but I did, anyway. "How long do you think your husband's been unfaithful?"

Maedean blinked, doing a perfect imitation of Poopsie earlier. *"Dwight?"* she said. "Are you kidding? Who in the world would have an affair with *Dwight?"*

Dwight, no doubt, would've loved to have heard this stirring testimonial.

"But, Mrs. Puckett, you said—"

Maedean took another long drag off her cigarette. *"I* don't suspect Dwight," she said. "Dwight suspects *me!"* Shaking her head, Maedean hurried on. "I mean, can you imagine? I don't know where he gets these crazy ideas."

I took in her low-cut neckline, her skintight leopard pants, and her high spike heels. As my daddy used to say, *Why advertise, if you're not in business?*

Maedean was hurrying on. "That's why I want to hire you, of course. If you could just follow me around for a while and report back to Dwight, it would convince him once and for all how wrong he is!"

I just looked at her again. Then, in a heartbeat, I came up with the kind of incisive, in-depth question that I believe I'm known for around these parts.

"Huh?" I said.

CHAPTER 2

Maedean was smiling at me. You might've thought that what she was saying actually made sense. "That's right. I want you to tail me night and day." She leaned over and gave Poopsie a quick pat on the head, apparently for emphasis. "I mean it, Haskell, I want you to watch my every move. I want you to to take pictures of me, too."

I reckon I still hadn't fully grasped what she was saying. "Pictures?" I repeated.

Maedean nodded, her small brown eyes eager. "That's right. I want you to take pictures of me shopping. And visiting friends. And, you know, walking Poopsie, that sort of thing. I want you to take *tons* of pictures of me."

I stared at her. The woman didn't need a private detective. She needed a press agent. "Mrs. Puckett," I began, "I really—"

Maedean interrupted me. "Call me Maedean. We're

going to be spending quite some time together, so we might as well be friendly."

The way I saw it, we weren't going to be spending any time at all together, but I corrected myself anyway. *"Maedean,* I really don't think that—"

Maedean interrupted me again. "I want my husband to know what I'm doing every minute of the day. I don't want Dwight to have a doubt in his mind how I'm spending my time. Matter of fact, I even want you to follow me when *Dwight* is with me. That way he'll know he's getting a totally complete report."

I continued to stare at Maedean. An essential feature of the entire surveillance process seemed to have gone right over her head. I realized, of course, that pointing out this little oversight was the same as signing up for more long hours of floor mopping downstairs. And yet as much as I dreaded more mop duty, I believe I pretty much drew the line at tailing somebody who could at any moment look over and *wave* at me.

I cleared my throat. "Maedean," I said, "as a general rule, when you do surveillance on a person, that person is not supposed to *know* you're doing it." I heard myself saying these words, and I still couldn't believe I was actually telling somebody this. As if it were news. "Fact is, that's pretty much the whole point of surveillance. You watch somebody when they *don't* know you're watching them, and that way you find out stuff they *don't* want you to find out." I cleared my throat. "I've never heard of surveillance working any other way."

Maedean didn't even blink this time. "Well, now you have," she said brightly.

I didn't blink, either. I may have been leaping to

conclusions here, but there appeared to be a good chance that on an IQ test, Poopsie could beat out his mistress. And Poopsie, let me tell you, did not appear to be any Rin Tin Tin himself. At that particular moment, Poopsie was sniffing the hem of Maedean's cashmere coat and then growling at the thing, as if maybe he'd mistaken it for some kind of extremely limp animal.

I took a deep breath and tried again, this time speaking very slowly and very distinctly. "Maedean, the person who gets tailed by the detective is *never* the one who hires the detective."

I didn't know how I could make that any clearer. Unless I drew pictures.

It looked like pictures might be necessary. Maedean did this little impatient flounce in her chair. "But don't you see?" she said. "This way is going to be so much easier on *you.*"

Now *I* wasn't getting it. "How do you figure?"

Poopsie was now trying to take a bite out of the hem of his mistress's coat, growling even louder than before. Maedean lifted the hem out of the dog's reach and said, *"This* way you won't have to worry about sneaking around and keeping me from finding out about you. Because I already know!"

I blinked this time. Obviously, I was going to have to be even more blunt. "Look, you can't tail somebody who knows—"

Once again she didn't let me finish. Poopsie had begun to take little leaps at the hem of the coat dangling above his head, evidently trying to bite it in midair. Maedean let go of the coat, reached down, and snatched Poopsie out of the air on his way up. "But, don't you see?" she said. "In *my* case it doesn't matter whether I know I'm being tailed or not." She deposited Poopsie onto her lap and said, her eyes still on the dog, "Because, in my case, there's nothing to be found out anyway."

Poopsie tried to jump to the floor, but Maedean once again caught him in mid-leap, depositing him still again in the middle of her lap. "In fact," Maedean went on smoothly, "my knowing that you're watching me is going to make everything go a whole lot smoother."

Poopsie had evidently given up on biting his mistress's coat, and now appeared to be intent on burrowing into her left armpit. Judging from the snuffling sounds he was making, he must've decided something was hiding in there.

All of this must've been a regular routine where Poopsie was concerned, because Maedean didn't even miss a beat as she dragged Poopsie out of her underarm, and deposited him again in her lap. "Say, for instance, you take a picture, and you're pretty sure that the lighting was bad or it was out of focus or something like that?" Maedean went on. "Well, that won't be a problem at all. Because you can just holler at me, and I'll let you take your picture all over again."

This time I didn't blink. I stared at her, slack-jawed. Lord. I could see it now. Me, concealed in the shrubbery around the Puckett house, snapping away with my Minolta, and then all of a sudden, standing up and yelling at her. In full view of her neighbors. Yelling something on the order of *"Yo, Maedean, howzabout doing whatever you were doing one more time so's I can take my surveillance photo again?"*

Oh yeah. Up to now it had been bad enough that

the only private eye in Pigeon Fork seemed to spend an inordinate amount of his time mopping floors. But *this* sort of behavior would, without a doubt, earn my detective agency exactly the kind of professional reputation I'd been hoping I had not already achieved.

"I mean it," Maedean was now saying. She tilted her Leno chin to one side. "I wouldn't mind a bit. You could take the same photo four or five times if you want." She punctuated this statement by giving Poopsie a little kiss on the top of his head.

The dog had given up armpit burrowing and coat biting, and had finally curled up on Maedean's lap as if that was what he'd wanted to do all along. When Maedean kissed him, Poopsie looked considerably more pleased with the entire situation than I was.

I gave Maedean an uncertain smile. Obviously, I was going to have to spell *everything* out for her.

"Look," I said, speaking even slower than before, "what I'm trying to tell you is that I'm not sure that my tailing you under these circumstances will convince your husband of anything. I don't think—"

Maedean interrupted me. "You're not being paid to think." She was scratching Poopsie behind one ear. The dog's eyes were closing as Maedean went right on without looking up. "I've got me a thousand-dollar retainer that says this will convince him, all right."

It was with considerable effort that I managed not to gasp. What did I say earlier about money talking? Poopsie's eyes may have been closing, but what money had just said to me, loud and clear, had popped my own eyes wide open.

Maedean hurried on, "And I'll pay twice your going hourly rate."

I'm ashamed to say that as soon as those particular

words were out of Maedean's mouth, I was actually thinking, Hey, what did I know? Maybe Poopsie could beat out Maedean's husband, Dwight, on an IQ test, too. I mean, don't they say that birds of a feather flock together? It was entirely possible that Mr. and Mrs. Puckett could *both* be birdbrains. What's more, if Dwight did happen to be every bit the birdbrain that his wife appeared to be, he might truly believe— even though Maedean knew she was being followed and photographed—that Maedean was still behaving *exactly* as she would have if she'd not known. Uh-huh. Sure. Lord. Could *anybody* really be that dumb?

Apparently, I hadn't leaped at Maedean's offer as quickly as she'd expected. She stopped scratching Poopsie's head, and started waving her hand in the air in a gesture of submission. "OK, OK, I'll give you a retainer of *fifteen* hundred dollars," Maedean said.

My eyes started doing that popping thing all over again.

"What's more, I'll write you a check right this minute." With Poopsie still on her lap, Maedean didn't have much room there for her purse. She grabbed it off the floor, anyway, and nearly set it right on top of Poopsie. Poopsie must've been accustomed to this kind of treatment because he just scrambled closer to Maedean's chest. The dog then just sat there, with his eyes still half-closed, while Maedean reached over him and pulled a leather checkbook out of her purse.

Using the part of her lap not occupied by Poopsie as a sort of desk, Maedean wrote out that check with lightning speed. I had to admire her dexterity. The last woman I'd seen spend money that fast was my ex-wife, Claudine—or, rather, Claudzilla, as I so fondly refer to her. If shopping ever gets to be an

Olympic event, believe me, Claudzilla is a shoo-in for the gold.

Maedean, however, looked as if she could probably take the silver. She was already tearing the check out of her book with a little flourish, and handing it to me. I don't know. I guess I hadn't really believed what she was saying until I saw that little slip of paper. On which was written, plain as day, One Thousand Five Hundred Dollars. I looked at that number as if I were hypnotized.

Maedean must've misinterpreted my pointed stare. "Oh, you don't have to worry," she said. "That check is good, all right. Dwight just inherited his family's farm, and not to be telling tales out of church or nothing, but our net worth just jumped right through the ceiling."

I pulled my eyes briefly away from the check and looked back over at Maedean. Of course. *Puckett*. I suddenly realized exactly who Maedean here was. Once it came to me, it seemed so obvious, I wondered why I hadn't put it together before this. After all, hadn't the obituary of Isom Puckett been in the *Pigeon Fork Gazette* only a few months ago? It had been right on the front page, too, set off from the rest of the paper in a black-bordered box.

I hadn't known Isom Puckett real well, his having been a lot closer to my dad's age than my own. But I did know that the big farm on the left that I passed on State Road 261 every night on my way home was the Puckett place. It was one of the largest working farms still left around here, and as I recalled, Isom had still been working it the day he died. He'd been stripping tobacco when he'd suddenly dropped dead of a massive heart attack. When I read his obituary,

I remembered thinking that it wasn't the worst way in the world to go, being taken right in the middle of an enormous, backbreaking job.

In addition to Isom, I also remembered Dwight, the oldest of Isom's two sons. I hadn't known Dwight well, mainly because he'd been four years behind me at Pigeon Fork High. If there is one thing that has held true right up until today, it's this: Seniors do not hang out with freshmen.

To tell the truth, I might not have remembered Dwight Puckett at all—I only vaguely remembered his younger brother, and I certainly couldn't remember his brother's name—except for one thing. As a freshman Dwight had made the basketball team. As a senior that year, *I,* on the other hand, had not. The sad fact was, I'd tried to make the team every single year for four years straight, and every single year I hadn't made it past the first cut.

So, yes, I remembered Dwight Puckett, all right. He'd been the tall, scrawny kid I'd envied when I was seventeen. If I remembered correctly, Dwight had gone off to college somewhere on a basketball scholarship, and he'd never been back. Until now.

I leaned forward a little and looked at Maedean with new eyes. So *this* was who Dwight Puckett had ended up marrying. It could very well be I'd finally been cured of that envying thing.

Maedean once again misinterpreted my look. "Hey," she said, "if I say that check is good, it's good." She gave her blond hair another toss. "Fifteen hundred dollars," she said, her tone enticing, "is nothing to sneeze at. I won't be going any higher, either. Fifteen hundred's fair."

Fair? It wasn't just fair, it was generous. I immediately stopped thinking about Dwight, and started thinking about fifteen hundred smackers. Talk about money yelling. And yet before anybody jumps to some unfounded conclusion about how mercenary I am, let me hasten to say that how loud Maedean's money seemed to be talking to me wasn't just on account of my being so tired of filling in downstairs as Elmo's chief mop pusher and soda jerk. No, when I looked at that check, it wasn't just the cash that I saw. I also saw my girlfriend, Imogene Mayhew.

Technically, I suppose Imogene is not exactly beautiful. With shoulder-length, wavy brown hair and a creamy complexion, though, she is real pretty in a big-boned, farm-fresh sort of way.

But before anybody jumps to yet another unfounded conclusion—that, since I see her when I look at money, then Imogene must be one of those women just interested in a man's wallet—let me once again hasten to say that you've got Imogene confused with my ex-wife. Claudzilla is the woman who ran up all my charge cards, and then left me. *Imogene,* on the other hand, is the woman who has never even so much as asked how much money I make.

Can you believe that? Imogene and I had been dating for all of six months now, and she'd never even asked once. Of course, one reason I suspected she hadn't asked here lately was that she knew very well that these days she was making a whole lot more than I was.

In fact, I reckon you could say about Imogene the exact same thing that Maedean had just said about herself and Dwight. Imogene's net worth had just jumped through the ceiling.

And when I say jumped, I mean *jumped.* When

Imogene and I met some six months ago, she was still struggling to make ends meet. She'd just gotten her real estate license the year before, and she was still trying to make it as a self-employed person. Just like me.

Imogene and I had run into each other during what had to be one of the darkest times of both our lives. I'd been looking into some strange break-ins around town—strange in that nothing whatsoever had been taken in any of them—and I'd ended up looking into the sad murder of Imogene's sister.

You'd think, having gotten acquainted under such terrible circumstances, the chances of Imogene and me ending up together were pretty much nil. And yet out of all that darkness, something bright and wonderful had happened.

When we'd first started dating a short six short months ago, it had seemed as if Imogene and I had almost everything in common. We'd both been born and raised right here in Pigeon Fork. We'd both left, lived in Louisville for a few years, and then—realizing how much we missed small-town life—we'd moved back. What's more, we were both University of Louisville basketball fans. Which, in this part of the country where most everybody is a University of Kentucky basketball fan, is practically the same as having the same rare blood type. Imogene and I also had one other real important thing in common: freckles. Believe me, it was real nice to finally have freckles in common with somebody a whole lot cuter than Howdy Doody. What all this comes down to, I reckon, is this: When I met Imogene, I'd felt as if I'd finally run into my soul mate.

That, however, was before Imogene sold the

McAfee place, and the Bishop farm, and two new houses in Twelve Oaks, the most prestigious subdivision in this area. That was also before she topped all of these sales by unloading the old Cunningham mansion down by the railroad tracks.

The closing on the Cunningham mansion had been just a little over two weeks ago. These days Imogene had herself so much extra cash, she practically jangled when she walked. Not that she was uppity about it. I'm here to tell you she certainly wasn't. I'm also here to tell you that I was real proud of her. Make no mistake about that. I knew Imogene had worked damned hard to be as successful as she was. But, I also have to admit, that all of a sudden, it seemed, Imogene and I didn't have quite so much in common as we used to.

I reckon that right there was the biggest reason why things had gotten so awkward between us lately. Imogene being so flush—and me, being not so flush—it really put a different spin on things. I've always heard that money changes everything, but I never believed it until now.

Now I know money changes even the little things. Like, for example, the last couple times Imogene and I went out to eat, Imogene actually tried to pay the tab.

I know, I know. It's the nineties, for God's sake, and this sort of thing is done all the time. The only problem is, it's not done all the time in Pigeon Fork, Kentucky.

I have no doubt that this kind of modern approach to dating flies just fine in big cities like Louisville or Nashville, but here in small-town America, things are still pretty old-fashioned. If you doubted that for even a second, you could just take a quick peek around downtown Pigeon Fork. I guarantee you'll see clothes there you haven't seen anywhere else since the fifties. We've still got your muumuu dresses, your wide ties, and your Elvis sideburns. We've also still got your hip-huggers, your saddle oxfords, and your pedal pushers. I fully expect one day to see somebody walking around downtown Pigeon Fork wearing one of those skirts with a poodle on it.

And, to tell the truth, it didn't help any that Imogene didn't even try to be subtle about paying for things. Last Saturday, for example, right after she and I had finished off two big plates of barbecued ribs at Frank's Bar and Grill, and Frank came over with the bill, why, Imogene didn't even wait until Frank had left. She just took the bill right smack dab out of Frank's hand, quick as anything. "Dutch treat," she said to me, giving me this real big smile.

I would've smiled back except that I was so surprised that Imogene had actually said those two words right out loud. *Dutch treat.* Within earshot of Frank, for God's sake.

Frank, of course, immediately started grinning from ear to ear. Turning to me, he said with a wink, "Why, Haskell, I didn't know you was Dutch."

Frank apparently thought that particular comment was so knee-slapping funny, it was worth repeating to just about every warm body in town. By the end of the next day, I'd had three different people ask me if I wore wooden shoes. Right to my face.

Even Pop Matheny of Pop's Barber Shop winked at me the very next day as I walked by his shop. Usually Pop is so totally absorbed in polishing the old-time barber pole he's got hanging outside his door that he doesn't bother to speak. This time, though, he stopped right in the middle of what he was doing and mumbled something about growing tulips. I'd been walking past him at a pretty good clip, and I hadn't been sure exactly what it was he'd said. Looking at the idiotic grin on his face, however, I knew I didn't want to ask him to repeat it.

Imogene tried to go *Dutch treat,* as she called it, all of five times in the last two weeks. I stopped her every time. I knew, of course, that Imogene was just trying to be nice and all, but let me tell you, it was embarrassing. It was even embarrassing just to talk about. In fact, I hadn't quite been able to bring myself to tell Imogene how I felt. For one thing, I knew how it made me look. If I didn't watch out, folks might actually get me confused with some of them animals on that swine farm out Highway 46. On the other hand, in the last ten days or so, I reckon I'd pretty much overdosed on comments about Dutch daffodils and Dutchboy Paint and Dutch elm disease. I'm sure that's why I did what I did yesterday.

After lunch, when once again Imogene tried to pick up the tab—and I mean that literally—she tried to pick it up off the table, I beat her to it. And all but ripped it out of her hand.

"I'll get that," I said. I myself was a little surprised to hear my voice. My tone was not kind.

When Imogene turned startled hazel eyes in my direction, I said something incredibly dumb. I said, "Hey, I can't have you wearing the pants in this relationship *all* the time, now, can I?"

Oh yeah, that was dumb; all right, I'd meant that little comment to come out sounding kind of teasing-like, but I don't reckon that's how it sounded at all. Imogene's hazel eyes went from very wide to slit-like.

She looked down at her plate real quick, but not before I saw her mouth set itself into a real thin line. Naturally, the first thought that went through my mind once she started looking like that was: *Uh-oh. I just stepped in it big-time.* Because, believe me, the look on Imogene's face was not exactly a foreign one to me. It was one I'd seen oh, say, about a zillion times on Claudine's face. That particular look, in fact, was one of the reasons I'd started referring to Claudine privately as Claudzilla.

Seeing that look on Imogene's face was enough to make my stomach knot up. What made it even more gut wrenching was knowing that, of all times to say something dumb, this was probably the worst, because lately there had been another man in Imogene's life.

Oh, Imogene has tried to assure me that I'm really the only man in her life, but what else would you call a guy who keeps sending Imogene a dozen long-stemmed red roses? Other than what I often called him—just to myself, mind you—that, of course, being, *asshole.*

Imogene has told me that this guy didn't interest her, but I've seen her face when the lady from the Bo-Kay Florist shows up with yet another delivery. Kids on Christmas Day don't look that tickled. So, to my way of thinking, if you'd say that Santa Claus is in kids' lives every December, then Randy Harned was definitely in Imogene's life. In fact, he'd been in her life every three or four days for the last month. Can you believe that? In November, a dozen long-stemmed red roses cost upward of fifty dollars or more, and old Randy was shelling out that much two and three times a week. Randy seemed determined, in fact, to outdo Santa.

33

I don't see how Imogene could help but be impressed. She told me that she'd only met Randy when he'd delivered water to her house a month or so ago, and that she didn't know what got him so interested in her all of a sudden. She also told me that he was just being sweet to her, that's all, but Imogene didn't know that I'd read several of the cards old Randy included with his damn roses.

These little messages, believe me, have become more and more nauseating. The last one took the cake. We'd been going out to see a movie—one that I intended to pay for, mind you—and after I arrived to pick Imogene up, I'd had to wait a spell in her living room while Imogene went to get her coat.

As soon as she was out of sight, I crossed the room in about two steps max. Written in red ink, the card said, "You are the flower in the garden of my life." It was signed with a little red heart and the words, "Love, Randy." Oh, brother. Granted I was a tad prejudiced, but this card sounded to me like something a blooming idiot would write. It also sounded like I was in deep, dark doo-doo, as my daddy used to say.

I mean, how in hell was I supposed to compete with this guy? It was painfully obvious that Randy Harned could buy and sell me. Fact is, when he'd showed up in town a few months ago, he must've had himself quite a bankroll because right away he bought the local water delivery company that was up for sale. Rumor has it, he bought it for cash.

Nowadays you couldn't turn around without seeing another one of Harned's water delivery trucks. You couldn't miss them even if you wanted to. They were big, and silver, and every single one of them had a gigantic Confederate flag painted on both sides. Underneath the flag, written in a real fancy script, were the words "The South will rise again." Underneath that little sentiment was HARNED WATER SERVICE followed by his telephone number: 733-WATR.

I'd actually heard folks around town saying how "distinctive" Harned's trucks are, but if you asked me, the part of that word that should be emphasized was the "stink" part. Those trucks of his were an eyesore, pure and simple.

I won't even get into how there are a lot of folks who find the Confederate flag downright offensive these days, being as how it reminds them of a time when a significant portion of the population wasn't being treated any too kindly. Not to mention, even if you really did want the South to rise again—a thing I can't say I personally would vote for—what did delivering water have to do with it? Did Harned actually believe that maintaining the water supply in this part of the country was somehow going to bring back the Confederacy?

Another thing that really rankled was that, even though the man had only been in Pigeon Fork a few short months, everybody in town seemed to know him. I reckon it's on account of his name being plastered on trucks rolling through town every hour of the day, but it was a little disconcerting to have folks who didn't know me from Adam actually call Randy by name.

Melba even knew who he was. In fact, she'd told me several times that Randy Harned was one real good-looking man. I personally didn't see it. He seemed kind of skinny to me, with hair too long and shaggy, and he had a mouth on him that would look a whole lot better on a woman. Melba, however, did seem to get all flustered every time Randy walked into the drugstore.

"Why, he looks just like Scully, the boyfriend of Jane Seymour's on that TV show about the woman doctor out West," she told me.

I deliberately watched that show, just to get a good look at this Scully character, and I reckon I had to admit it. Randy Harned did bear a passing resemblance to the boyfriend guy. Only Harned didn't wear Indian clothes like Scully, of course. Harned always seemed to be wearing black—black jeans, black shirt, and black boots. Like maybe he thought he was related to Johnny Cash or something.

From what I'd heard—and believe me, I'd tried not to ask—Harned was a Louisville transplant, just like me. *And* just like Imogene. The thing about Randy, unfortunately, that was not a bit like me got painfully obvious every time flowers showed up for Imogene.

Imogene has always insisted that whether you have money or not didn't really make any difference to her. And yet, I couldn't help but wonder. Imogene has also told me that she and Harned have never gone out, and that she wasn't even tempted. I wanted to believe her. I really did. And yet, how long could I expect Imogene to keep turning down a guy who could give her just about everything she ever wanted?

Compared to Randy Harned, I knew how I had to look. Like a loser. That's why—more than anything else—that fifteen hundred dollars in Maedean's hand was so all-fired mesmerizing. I knew, without even thinking about it, that if I earned a decent living for a change, it would make all the difference in the world to me and Imogene. Taking Maedean's job meant that Imogene and I could weather this little storm of ours.

And that our relationship would go back to the way it was.

Given all this as fact, who exactly was I kidding? For a fifteen-hundred-dollar retainer, I would've agreed to tail Poopsie. Even if Poopsie *did* know I was tailing him.

"Maedean," I said, coming around the front of my desk and extending my right hand, "you've just hired yourself a detective."

Poopsie, of course, growled again when he saw my hand heading toward his mistress. I started to snatch my hand back, but Maedean got quickly to her feet, holding Poopsie out of snapping range. Grabbing my hand with her free one, she said, "Great!" Beaming at me.

Poopsie let out several snarls while his mistress and I shook hands. The dog seemed to be registering his disapproval of the entire deal.

Hey, I can't say I blamed him.

CHAPTER 3

Maedean and I had no sooner finished shaking hands than she said, "OK, get your camera. I want to give Dwight a full report ASAP."

She didn't say that last phrase the way most folks I know say it—by pronouncing each letter. No, Maedean said it, "A sap." Which at the time seemed real appropriate. Considering that this was a pretty accurate description of what I was feeling like at that particular moment.

In one smooth motion Maedean picked up her coat, her purse, and clutching Poopsie tightly to her chest, headed for the door. "I'll wait for you out front, OK?" Without giving me the chance to answer, she added, almost as if she were talking to herself, "When I get home, I think I'll change into my red jumpsuit. That'll show up a lot better in the pictures than what I'm wearing now, don't you think?"

I kept my face real still after that one, afraid that any change in my expression would betray what I really wanted to reply. Which was, of course, *What the hell do you think this is—a photo layout for some women's magazine?*

"Good idea," I said instead.

Maedean gave Poopsie a quick kiss on top of his little golden mop head, as if the dog had come up with the right answer again, and she hurried out of my office.

I, on the other hand, just stood there for a long moment, wondering what in the world I'd gotten myself into. It occurred to me, as I stood there, that if any of my old cronies on the police force back in Louisville ever got wind of this particular job, my life would not be worth living. With that happy thought, I ran around my office and got my camera bag, my telephoto lens, and the little 3×5 notebook I always use when I conduct a real surveillance. I also made sure my Minolta was loaded with a fresh roll of film.

As it happened, the film in my camera was not exactly fresh. I'd taken a few shots of my own dog, Rip, a couple days before. I'd taken these pictures in self-defense, to my way of thinking. It had crossed my mind—once it had gotten to be November—that Christmas was right around the corner. And, of course, I couldn't help remembering what fun I'd had last Christmas—pulling card after card out of my mailbox, all containing snapshots of the sender's family.

At the time I couldn't believe it. Either every photographer in America had been having a Christmas special, or else every one of my friends and relatives had decided that, being as how I didn't have any of my own, I needed reminding what children looked like. By the time Christmas had gotten here, I'd been feeling a lot like what Bob Cratchit, no doubt, would've felt like if his entire family—including Tiny Tim—had never been born.

That's why a couple days ago I'd decided that this year I was going to fight fire with fire. In every one of my Christmas cards, I, too, intended to enclose a photo of my own adorable family—that is to say, my dog Rip. I'd wanted to take Rip's picture with a cheery red Christmas bow around his neck, but Rip wouldn't have any of that. I tried several times to tie the thing on him, but it got to where when I approached within a foot of him with the bow in my hand, Rip would snarl under his breath. Rip is half German shepherd, half big black dog, so when he snarls, he's sort of like E. F. Hutton. You listen.

I ended up just taking pictures of Rip with the expression on his face that I see most often. A tongue-lolling grin. I knew, of course, that this particular expression meant, "Where's dinner?" But maybe all my married friends and relatives would think it meant, "Happy Holidays."

Even counting the Rip Christmas assortment, though, I still had over thirty shots left on the roll of film in my camera. Surely, that would be enough to last out the night. Unless, of course, Maedean decided she looked so great in her red jumpsuit that she wanted me to take enough shots so that she could enclose them in *her* Christmas cards.

Before I left, I stopped in at Elmo's to let Melba know that I'd just been hired to do some surveillance work, and that I'd be out of the office for a while. I was in the middle of telling Melba to take any messages and that I'd be checking in with her every so often when Melba interrupted me to ask, "Who are you tailing?" Her tiny blue eyes traveled toward the front of the drugstore, in the direction, no surprise, of Maedean's Corvette.

I acted as if I hadn't even heard Melba. Melba, you see, is the unofficial head of Gossip Central in Pigeon Fork, and as such, she would've, no doubt, loved to have spread this latest news. All about how I was so inept that I now required the folks I tailed to know in advance that I'd be tailing them.

"I'll be in touch." I said this so fast, it came out sounding like one word. Then, before Melba could ask me anything else, I got out of there.

I did notice, however, that Melba's eyes narrowed some and then followed me curiously all the way to the front of the store. I all but ran out the door.

I keep my truck parked in the alley between Elmo's and the Dry Goods Store next door, so it was only a few steps away. In a matter of minutes, I was pulling up right in back of Maedean's Corvette. As promised, Maedean had waited for me, her motor running, directly in front of the entrance to the drugstore.

Maedean waggled her fingers at me in the rearview mirror as I pulled up behind her. I just looked at her for a second. And then, what the hey, I waggled my fingers in return. Once again, of course, feeling like what Maedean had mentioned earlier. A sap.

It didn't help to notice that, as Maedean pulled out onto Main Street with me right behind her, Melba had moved to stand once again at the left front window, looking first at Maedean and then over at me. Patting her beehive speculatively. I did not wave at Melba as I drove by. Maedean, however, did. I all but cringed when I saw Maedean do it.

Following right behind Maedean's Corvette, out of downtown Pigeon Fork, and right on past where Main

Street becomes a state road, I was almost convinced
that this was the stupidest thing I'd ever agreed to
do in my entire life. Fortunately, however, I had my
marriage to Claudzilla to look back on. In the stupidity department, it was going to take an awful lot to
beat that one out. I had to admit, though, that the
current Maedean Mission was certainly giving it a run
for its money.

Not surprisingly, Maedean had been right. Following somebody who knows you're following them is a
whole lot easier than following somebody who doesn't.
A couple times on the way, I might've lost Maedean,
being as how that Corvette of hers could really move.
Those times, however, when Maedean completely disappeared over a crest in the blacktop up ahead, she
thoughtfully pulled over to the side of the road and
waited for me to catch up.

It was a little disconcerting to have her once again
waggle her fingers at me in her rearview mirror as I
came up behind her, but I kept telling myself, What
did I care? If Maedean Puckett wanted to spend her
money being tailed to the tune of fifteen hundred dollars, who was I to stop her? Besides, I believe I had
tried. The woman just wouldn't listen.

I'd been expecting the Pucketts to live someplace
like Twelve Oaks, the prestigious subdivision I mentioned earlier. All the moneyed folks in Pigeon Fork
seem to pretty much gravitate there. It's almost as if
money is a kind of magnet, attracting others similarly
endowed. I myself have never felt the least bit drawn
there.

When Maedean and I sailed right past the left-hand
turn onto Highway 46 that led to Twelve Oaks, however, I amended my guess. Maybe the Pucketts had

found themselves a real nice house for sale on some really expensive, extremely private piece of land—a choice I myself could've gone for in a big way.

I'd pretty much made up my mind that this had to be what they'd done, so I was a tad surprised to see Maedean turn up ahead. I followed right behind her, turning into the winding gravel driveway leading to old Isom Puckett's farmhouse—the same farmhouse setting off State Road 261 that, as I also mentioned earlier, I passed every night on my way home.

Apparently, when Maedean said she and Dwight had inherited the place, she'd meant it literally. She and Dwight appeared to be actually living these days in the house that had once been Isom's.

From the road, anybody driving by can see the farmhouse sitting up there on the hill in the distance. A white, Victorian-style frame with turn-of-the-century gingerbread decorating every gable, every eave, and every corner of the wraparound porch, the house looked as if it belonged in a storybook. It had two porch swings, five chimneys, and a pebble walk leading to the front door. It also had one of them cupola things on the second floor. With a brown-shingled conical roof, that thing looked for all the world like a giant, upside-down ice-cream cone sitting up there on top of the house.

When old Mrs. Puckett was alive, the pebbled walk had been bordered on both sides with flowers. At least that's what I've heard. Now, following Maedean up the gravel driveway and taking in the general dilapidated condition of the grounds, it struck me just how long ago that must've been. In fact, as best as I could recall, Dwight's mom had died of cancer shortly after Dwight had gone off to college. I wasn't absolutely sure about the time she'd died, but I did remember the cause on account of it being the same thing my own mother had died of. Now the only things that even hinted at how things had once been around here were a few scraggly orange flowers blooming forlornly near the front steps. This close to the house, I could also see that the exterior of this place sure could use a good coat of paint.

I took a deep breath, feeling unexpectedly sad all of a sudden. Poor old Isom Puckett must've been feeling mighty poorly for some time, to let his house get in this kind of shape. It made you wonder where his two sons had been when all this had been happening. Even as run-down as the place was, though, I knew very well that if Imogene had been trying to sell it to somebody, she would've described it as quaint and charming. I believe I might've agreed with her.

Maedean, on the other hand, had an entirely different description for the place. She braked right in front of me, just a little beyond where the pebbled walk met the gravel driveway, got out of her Corvette, and with Poopsie in her arms, walked back to where I'd stopped, just a few feet behind. "Well, here we are," she said, with a disparaging glance at the farmhouse, "at the family dump."

I just looked at her. Now what was a person supposed to say to that, for God's sake? *And what a charming dump it is?* Somehow, I knew I didn't want to hear what Maedean would say in return. Sitting there in my truck, I tried to come up with something more appropriate, but nothing occurred to me. Under other circumstances I'm sure I'd have been able to think of something, but to tell you the truth, right then I was a tad distracted.

I was real busy, casting nervous glances toward the farmhouse, wondering if Dwight Puckett himself was about to walk out the front door. If Dwight did appear, how in hell was I going to explain what I was doing here? Somehow, when Maedean and I were back at my office, this whole setup hadn't seemed quite so ridiculous as it seemed right now—as I was facing head-on having to explain it to a third party. Who, not incidentally, was financing it.

Maedean apparently noticed the direction my eyes kept heading. Waving a hand carelessly in the air, she said, "Now, Haskell, don't you worry. There's nobody home right now." She scratched Poopsie between his ears. "Fact is, Dwight went out to the store, and I'm pretty sure he won't be back for a couple more hours."

I stared at her. Pretty sure? She was only pretty sure? I tried to look as if what she'd just said had certainly done away with any worries I might've had, but I couldn't help wondering exactly how long Dwight's shopping trip could take.

If, of course, it had been Claudzilla we were talking about, I wouldn't have had the slightest worry. I'd have known she was gone until the last store closed.

But this was Dwight. A man. Pardon me if I sound sexist, but most men I know aren't really into what Claudzilla used to refer to as "the shopping experience." Of course, as far as Claudzilla was concerned, it was not just an experience—it was pretty much the entire life.

Maedean was now giving me a conspiratorial wink over Poopsie's golden head. "You don't have a thing to worry about. You and I will have plenty of time."

For a woman who was trying to convince her husband that she was not unfaithful, Maedean sure had a sultry way of talking. She also had a sultry way of moving. As Maedean spoke, she sort of shifted her weight and leaned toward my truck. I wasn't sure if she meant to do it, but when she moved, she gave me a pretty much unrestricted view down that low-cut neckline of hers. I moved uneasily in the front seat of my truck, actually wondering for a second there if Maedean might not have more in mind than a photo session.

It even flashed through my mind to make it clear to Maedean that I did happen to have myself a girlfriend. Fortunately, however, before I had a chance to actually say anything out loud—an action which would've, no doubt, guaranteed my entry into the Stupidity Hall of Fame—Maedean hurried on. "Oh, my, yes," she said, "you and I will have loads of time. What's more, I've found you the perfect spot to sit and watch me."

I tried to nod and look as if I certainly appreciated her efforts, but frankly, for a second there, the only thing that went through my mind was relief. Relief that Maedean wasn't really making a move on me. And even more relief that I had not opened my big mouth and made a total fool of myself.

"It's right over there, on the other side of the driveway, where those shrubs have grown up real thick." Maedean patted Poopsie again, looking positively delighted with her find. "Why, you can stand over there and watch me for hours, and nobody'd ever know you were there."

I was nodding the whole time she was talking, but I was starting to feel real weird. Maybe it was the view Maedean had just given me down her shirt. I don't know, but it was getting clear to me that my job description was starting to sound real close to that of a Peeping Tom. A Peeping Tom whose peeping the victim not only knew about, but encouraged.

Maedean turned out to be true to her word, though. The place she directed me to was perfect for the purpose we had in mind. Hidden by low-hanging evergreen branches that had apparently never recovered from last year's snow, it afforded an unobstructed view of the front of the house. And yet, if you were standing within three feet of those shrubs, you'd never know that I or my truck was there. Unless, of course, you were Maedean.

The place was ideal, all right, but I sure hated to back my truck in there. Not only because I was feeling like a Peeping Haskell, either. I also hated to do it for another reason: My truck was nearly brand-new.

On my last case, I'd also been driving a nearly brand-new Ford pickup—which I'd totaled. It hadn't been my fault—somebody had done me the colossal favor of eliminating the brake pedal as one of my driving options. The upshot of all this was that my Farm Bureau auto insurance had paid to replace my nearly new truck with yet another nearly new one. One, mind you, with a scratch-free, dent-free exterior and a truly terrific paint job—burgundy with a metallic flake. Backing my nearly new burgundy truck into what looked to be a tangle of twigs and low-hanging branches made me wince, but I did it, anyway. I am a professional, mind you. I even managed to back it in without glaring at Maedean.

Maedean, for her part, continued to be helpful. "OK," she said, "I'm going to run inside now and stand in front of the windows a lot. So's you can get some real good shots."

The Peeping Tom feeling was back. "Great," I said without enthusiasm.

Maedean, though, was enthusiastic enough for the both of us. "Goodness me," she said, pointing Poopsie at me, "Dwight is going to be so pleased with your report. He's just going to be tickled pink!"

You might've thought she was talking about a surprise birthday present she was giving the guy. I swallowed, as another wave of uneasiness hit me. What on earth was Dwight going to think of this? This is again what I mean by money talking. Money had apparently spoken to me so loudly back at my office, it had completely drowned out all thoughts that Dwight might not be all that pleased to discover just how his wife had chosen to spend fifteen hundred of his precious dollars. Unless I missed my guess, there was the distinct possibility that Dwight could be pissed. What's more, as I recalled, the guy was significantly bigger than me.

I took a deep breath. "You know, Maedean," I began, "I'm still not sure that this is a good—"

Maedean must've known where I was headed with this, because she cut me off. "Oh, for God's sake," she said, her tone irritated. "You've got my check, and you're not backing out on me now. We've got a deal, and that's that." She started to turn on her spiked heel and head for the house, but I reached out and grabbed her arm. This was not a real smart thing to do. Poopsie went for my hand as if it were a fresh-cut sirloin. I jerked my hand back.

Maedean, I noticed, did not look all that upset that I'd nearly been chewed. "What already?" she said.

I wasn't sure how to put what I had to say. "Look, we do have a deal, just like you say. But if it turns out that your husband isn't much impressed by what we've got to show him after a day or so, well, I'll be glad to call it quits, OK? And only bill you for the hours I've worked until then."

Maedean, I must say, was real impressed by my integrity. "Yeah, yeah, yeah," she said, waving her free hand in the air, as if trying to dispel smoke. Having said that, she headed for her house without looking back.

Maedean was moving at a pretty good clip, but as soon as she put her key into the lock, she just stood there, absolutely motionless for a good minute or so. As if maybe she was practicing to be a mannequin. It took me a second to realize what she was up to. And then, of course, it hit me. Maedean was *posing*. Maedean was standing there, in front of her door, without moving a muscle, waiting for me to snap the picture. I blinked a couple times, and then, of course, there really didn't seem to be anything else for me to do. I took the picture.

Glancing at my watch, I also made a notation in my spiral notebook: 3:45 P.M. *Subject entered residence*. After I'd finished writing, I just sat there and stared at that notebook page. It was right about then that I began to repeat to myself the three words that would become almost a litany for me during the next twenty-four hours. It's her money. It's her money. It's her money. It was also, of course, Dwight's money, but I decided that was a whole line of thought I didn't need to get into.

Having given me one excellent photo opportunity, Maedean immediately moved on to another. Opening the door, she stood stock-still again. Giving me a coy smile over her left shoulder. I snapped that one. Then in the next few minutes, I snapped several more, as Maedean, in her enthusiasm, struck more poses than all those women in the Cover Girl TV commercials put together.

Maedean then disappeared for a few minutes. When I saw her at a front window next, she'd changed into the bright red jumpsuit she'd mentioned earlier. I couldn't help but stare. What do you know, Maedean had been right again. That red outfit probably *would* show up better in my photographs than what she'd had on earlier. I suppressed a sigh, and then, what the hell, I started snapping pictures again. What can I say? Maedean kept coming up with Kodak moment after Kodak moment. There was Maedean, holding Poopsie, reading the mail. Maedean, holding Poopsie, watching TV. And Maedean, holding Poopsie, looking out the window.

Every Kodak moment, oddly enough, seemed to include Maedean holding Poopsie. In fact, I got downright tired of making that particular notation in my notebook. After a while I just started recording the time and putting down, *Subject in living room, ditto. Subject in dining room, ditto. Subject in kitchen, ditto.*

I probably would've taken even more pictures of *Subject in some room or another, ditto,* except that in the next hour or so I had to interrupt my picture taking three different times. The first interruption was when I had to tell Maedean to stop looking in my direction. I put up with it for a while, but finally, I'd had enough. I got out of my truck, stepped out from the overhanging branches, made my way across the road to the house, and knocked on the front door.

Would you believe, Maedean actually asked, "Who is it?"

I swallowed my first response. Which was, "The Avon lady." Instead, I said in an unbelievably agreeable tone, considering how I was feeling, "Maedean, would you please open up?"

When Maedean complied, I even managed to smile at her. "You know," I said, "it doesn't help to have a good hiding place if you've got somebody in the house who keeps looking at the exact spot in the woods where you're hiding." I tried to sound real casual, as if I were just pointing out a tiny, insignificant detail that might not have occurred to her.

"Oh," Maedean said. "You think maybe I shouldn't be looking your way at all?"

I nodded. "I think so."

On my way back to the truck, I did overhear Maedean saying to Poopsie, "Picky, picky, picky," but I didn't care. As long as I got her to stop staring at me.

My second trip to the house didn't go nearly as well. This time I had to tell Maedean to stop smiling. It took me a while to notice, but eventually I realized that in every single shot I'd taken, Maedean's expression never varied. She always had this coy smile on her face. She wasn't even smiling at Poopsie, for God's sake. She was just smiling. Period. I did not, of course, have to ask Maedean why on earth she'd suddenly gotten so damned happy. I knew. Maedean was smiling, because she was well aware that she was having her picture taken.

Watching Maedean smile at nothing in room after room was more than a little disconcerting. In fact, by the time I'd snapped Smiling Kodak Moment No. 15, Maedean was starting to look like a shoo-in for the lead in *One Flew Over the Cuckoo's Nest*. There was no way, once you saw all those self-conscious smiles, that you'd ever think that this woman didn't know she was being observed. And, correct me if I'm wrong, but wasn't that the impression these pictures were supposed to give?

This time, when I went to all the trouble of getting out of my truck and walking across to the house just to suggest that she ix-nay the grin, Maedean rolled her eyes. "Oh, for God's sake, I'm going to look awful if I'm not smiling," she said testily. "Why, I'm going to look real plain!"

I've been told by Claudzilla more than once that I didn't know the first thing about women, and that could very well be true. I did, however, in this instance know better than to tell Maedean that it would be preferable to look plain than to look like somebody who could stand a few doses of electroshock therapy.

Instead, I said evenly, "Maedean, you could never look plain."

God. I'm good.

Maedean smiled so wide, you could see her back teeth. While I had her smiling for real, I hurried on. "But, you know, Maedean," I said, "I think we've got enough of you smiling. Now we should show your serious side."

Maedean cocked her head to one side, considering what I'd said. At that moment in Maedean's arms, Poopsie was doing the same thing. I did not, however, point out this remarkable similarity. Finally Maedean said, "You know, you could be right."

Unfortunately, Maedean's serious side turned out to be a little more serious than I'd anticipated. For the next several frames, Maedean stood in one of the front windows of the old farmhouse and looked as if she'd just heard the sun was going to nova in the next five minutes. I stared at her through the lens, and contemplated whether it was worth it to get out of my truck and head back to the house again. I decided it wasn't. If Maedean wanted to look like maybe we should take away all her belts and any and all sharp utensils, it was her business. Besides, given the choice of depressed or demented, I decided depressed was a definite improvement.

I returned to the house only one more time, but this one was the worst. This time I had to tell Maedean to stop posing.

As tired by then as I was of trotting across the street to Maedean's front door, it had to be done. For two reasons. One, because Maedean was looking damned unnatural in frame after frame, lounging motionless against the mantel in the living room, and against the table in the kitchen, and against the banister in the foyer. And, two, because I was having real trouble deciding when to take the damn picture. No sooner would I decide, OK, she's not going to move for a while, and I'd start to snap it, when Maedean would suddenly change her pose. I finally decided I'd better tell her to quit posing, or a whole lot of the photographs were going to be blurred.

This time Maedean not only rolled her eyes, she pouted. "For Pete's sake," she said, "I was just trying to help out. I was merely letting you know when would be a good time to take the picture, that's all, but oh no, you don't appreciate it one bit, nope, you just—"

I'd pretty much had it by then. I interrupted her. "Maedean, if the pictures are fuzzy, Dwight's not gonna know it's you."

I could tell Maedean wanted badly to argue with

me some more, but even she had to admit that particular point was well taken. Maedean had actually started to nod her head when I heard the sound of tires crunching on the driveway. A car was headed this way.

Maedean's eyes met mine. "You don't think it could be—"

That's all she had to say. I turned and ran as fast as my feet would carry me, straight out her back door. Once outside, I circled around the house, and I hid behind some bushes in the side yard. There I decided I didn't have a prayer of making it across the driveway to where my truck was hidden without the driver of the approaching car seeing me. So, when the car pulled to a stop in back of Maedean's Corvette, I hunkered down in the shrubs and just watched. Feeling, of course, more and more like a Peeping Haskell.

The car was a sleek black BMW.

The driver was Dwight Puckett.

I guess, in a way, I was sort of hoping, since this guy was supposed to be swayed by the surveillance report of a detective hired by the person under surveillance, that Dwight would look like a person who'd taken one too many basketballs to the head. That maybe he'd have the studied look of somebody who, in order to remember how to walk, had to mouth to himself, "Left. *Right.* Left. *Right.* Left. *Right.*"

Dwight's mouth, however, did not seem to be moving at all as he walked up to his front door. My heart, I admit it, sank. For a second there I even tried to tell myself that maybe this wasn't Dwight after all. He *had* changed an awful lot. He was still tall, of course—at least six feet five—but he was no longer the least bit scrawny. In fact, he looked as if maybe he'd swallowed one of the basketballs he'd played with, and the thing had lodged right around his midsection. This guy also had a hairline that had receded so much that a good three quarters of his face now appeared to be forehead. He also had thighs that looked as if they'd been inflated with a bicycle pump. And a double chin.

Oh yeah, this guy hadn't played basketball in quite a while. But then again, I already knew that. As I recalled, Dwight had played college basketball for all four years, but he hadn't gone on to play pro ball anywhere. Although I couldn't recall exactly what college he'd been with, I did remember seeing him once during the NCAA finals on TV. His team had been beaten in the second round. Still, he'd sure done a lot better, basketball-wise, than I had. He'd made it to the NCAA, for God's sake. Once his basketball career was over, I'd heard he'd started working as a car salesman somewhere in Tennessee.

Oh yeah, as much as he'd changed over the years, there was no real doubt in my mind that this here was Dwight, all right. He still walked slightly pigeon-toed, just like I remembered, and he was still swinging his arms a little too widely at his sides. Back in high school, everybody had known to give Big Dwight a wide berth when he came striding down the hall.

I watched that familiar walk, and it occurred to me that this was probably the first time in my life I'd ever laid eyes on the guy that I hadn't been envying him a little. Wearing a plaid wool coat, blue jeans that looked brand-new, and carrying a shopping bag by the handle, Dwight for the first time in my life looked like just another guy to me. Just another guy who was a whole lot taller than me.

About halfway up the pebbled sidewalk, Dwight stopped dead in his tracks and took a long, long look around him. For a split second I was afraid I'd given myself away, but Dwight's eyes went right past me. Or, rather, right past the shrubs I was hiding behind. His eyes, instead, took in the rolling hills in the distance, the trees still in the process of losing the last of their leaves, and the sky now streaked gold by the setting sun. The guy looked at all these things, and slowly smiled.

I found myself smiling, too. Because Dwight here was looking exactly as I knew I myself had looked right after I'd gotten back in town. Those first few weeks I reckon I'd spent hours, just standing and staring. I'd been that glad to be back. Oh yeah, I knew exactly how Dwight felt.

When Dwight turned back toward the house, the smile he'd been wearing faded. I wondered if the reason he suddenly looked so somber was because inside he knew Maedean was waiting. The woman he suspected of being unfaithful. Lord knows, I knew exactly how he felt in this instance, too. Claudzilla had been kind enough to let me know, on her way out the door, that all those times I'd suspected she was running around on me, I'd been right. What a gal.

Maedean must've been watching Dwight just like I was, because the second he stepped onto the front porch, the front door swung open.

"Dwight, honey!" Maedean's voice was a trill of delight. "I'm so-o-o glad you're finally home!" Before Dwight could answer, Maedean threw herself into his arms and planted her mouth on his.

I would've liked to have believed that this was the way Maedean always greeted her husband, but somehow, I doubted it. For one thing, just before Maedean connected, I got a split-second look at Dwight's face.

He looked as if he'd been poleaxed. He even looked briefly as if he wanted to pull away, but by that time Maedean had wrapped her arms around his neck.

I blinked. This was the first time all night Maedean hadn't been carrying Poopsie. It was a good thing, of course. Poopsie would've definitely been crushed. The kiss went on and on. Long enough, in fact, for a truly uncomfortable thought to occur to me. Could Maedean be posing again?

CHAPTER 4

As Maedean continued to wildly welcome Dwight home, I continued to wonder. Could this enthusiastic greeting really be another one of Maedean's poses? Or was I just being cynical, on account of my own bad luck in the marriage department?

Hell, maybe Maedean was simply trying, in her own special way, to convince her husband that she could never be unfaithful to him. Watching the lip lock she was presently putting on Dwight, I'd say she had one powerful argument.

Besides, surely Maedean had noticed that I didn't have my camera with me when I'd walked over that last time. Surely, too, Maedean could not fail to realize that I'd not had time to make it all the way back to my truck. She had to know I wouldn't be able to document this touching moment with Dwight.

And if she knew I couldn't take her picture, didn't it logically follow that this couldn't possibly be another one of her poses? I actually felt relieved once all this occurred to me. I reckon, for Dwight's sake, I'd been sort of hoping that this little scene was for real.

Dwight must've had his own doubts, though. He was the first to break away, and when he did, I got another good look at his face. He was staring at Maedean goggle-eyed. Judging from his expression, I'd say Dwight would definitely vote with me with regard to the lead in *One Flew Over the Cuckoo's Nest*.

Dwight's eyes continued to be riveted on Maedean as she took his elbow and, more or less, pulled him inside. "I'm going to make us a real nice meal," Maedean said as she practically dragged him bodily through the front door. "Fried chicken, mashed potatoes, black-eyed peas, and biscuits—"

Maedean was reciting the supper menu a lot louder, it seemed to me, than absolutely necessary. It apparently didn't do her much good, though, because on the way inside, Dwight said, as if he was sure he couldn't possibly have heard his wife right, "You're—you're going to make *what?*"

It didn't exactly take a detective to conclude that Dwight wasn't any more used to having Maedean cook his dinner than he was to having her plant one on him the second he got home.

Standing there in the shrubs, I smiled to myself. If nothing else, my serving as a witness seemed to be encouraging Maedean to behave in ways to which old Dwight was clearly unaccustomed. The way things were going, it looked as if Dwight might very well end up getting his money's worth after all.

I took one last glance toward the Puckett front porch, to make sure that the happy couple had indeed disappeared indoors. That done, I hurried across the road to my truck. There I opened the door on the driver's side as quietly as I could, and I scooted inside.

Once I was back in my truck, my choice of activities got real limited. Not counting those few times that I briefly left my post, in order to—as my daddy used to say—answer Nature's call, I just sat there, pretty much watching the trees grow, for the next five long hours.

Nature's call was the only thing that broke the monotony.

This is the thing that all those private eye television series and Sunday mystery movies never show you. In fact, a significant part of this job often involves keeping your butt connected with the front seat of your vehicle for interminable lengths of time. Sometimes this job can be so unrelentingly boring that taking a leak starts looking like excitement.

To interrupt the tedium more than anything else, I took a couple more pictures. I knew when I snapped them, though, that they wouldn't amount to much. Maedean was not standing right next to the windows anymore, so you couldn't see her real clear. And, of course, Dwight was actually behaving like a person who didn't know he was being watched—a unique concept, if ever I heard one. Evidently, someone who is unaware that he is the subject of surveillance does not spend any time at all standing directly in front of a window. What a surprise.

I got a few shots of the Pucketts sitting down to eat at the dining room table, and later, sitting side by side watching TV in the living room. That, however, was about it. When all the lights in the Puckett house went out around eleven, I made a note of it in my notebook. Then I waited around for another hour just to make sure nobody would hear my truck start. Finally, with a thankful sigh, I headed home.

One thing about conducting a surveillance that's not a real surveillance is that you can take a break to feed your dog. This had to be one of the perks of this particular job. It could very well be the only perk, but I'd say it *was* a perk, sure as shooting. My dog Rip, oddly enough, seemed quite a bit more delighted with this perk than I was. Of course, anybody else—who didn't know Rip as well as I did—might've thought he wasn't delighted at all.

The A-frame I live in is only about five minutes from the Pucketts' front door. So in no time at all, I found myself heading up the steep hill that leads to my own home sweet home. About halfway up, I could already hear Rip carrying on.

Rip and I live in the middle of five acres of dense woods, and our driveway is so steep even Jehovah's Witnesses steer clear of it. It's, no doubt, because we get so few visitors that Rip seemed to have made up his mind a long time ago that the only barking practice he was ever going to get was when *I* showed up.

Rip was doing his full routine when I pulled up in front of the house. He was snarling and barking and dancing back and forth up there on the deck. To look at him, you might think that this is why I named him Rip. With all his antics, Rip seemed as though he'd just as soon rip my heart out as look at me. This is, believe me, far from the truth.

I named him what I did because I'd had two other puppies before Rip, both of which died when they were only months old. To this day I still have no idea why. I took them both to the vet, got them both all their shots, and still they died. When I finally got Rip,

I'd been so sure he was going to go the same way the other two had gone that I just wrote R.I.P. on his doghouse.

Rip, however, is now two years old, and other than having a few idiosyncrasies peculiarly his own, he seems to be doing just fine. Of course, one of Rip's idiosyncrasies is his bark-at-the-guy-who-lives-here routine. By the time I'd pulled in front of the house, you might've thought that in the short time I'd been gone, Rip had completely forgotten who the hell I was.

When I hit the automatic garage door opener and started to head into the garage, Rip went into full rage, baring his teeth, growling ferociously, and even slobbering some. I admit it, I was impressed. This was probably Rip's best performance in a month of Sundays. I wasn't about to let him know it, though. Lord knows, if I ever praised him for barking at me, he was liable to start doing it at all hours. Then, I'd have old Rip waking me up at three in the morning, acting as if I were a total stranger who'd somehow snuck into the house and gone to sleep in my bed, like maybe Rip had mistaken me for some kind of male Goldilocks. Oh no, I knew better than to do any praising. Even if Rip's current performance was indeed spectacular, and in competition would no doubt earn him extra points for degree of difficulty.

Instead, I said to Rip exactly what I always say as soon as I get home. "Rip! No! It's me, boy. Come on now. Hey! It's me! No! Bad dog! No! Rip, quiet! Come on, shut up!" It never does any good. Sometimes, I suspect that Rip is under the impression that any day now they're going to do a remake of *Cujo,* and he wants to make sure he'll be ready to try out.

My garage isn't attached to my house, so it always takes me a little bit of time before I head up the steps to my deck. I've got to make sure that I've turned off my headlights, that I've remembered to hit the button to lower my garage door, and that I've got everything I wanted to carry into the house. This time I grabbed up my Minolta, intending to load it with fresh film and attach a telephoto lens before I headed back to the Pucketts' place. All this time, naturally, Rip was practicing his *Cujo* performance.

The minute I placed my foot on the bottom step leading to my deck, Rip apparently felt compelled to demonstrate his versatility. He switched movies. Now that silly dog was doing *Lassie Come Home.* Only I reckon, in Rip's mind, *I* was playing the part of Lassie. Rip, on the other hand, was playing the hysterical pet owner, giddy with joy that his pet had finally returned. I had to hand it to him. If I hadn't known that he would've behaved exactly this way whether I'd been gone ten minutes or ten years, Rip's delirious tail wagging and ecstatic jumping in the air would've brought a tear to my eye.

It also didn't help to know that Rip had another very practical reason for being real glad to see me. According to the vet back in Louisville that I took him to when he was a puppy, poor Rip is psychologically damaged. Meaning, in layman's language, that he's a nut. Rip's nuttiness takes the form of being afraid, ever since he opened his eyes, to go up and down steps.

I'm not sure how he got this way. I got Rip when he was only eight weeks old. You wouldn't think he would've had time to get himself traumatized, but something must've happened to permanently scar his canine psyche. Maybe his mom used to carry him up and down steps, bumping his head on every step as she went. Or maybe heights make him feel a lot like he's about to do a Thelma and Louise into the abyss. Whatever the reason, old Rip steadfastly refuses to go up or down any stairs.

Being as how the A-frame we live in is surrounded by a large deck, Rip's total lack of stair-climbing ability is no small problem. The only way you can get off my deck is to go down steps, unless you want to hazard a twelve-foot jump to the ground—the prospect of which, I believe, scares Rip even more than stairs.

I reckon what I should've said earlier was that Rip's stair-climbing inability is no small problem for *me*. Because I, of course, am the one who several times a day carries him off my deck and into my side yard—so that Rip can do his business there instead of doing to my deck what Poopsie had done earlier to my magazines.

I'll admit, when Rip was still a puppy, I thought having to pick up that little, roly-poly fur ball and carry him downstairs was real cute. Back then, though, I hadn't exactly thought the entire thing through. Today that dog has got to weigh all of sixty-five pounds. Picking him up is a lot like hoisting a huge sack of potatoes. A huge sack of *squirming* potatoes trying to lick your face.

Now, as I approached the top of the steps, Rip— just like always—scooted as close to the edge of the steps as he dared. There, he gave me pretty much the same look I'd seen on Maedean's face when she opened the front door and saw Dwight standing there. I stared at Rip. If he tried to put a lip lock on me when I picked him up, there was a good chance I might not ever pick him up again.

As it turned out, I didn't have to worry. Rip's attention was pretty much elsewhere. In fact, he'd actually started doing this unbelievably pathetic whine by the time I'd gotten him to the side yard. The whine seemed to be saying, "Good God, man! Do you have any idea how long you've been *gone?* I'm desperate here! *Move your ass!*" It's this kind of tender moment that pretty much cements Rip's and my relationship. That and, oh yes, his total dependence on me for food.

After I'd carried him back up to my deck, Rip followed me inside and started doing an even more pathetic whine while I opened a couple cans of dog food and dumped them into his bowl. Rip's whine was, once again, easy to interpret. "I've given you the best years of my life, and *this* is how you treat me? I'm damn near *starvation,* but do you care? Oh *no*—" Sometimes, Rip reminds me a whole lot of Claudzilla. Only Rip isn't quite as hard on my credit cards.

After I made myself a quick ham sandwich, gulping it down with an even quicker Pepsi, I was tempted to crawl into bed and grab a little shut-eye. I knew, however, that if I did Maedean would no doubt wake up and discover that her fifteen hundred smackers were not going as far as she'd expected.

So, instead of the nap, I took a shower, changed into a fresh shirt and jeans, and headed back into the kitchen to fix me some surveillance snacks. I've got one of those insulated coolers—the kind folks generally take on picnics, only mine is small enough to sit on the seat beside me in my truck. I packed it to the brim with ham and cheese sandwiches, Pepsi, potato chips, Fritos, M&M's, and Oreos—all the things no detective conducting an all-day stakeout should be without. I carried the cooler out to my truck, grunting pretty good on account of that thing now had to weigh almost as much as Rip.

My surveillance snacks taken care of, I grabbed my fleece-lined denim jacket and carried Rip, whining his head off, out to the side yard. Ignoring his whines, I filled his bowls with water and dry food, and I headed back to the Pucketts.

When I left, Rip whined louder than ever. I would've liked to have believed that he was doing this because he truly hated to see me go. I was pretty sure, however, that the main reason for his dismay was that Rip knew it was bedtime, for God's sake. And bedtime to Rip meant that he was supposed to be lying at the foot of my bed, all warm and cozy, sawing logs.

Sleeping outside *under* the stars was not Rip's idea of four-star accommodations. What's more, even though he had his very own redwood dog house in the side yard—complete with shingled roof and wall-to-wall layers of blankets, that I built with my own hands, mind you—Rip rarely went into the thing.

I guess this was something else I should've thought through. I mean, it's a bad sign if, the entire time you're building your dog a dog house, he's sitting by your back steps, waiting for you to get done and carry him indoors.

Naturally, the very day I finished his house, I'd ended up letting Rip sleep inside, just like always. In my living room, he'd outdone himself that night, licking my face and wagging his tail. I realize now, of course, that he was just trying to tell me how pleased he was that I'd finally built me a little place of my own so that he could have the big house all to himself.

I guess I'd known then that I wasn't going to win this one. Tonight, in fact, I would've left Rip inside except that I had no idea how long I was going to be gone. If Rip had been desperate when I'd gotten home tonight, there was no telling how hysterical he'd be by the time I showed up tomorrow.

Rip's whine had grown to a piteous yowl by the time I was halfway down my driveway. He seemed to be saying, "Hey, you're not leaving me out here in the *wilderness,* are you? *Hey!* It's *damn* cold out here!"

If I had not been outside myself, Rip might've convinced me. I could tell, however, that Kentucky's roller-coaster weather had already started on yet another upswing. It didn't feel as if we'd even be getting any frost overnight.

The way Rip was carrying on, however, you'd think all of Kentucky should immediately start watching for a glacier to slide by. I hated to hear Rip this upset, so right away I did something about it. I turned on the radio. Loud. I know. I'm mean. I kept the radio going until I turned into Maedean's driveway. It was a good thing, too. I was pretty sure, without back-to-back golden oldies blasting in my ear, I might've nodded off on the way.

I did nod off once I was hidden again among the overhanging branches across from the Puckett front door. I do want to make clear, however, that this is *not* the sort of thing that usually happens when I'm conducting a surveillance. Knowing, however, that the person under surveillance in this case already knew that I was there pretty much took away any incentive I might've had otherwise to keep my eyes open. Even still, I was a little surprised the next morning to find that I'd actually been asleep. On a stakeout, for God's sake. I was also a little surprised to be awakened by Dwight starting up his BMW.

It took me a second to realize where the hell I was. Right after I realized that, though, I realized something else. Trucks are not meant to be slept in. When I moved, everything ached. Apparently, in my sleep I'd tried to get into a more comfortable position and failed miserably. My left leg was jammed diagonally under the dashboard, and my right leg was wedged between the cooler and the back of the seat next to me.

It was hard to figure out how I'd contorted myself into such a position, and it was going to take some doing to get out of it. While I was trying to get my legs back to where they belonged—under the steering wheel within actual reach of the pedals—I watched Dwight turn his BMW around and head back down the driveway.

I checked my watch, still feeling disoriented the way you do when you've been awakened too suddenly. Eight-thirty. Most stores around these parts aren't open this early. If Dwight was off on another shopping trip, the store he was headed to must be quite some distance away. It also must be having a sale or something. He kicked up gravel and clouds of dust as he roared away.

The way he was careening down the road could give you the idea he couldn't get away fast enough. It could also make you think that fifteen hundred dollars' worth of surveillance might not be enough to get Dwight in a good mood. Could it be that, when it came to getting her marriage back on track, Maedean was beating a dead horse?

I didn't have much time to think about that one,

though. Right away Maedean appeared, carrying Poopsie as usual. She was wearing her cashmere coat again, but she hadn't buttoned it. So that you could see that she was also wearing a bright yellow sweater and skintight blue jeans. The silver tips on the toes of her cowboy boots sparkled in the early morning light as she walked purposely toward her Corvette.

If Dwight had been in some kind of snit, you couldn't tell it by looking at Maedean. She was smiling and kissing the top of Poopsie's head as she went.

She waggled her fingers in my direction as she got in. I did not waggle my fingers back. I would've liked to have said that I didn't because I was trying to maintain some semblance of dignity. The truth was, I knew she couldn't see my fingers waggle through the overhanging branches, so why bother?

I started my truck and pulled out in back of Maedean.

For the next eight hours—how do I put this—the excitement never stopped. First, I was treated to the thrill of watching Maedean get her hair done. Snapping several shots using my telephoto lens, making several entries in my notebook, and munching surveillance snacks, I documented how Maedean, even when she was having her hair done, continued to hold Poopsie on her lap.

I also documented how Poopsie continued to growl at Ruta Lippton, the sole proprietor of the Curl Crazee Beauty Salon. The dog also snapped at her every time Ruta got within snapping range. I knew Ruta pretty well, being as how she was a victim in one of those strange burglaries I'd mentioned earlier. When all that had been going on, Ruta had never struck me as a particularly tolerant sort, and once again she demonstrated it.

While Maedean was getting her hair shampooed, leaning all the way back with her eyes shut—so that Ruta knew Maedean couldn't see—Ruta stuck her tongue out at Poopsie. I did not snap that picture, however. It seemed like information Maedean didn't really need to know. When Ruta did what she did, Poopsie didn't look the least bit offended, but it evidently did a world of good for Ruta. She was still smiling when Maedean walked out of the Curl Crazee two hours later, her coif completely, I suppose, re-coiffed. Personally, I couldn't tell the difference between Maedean pre-Curl Crazee and Maedean post-Curl Crazee.

After watching Maedean get her hair done, I was treated to an even bigger thrill—watching Poopsie get *his* hair done. Poopsie did his best to liven things up—by trying to bite the hand of the one who shampooed him. The pictures I took with my telephoto through the front picture window were certainly a tad more interesting than the ones I'd shot at the Curl Crazee. Mostly because I caught the woman who was sudsing up old Poopsie actually screaming a couple of times as she snatched her hand away from Poopsie's tiny, pointed teeth.

For all his snarling and snapping, Poopsie came out of the place, looking downright smug. He also looked like a brown mop that had been inadvertently put through the fluff cycle on a dryer, but from the way he was holding his head, he seemed to be looking down his nose on the rest of the unkempt animal kingdom.

Poopsie's sudden boost in self-esteem might've had

something to do with the way Maedean was cooing to him, burying her face in his fur, "Oh, Poopsie, sweetie pie, you look so-o-o handsome." My reaction to that little display could be summed up in two words: *Gag me*.

After that, the excitement pretty much continued as I watched Maedean have a leisurely lunch at Lassiter's, the only restaurant in downtown Pigeon Fork. I, of course, had my own lunch, right out of the old surveillance cooler. I then watched Maedean drop off several dresses at the dry cleaners located directly across from Pigeon Fork High. And then, fighting yawns and downing Pepsis to stay awake, I watched Maedean stop in at several yard sales displaying a whole lot of what my daddy used to call Arts and Crap.

Arts and Crap generally consists of things folks around these parts have made by hand—things like pot holders in the shape of ducks, refrigerator magnets in the shape of pigs, and toaster covers in the shape of chickens. Farm animals, for some reason, seem to be a recurring theme in the local Arts and Crap industry. Frankly, I myself wouldn't have given a plug nickel for any of it. Judging, however, from the bulging sacks that Maedean carried back to her car, Maedean had given quite a bit more than a nickel.

I wrote down every stop in my notebook, recording the time and location—more to have something to do than anything else.

Once Maedean had loaded up on Arts and Crap, she headed toward downtown Pigeon Fork. Following Main Street right through the middle of town, Maedean's Corvette started picking up speed once she passed Lassiter's Restaurant.

I might've lost Maedean except that after she got to Highway 11, the road stretched out straight ahead of us. I could still see her whether she was just one or all of five miles ahead.

Ten minutes later, Maedean made a sharp right-hand turn into a long driveway that wound through some trees, and ended up in front of a large, two-story log cabin.

You see a lot of log cabins here in Crayton County. Mostly, they've been built from kits. I myself have always found the whole cabin-kit concept a little too much like trying to build yourself a home from Lincoln Logs. Apparently, though, quite a few folks around these parts don't find this idea as daunting as I do.

This particular log cabin I was pretty sure I'd seen advertised in the back of one of those *Home Ideas* magazines up at Stop & Shop grocery. Bigger than most with a low front porch stretching across the front and a massive creek-stone fireplace covering most of the left side, it managed to look both rustic and modern at the same time.

I'd been afraid when Maedean turned into the long driveway that anybody could see me following her, but as it turned out, everybody there was already inside when we pulled up in front. I was also afraid my truck would stick out like a sore thumb, but I was wrong about that, too. There were about twenty cars and trucks, parked here and there around the cabin. I pulled my own truck between a red Chevy pickup and a stand of evergreens, and, turning off my engine, tried to decide what in the world had brought all these folks out here on a Monday night.

Prayer meetings are usually held on Wednesday

nights, so that pretty much eliminated that. Generally, showers and birthday parties are held on weekends, so those were probably out, too. I reckon I could've asked Maedean, but she was still in the process of parking her Corvette, trying to sandwich it between a Toyota pickup and a Ford Ranger. I sort of hated to distract her while she was busy.

I looked through my telephoto into the cabin's windows, and realized that there didn't seem to be anybody inside but women. For a second I thought I was looking at a Tupperware party. And yet the women were sitting in groups of four at several card tables. Some of them were rolling dice. All of them were holding cards—and drinks.

As I watched, a tall woman with dark brown hair pulled back into a bun at the nape of her neck, walked into the living room, carrying a tray of crackers. Each cracker had pink stuff or green stuff dabbed on top. These were, of course, what my secretary, Melba, often calls can-apes." That's "can," as in Campbell's soup can. And "apes," as in *Planet of the*. I've never quite had the courage to tell Melba how canapés is really pronounced.

The lady with Melba's can-apes extended the tray toward four women sitting at a table very close to the front window. When the can-ape lady did this, I could clearly read her apron. It said, *Bunko Squad.*

I knew then, of course, what this little gathering had to be. A bunko party. That's right. Bunko. It sounds like something you could possibly get arrested for, but in actuality, bunko is a game played by a large portion of the female population in this part of the country. Going to a bunko party is a lot like going to a bridge party, only bunko does not require the kind of attention span you might need for bridge. To play bunko, I've been told, you don't even need to know the rules.

I myself have never been to a bunko party, being as how men are pretty much never invited to these things. I've also been told that the reason men aren't welcome is that men are often the main topic of conversation.

I've been told all these things by Melba, who is a bunko artist. In more ways than one, I believe. According to Melba, the rules of bunko are deliberately kept mind-numbingly simple so that the game will, in no way, interfere with the real reason bunko parties are held. Which is, of course, to drink great quantities of alcohol, to trash men, and to catch up on the latest gossip.

By the time Maedean finally got her Corvette parked, it was about six-thirty. As best as I could tell, looking through my telephoto, the bunko party seemed to be in full swing. Maedean must've known she was late, because she grabbed up Poopsie and ran inside, without waggling her fingers at me once. Thank God, I might add. In all honesty, I don't believe I'd ever been so tired of watching a person's fingers waggle.

For the next six—yes, I said *six*—long hours I sat there, looking through one of the cabin's front windows through my telephoto. At least most of the time I was looking through the telephoto. A couple times I put the thing down to rest my arms. And to make another notation in my notebook. Notations that, after a while, went like this: *9:30 P.M. Subject and dog still at bunko party.*

I didn't always watch Maedean through the telephoto, because even with just the naked eye, it wasn't hard to spot the blond in the yellow sweater, holding the little brown dog.

Once again, there wasn't a thing for me to do, except sit.

And sit.

And sit some more.

Shortly after eight, I was so bored that to break the monotony, I started taking pictures. Just as if what Maedean was doing actually warranted recording. Over the next few hours, I must've snapped about ten shots or so. Mainly so that the clicking of the camera would keep me awake. And, yes, to feel as if Maedean—and Dwight, too, for that matter—were getting something for her money.

The bunko party started breaking up a little after midnight. After five or six females had come out the door, Maedean herself finally showed up, holding Poopsie as usual. She said her good-byes and then headed for her car. I pulled around the red Chevy, and hit the road right in back of her. This time I didn't lose her once. Of course, knowing where she was headed helped some. We got to the Puckett farm about twenty minutes later, and then—just as if I was on a routine surveillance—I pulled out my little 3×5 notebook again, to make yet another boring entry. Maedean was headed up the sidewalk, clutching Poopsie to her chest, as I began writing: *1:15 A.M. Subject arrived at residence.*

It had gotten quite a bit colder, but Maedean didn't seem to be in any hurry to get indoors. Dwight's BMW was parked in the same place it had been parked the night before, so Dwight was obviously home. And yet, Maedean didn't seem anywhere near as eager to see him tonight as she'd been the night before.

I'd finished my entire entry by the time Maedean wandered up to her front door. As Maedean was slowly turning her key in the lock, I started idly wondering how old Rip was doing. Surely, Rip had been able to bring himself to go into his doghouse by now.

My eyes fell again on my notebook, and stifling a yawn, I'd been about to add, in the interest of being thorough, *Subject was alone, except for Poopsie.* I didn't get the chance, though. I'd only written, *Subject was* . . . And then Maedean started to scream.

CHAPTER 5

When Maedean started screaming, I must've jumped a foot, dropping both my pen and my notebook. I didn't stop to pick them up, though. My pen was still bouncing off the floor of my truck as I flung open the door on the driver's side, and started running as fast as I could toward the house. Maedean was still screaming, standing just a couple steps inside her own front door, clutching Poopsie to her chest. Her back was to me, but Maedean seemed to be staring at something on her left.

As I recalled from my earlier visits, the foyer opened into the living room on the left. Evidently, whatever it was that was making Maedean scream was in there.

My heart started doing a dull thud.

I tried to pick up speed, cutting across the driveway, but it seemed suddenly as if my legs had grown unnaturally heavy. It seemed to take all the strength I had to move one and then the other.

It felt like an eternity before I finally crossed the driveway and got to the pebble walk. Once I got there, I was only about twenty feet from Maedean, and yet somehow she still seemed miles away. Even her screams seemed to be coming from somewhere a long, long way off.

It flashed through my mind as I continued to run toward her, that maybe Maedean was just reacting to a little memento Poopsie had left in the middle of her living room. That could be it, couldn't it? A little memento Maedean hadn't noticed on her way out this morning? I hoped this was true, but I had to admit, the odds didn't look good. For one thing, Poopsie also seemed to be reacting now to the same thing that was making his mistress scream. The dog had started to growl a little, staring fixedly into the living room. It seemed unlikely that old Poops would be growling at an error of his own making. Lord knows, he hadn't seemed to mind at all the error he'd left earlier on the magazines in my office. If anything, he'd seemed proud.

I was almost up to Maedean now, and she'd apparently run fresh out of screams. She was just standing there, her eyes still riveted to whatever it was in her living room. Maedean's body apparently was riveted, too. She didn't budge when I tried to get past her. I actually had to shove her a little to one side so that I could get a good look at the thing she couldn't seem to pull her eyes away from.

When I finally saw what it was, my breath caught in my throat. It was, oh God, *Dwight.*

He was lying on his back on the hardwood floor, arms askew, one leg crumpled under the other in a position that would've been painful had Dwight been able to feel it. Dwight, however, looked pretty much beyond feeling anything. His eyes were fixed and staring, his mouth was slightly open, and his skin looked like pale yellow wax. With his arms spread out like that, you couldn't miss the ugly red smear staining the front of his denim shirt.

For a split second, I froze. And I just stared at him, with my throat hurting real bad. This was the guy I'd envied in high school. The guy who only yesterday had looked so happy to be back home.

I started moving again. I ran straight to Dwight's side, dropped to my knees, and started frantically feeling for a pulse in his throat.

Nothing. Not even a flicker. In fact, as soon as I touched him, I knew there wasn't anything that could be done for him. Poor Dwight felt as if he'd recently spent some time on that glacier Rip had been whining about earlier.

"Is he—? Is he—?" Maedean couldn't seem to bring herself to say the word out loud.

I guess I couldn't, either. I just looked at her and nodded. In fact, my best guess was that poor Dwight had been dead for hours. My throat was killing me, but I managed to say, "I'm real sorry, Maedean."

I wasn't at all sure Maedean even heard me. The moment I'd nodded, she'd begun screaming again with renewed energy.

I'd been under the impression, as I mentioned before, that Maedean had pretty much run out of screams. So I wasn't any more prepared for this latest onslaught than I'd been for the first. When Maedean let loose, I must've jumped a foot all over again.

Clutched tightly against Maedean's chest, Poopsie evidently hadn't been prepared, either. The little dog gave a start, and would've leaped right out of Mae-dean's arms, except that Maedean—in the middle of her screaming—grabbed at the animal as if it were some kind of fluffy life preserver.

While Maedean was pretty much occupied, not only continuing her wailing but also hanging onto the still-struggling Poopsie, I turned back to Dwight. This close, I could see that there was an ugly, dark hole smack dab in the middle of the red smear on his shirt. It wasn't hard to figure out what had happened. I'd seen wounds like this one before.

Dwight had been shot.

What's more, it looked to me as if whoever had shot him had terrific aim. Dwight's killer appeared to have gotten him right in the heart. I stared dully at that awful wound.

And, then, I found myself staring at something else. There was a handkerchief in Dwight's right hand. Dwight wasn't exactly gripping the thing, of course. In death his hand had relaxed. So the hanky was more or less just lying on top of his open palm. Still, it looked as if Dwight might've been holding the hand-kerchief when he'd breathed his last.

It also looked as if maybe Dwight had gone to some effort to get hold of the thing. There was a trail of blood across the floor. The kind of trail that might've been made if Dwight, after he was shot, had dragged himself a ways to reach it.

Lord. Had Dwight really pulled himself across the room, bleeding, in order to get a *handkerchief?* But why? Surely, if you've got a hole in your chest, you wouldn't be all that concerned about the sniffles. Of course, maybe he'd been intending to use the thing to press against his wound, to try to stop the bleeding.

Then again, Dwight had ended up lying right in front of a table that held a phone. This particular phone was, of all things, a Mickey Mouse phone—one of those large, colorful, plastic figures where Mickey appears to be holding the receiver for you.

Mickey's happy grin was downright disconcerting as several more questions chased themselves through my mind. Had the poor guy used his last ounce of strength in a vain attempt to phone for help? This *was* what it looked like. Judging from the position of his body, it looked as if Dwight might've tried to pull himself up, leaning against the table, and then collapsed. That could easily have been how he'd finally ended up on the floor on his back. And yet if he'd just been going for the phone, what was he doing with a handkerchief in his hand? Was he already holding it when he was shot? Lord. Had the gunman pulled the trigger while Dwight had been blowing his nose? Somehow, that seemed even more cruel than just plain shooting him.

I was standing there right by the phone, so all I had to do was let Mickey hand the receiver to me. I knew, of course, that I should be calling 911 right this minute. And yet before I made that call, I just wanted to take one real good look at Dwight's handkerchief. I took a few steps closer to Dwight, leaned over, and peered at the thing.

Now I could see that the handkerchief was linen, and that it had a narrow band of crocheted lace all around the edge. Not exactly the sort of handkerchief an ex-jock would carry.

I moved even closer. There *was* another possible scenario—that Dwight had known from the beginning that he only had a few seconds left. Realizing this, he'd dragged himself to the table, not because of the phone, but because he knew *that's* where this particular handkerchief was.

Had Dwight been trying to leave a clue to his killer's identity?

I bent to peer at the hanky even closer, and that's when I saw them. There were *initials* embroidered on one corner of the handkerchief. In a silky white thread, stitched on a white linen cloth, they didn't exactly jump out at you. Once you saw them, though, they were unmistakable.

The initials were plain as day—*M.P.*

My mouth went dry. It didn't exactly take a detective to figure this one out. Now, let me see, whose name could those initials possibly stand for? I turned slowly to stare at Maedean.

At that moment, she'd given up on her screaming, and was gazing heavenward, wailing, "Why, God? *Why?* What did my wonderful, wonderful, wonderful Dwight do to deserve *this?*" Maedean sounded so genuinely heartbroken that I felt kind of bad for even thinking for a split second that she might somehow have been involved in her husband's death. *I'm probably leaping to conclusions here,* I actually told myself. *After all, there's got to be a ton of people in the world with the initials M.P., doesn't there?* Talk about your blind optimism.

I even went on to think, *I mean, just because Maedean Puckett happens to have a name with those exact same initials doesn't necessarily mean that this is her handkerchief, does it?*

I might've actually continued following this moronic train of thought, except that Maedean herself kindly cleared the whole thing up for me. Right after she finished wailing, "Why? Why? *Why?*" she dropped her gaze. And apparently at that moment laid eyes on what Dwight had in his hand for the first time.

Maedean actually staggered backward for a moment, as if she'd been struck. "Oh, my God!" she yelled. From the way Poopsie shuddered, I believe she yelled this directly into the dog's right ear. "That's *my* hanky!" She pointed with her free hand. "Right there in Dwight's hand!"

I started to ask Maedean if she was sure, but she thoughtfully cleared *that* one up for me, too—before I could even open my mouth. "Those are my initials right there on the corner!" she said. Staring wild-eyed at me, Maedean managed to sound even more upset than she had before. Which was going some. "Oh, my Gawd!"

Poopsie had evidently gotten real tired of being yelled at. He whined some, and then lowered his fluffy head until it was almost between his paws. I think he would've put his paws over his ears if he'd only known how.

With Poopsie lying low, Maedean turned to me. Pointing at the handkerchief with a trembling forefinger, she said, "Haskell, my hanky being right there could make somebody think *I* had done this!"

I just looked at her.

She did have a point.

Except, of course, for one tiny, little thing. I *had* been personally watching her all day long. While pulling a trigger did only take a few seconds, driving here from any of the places Maedean had been today would've taken, at the very least, several minutes. I was pretty sure that Maedean hadn't been out of my sight long enough to swat a fly, let alone get all the way home and shoot a gun.

I was also pretty sure that had Maedean disappeared for several minutes at any time during the day, I would've noticed.

"Maedean," I said, "don't forget, I've been watching you all—"

Maedean was not listening to me. Instead, she was starting to pace, her high heels making little explosions on the hardwood floor. "How could something like this have happened? How could it? *How?*"

For some strange reason, I actually thought—being as how his body was lying right there in front of us—that Maedean was talking about the unfortunate murder of poor Dwight. I started to say, "Maedean, I can't tell you how sorry I—"

Maedean cut me off. Clutching Poopsie so tight to the front of her cashmere coat that his little black beady eyes seemed to bug out a little, she said, "How on earth could *my* handkerchief have ended up in Dwight's *hand?*"

I stared at her.

Maedean had stopped pacing, and was now pulling a cigarette case out of her coat pocket. Extracting one, she managed to light it without even singeing Poopsie. She also managed to light it even though her hands were trembling—bad. It was a tad disturbing that my client now seemed significantly more upset about the current condition of her handkerchief than the current condition of her husband.

Call me what Maedean had indeed called me earlier. Picky, picky, picky.

"Where did you leave your handkerchief last?" It seemed like the obvious question to ask.

Maedean looked at me as if I'd just asked her the current location of Jimmy Hoffa.

"Now, how would I know?" she said. Her tone had turned testy. She took a long drag off her cigarette, and exhaled a cloud of smoke directly over Poopsie's head. From where I stood, it looked like the dog's ears were smoldering.

"I suppose I could've left my hanky on that table"—Maedean pointed her cigarette at the table next to Dwight's body—"but I sure don't remember doing it. I might also have left it on my dresser upstairs, or in one of my jacket pockets, or even on the couch. I tell you, I don't remember." What can I say? Maedean would've made the perfect witness at a Senate hearing.

"You don't have *any* idea where you—"

Once again Maedean didn't let me finish. "Do you know how this looks?" Maedean's eyes were getting wild again. "It looks as if Dwight is pointing the finger at *me!*"

I stared at her again. Maedean, who only moments ago had seemed near hysterics after finding Dwight's body, now appeared to be handling her grief remarkably well—oddly enough.

In fact, she no longer appeared to be grieving at all. What she appeared to be doing was fuming. Eyes flashing, mouth pinched, Maedean took another drag off her cigarette and snapped, "The nerve of that man!"

I guess all this was such a surprising turn of events that I was having a little trouble digesting it all. "What man?" I said.

Maedean gave me the sort of annoyed look a teacher might give to a student who'd fallen asleep in class. "Dwight, of course!" she snapped. "I mean, it's pretty obvious what's happened here, isn't it? Dwight went and got my hanky just to get me in trouble!"

The woman actually said this with Dwight lying on the floor not five feet away. It seemed to me, in the race for who was in the most trouble, Dwight clearly had the edge. I did not, however, point this out to Maedean.

I also did not tell her, as I looked back over at that awful chest wound, that I found it hard to believe that Dwight had the strength to do *anything* after he'd been shot. It was difficult to believe, in fact, that he'd moved at all. Unless, of course, you counted his abrupt drop to the floor.

Maedean's voice had turned petulant. "What a mean, mean, *mean* thing for Dwight to do!"

I blinked at that one. This was an abrupt about-face. Whatever happened to Dwight being wonderful, wonderful, *wonderful?* Correct me if I'm wrong, but wasn't this the guy that Maedean cared so much about that she was willing to spend a good chunk of change in order to document just how faithful she was being to him?

Not to mention, Maedean seemed to be overlooking a distinct possibility. "Maedean," I said, "your hanky could've been *put* in Dwight's hand, you know. By whoever it was who—"

Once again Maedean interrupted. She took another long drag, gave her blond hair a toss, and said, "Oh no, it was Dwight, all right. It's just like him to do something like this to me. He could be *so* cruel!" She started pacing again.

I couldn't help staring at her. The woman seemed clearly to be overlooking the fact that, no matter what she thought Dwight might be doing to *her,* he himself was absolutely, positively dead—a thing that had to be a real inconvenience on Dwight's part. In fact, it appeared to me that, of the two of them, Dwight had significantly more to be angry about. I wasn't about to mention it to Maedean, but the phrase *totally self-centered* did spring to mind.

Maedean must've noticed the way I was looking at her, because she lifted her Jay Leno chin defensively. "Oh, you needn't give me that holier-than-thou look! *You* didn't live with him. Believe me, Dwight could be *such* an asshole!"

I was beginning to hope that the grieving widow would not be called upon to say a few words at the funeral, or, indeed, to suggest anything to be engraved on the headstone.

Maedean was now pacing, holding Poopsie with one hand and wildly gesturing with the hand holding the cigarette. "God Almighty, I knew Dwight was always in a snit about *something,* but I never—"

I'd pretty much heard enough. I turned my back on Maedean, went over and took the receiver out of Mickey Mouse's hand.

Maedean was hurrying on, "—No, I *never* thought Dwight would carry a grudge this far!"

This last got my attention. I gave the receiver back to Mickey, and turned back toward Maedean. "Grudge?" I said. "What kind of grudge would Dwight have against you?"

Maedean took a moment before she answered. She covered it by taking a drag off her cigarette, but she was clearly taking the time to think. "Well," she finally said, "it wasn't anything really. Just little stuff like, uh, the way I, uh, did his laundry. *That* kind of thing."

I nodded, as if I bought it, but to tell you the truth— which I was pretty sure Maedean herself was *not* doing—I was thinking: She'd taken some time, and *this* was the best she could come up with? Apparently, I'd been right on the money earlier. Poopsie *was* smarter than his mistress.

Maedean now squared her shoulders and pointed her cigarette at me. "Well, Haskell, now that you know that Dwight's trying to frame me, I guess you also know what you've got to do!"

I just looked at her. Dwight didn't appear to be open for discussion on the subject, so what exactly did she think could be done at this point?

Maedean was nodding her blond head emphatically. "You've got to stop him!"

I may have been wrong, but it appeared to me that, no matter what Dwight might've been up to, he'd already been stopped.

"Well?" Maedean said.

"Well, what?" I said. What did she think were my options? Did she expect me to take out a restraining order? Somehow I got the feeling that Dwight would comply with it.

Maedean's voice was getting shrill. "Well, you've got to get me my hanky, *that's* what! We can't leave the damn thing in his hand! Everybody will be jumping to terrible conclusions!"

I'd already said it once, but I thought it bore repeating. "Maedean, you seem to be forgetting that I was watching you all—"

Maedean waved her hand as if what I was saying was insignificant. "Look, Haskell, you're still working for me, remember? And I'm telling you to get me my handkerchief!"

I stayed right where I was. Mainly because I was certain my job description did not include tampering with a crime scene. "Maedean," I said, and I believe I was demonstrating quite a bit of patience here, "we've got to leave everything just as it is. Understand? The sheriff won't look any too kindly on us messing with evidence."

Maedean glared at me. *"Evidence?* This isn't evidence! You know I couldn't have done this! You said so yourself—you were watching me all day!"

I blinked at that. So she had been paying attention, after all.

Maedean was now pointing Poopsie's nose in my direction. "Besides, Haskell, we're not going to *tell* the sheriff what we did." Her tone implied I should've known this without her having to mention it. "So get me that handkerchief. Now!"

She could've been giving orders to Poopsie. You know, something on the order of: *Haskell, fetch!*

I thought I'd demonstrate just how badly trained I was. I didn't move a muscle. "Maedean," I said, "what you're asking me to do is called obstruction of justice. People go to jail for that sort of thing."

Maedean stopped pacing and just looked at me.

"Then, I'm going to have to do it myself?" Her voice was so quiet that even Poopsie seemed to pick up on it. He began to move restlessly in her arms. "Is *that* what you're telling me? I'm going to have to actually touch Dwight and get my handkerchief *myself?"*

From the expression of distaste on Maedean's face, I believe I could assume that Maedean found the prospect of making any kind of contact with Dwight in his present condition to be particularly repugnant.

I shook my head. "No, you're not." Relief washed over Maedean's face. Until I went on, *"Nobody's* touching anything until the police get here." I turned and moved toward Mickey, intending to phone 911 before another second passed.

I'd say Maedean's reaction to all this was mixed. First, the relief on her face was rapidly replaced with cold fury. She cleared her throat, closed her eyes as if steeling herself, and then she started toward Dwight with an air of grim determination. "If you don't have the guts to get the damn thing, I guess I'll have to!"

I reckon there was still enough of the cop in me that I couldn't stand idly by and let her compromise a crime scene. I gave up on going for the phone, turned, and when Maedean started to go by me, I reached out and grabbed her arm.

This, I immediately found out, was a mistake.

Poopsie let out a growl, and went for my hand faster than that white shark went for the swimmers in all those *Jaws* movies.

Poopsie's tiny white teeth might even have been sharper than that shark's. Fortunately, however, he missed bare skin and instead chomped down on the cuff of my denim coat. While Poopsie tore at my cuff, I let go of Maedean's arm. Poopsie, however, did not let go of me. Not even when I lifted my arm until he was more or less dangling from my wrist like some kind of furry watch fob.

"Don't you hurt *him!*" Can you believe that this was what Maedean actually said? To *me?* "Don't you hurt my sweet baby dog!"

Her sweet baby dog was at that moment snarling and drooling down my sleeve.

Maedean rushed toward me, pried Poopsie off my cuff, and then glared at me. "I'm going to report you to the cruelty to animals people!"

I met her glare head-on. "I'm going to report *you*

to the police—if you so much as take one more step toward that handkerchief."

That pretty much took the wind out of Maedean's sails. She made a good show of it, though. She gave her hair another toss, threw me a defiant glare, and stalked across the living room, and on out into the foyer. On the way she told Poopsie what a "brave, brave, *brave*" dog he was.

Like I said, it was a good show. But I knew that's all it was. Just before Maedean had glared at me, I'd seen something in her eyes—something that was pretty much unmistakable.

Fear.

So, the question was, what was Maedean afraid of? If I'd been watching her all day, and there was no way she could've done this, then, why was she so insistent that we remove her handkerchief?

I stared at her, my stomach starting to hurt real bad. Was it possible that Maedean had hired somebody to do away with her husband? Was that why she wanted to make sure that nothing at the crime scene pointed in her direction?

I turned back toward Mickey Mouse, intending to finally make that 911 call. As soon as I moved, Maedean did, too. When she got to the doorway, she stopped and said, "Uh, Haskell, since you're still working for me, whatever we talk about is still confidential, isn't it?"

I was pretty sure she had the client/private eye relationship confused with the client/*attorney* relationship. Not to mention, since the job she'd hired me to do entailed snapping photographs to show to a man who was no longer capable of looking at them, I'd say my employment was pretty much over.

Maedean apparently didn't exactly see it that way. "I mean," she was going on, "you're still a *private* detective, aren't you? So, we don't have a problem, do we?"

That one made me gulp a little. Lord. She didn't consider a dead husband a *problem?*

Or—and this was a terrible thought—had Dwight's death *solved* all Maedean's problems? My stomach was starting to feel as if somebody had just tossed down a few burning rocks.

Maedean was still petting Poopsie, still smoking, and still glaring at me. "I asked you a question, Haskell, and I expect an answer. Are you a *private* detective, or what?"

I didn't answer. Instead, I took the receiver out of Mickey Mouse's hand, turned my back on Maedean, and started dialing 911. While Mickey grinned at me, I requested an ambulance. I also mentioned that maybe the coroner ought to drop by, too.

All the time I was talking on the phone, I'm not sure what Maedean was doing. I reckon she was just standing out there in the foyer, holding Poopsie and trying to endanger my health with secondhand smoke. Being as how I'd suddenly gotten pretty sick of the sight of her, though, I didn't look.

Having made two phone calls, I decided I ought to make one more. Although I knew that the 911 operator would notify Sheriff Vergil Minrath, too, I thought it might be a good idea if old Verg heard it from me before he heard it from anybody else.

I decided this, because Vergil's nose has been a tad out of joint ever since I moved back in town. The sheriff actually seems to be under the impression that

I've come back to Pigeon Fork just to show him how criminal investigation is done in the big city.

Being as how Vergil is so sensitive and all, it would not be a good thing if Vergil ever got the notion that I was not letting him know pretty quick about any crimes I run across. I wasn't sure what he'd do, but I knew it wouldn't be pretty.

Besides, I didn't want to upset Vergil any more than he already was. Vergil, you see, is what I suppose you'd call a friend of the family. He was my dad's best friend as far back as I could remember, and he'd no doubt still be Dad's best friend today if my dad were still alive.

Unfortunately, my dad died some nine years ago. Just a year, in fact, after my mom passed away from cancer. Back then Vergil and I had both agreed—Dad had died from grief. With both my mom and my dad gone, old Verg is just about the closest thing I've got left to a parent. I reckon I owed him a personal phone call.

It was almost one in the morning, so naturally, I dialed Vergil at home. The 911 operator hadn't beat me to the call yet, because Vergil was obviously still asleep when he answered. "Whuf?"

That, I'm pretty sure, is exactly what Vergil said.

What *I* said was, "Vergil?"

That was all I got out. Vergil, being the true family friend that he is, greeted me with the kind of warmth you'd expect from somebody you think of as a third parent.

"Oh, God, no," Vergil said.

93

CHAPTER 6

Vergil's response over the phone didn't sound real promising, but I was hoping that maybe Vergil had my voice mixed up with somebody else's. "Uh, Vergil?" I said.

"Oh, God, tell me this isn't Haskell."

OK, so much for him being confused.

"Well, yeah, Vergil," I said, "this *is* Haskell."

"Oh, God, no," Vergil said again.

I took a deep breath. It was true that, in all the months I'd been back in Pigeon Fork, I'd never phoned Vergil except in situations much like this one now. Still, I didn't think Vergil had any call to sound as if he were talking to the grim reaper.

"Oh, Lordy, Lordy, Lordy," Vergil said. "Tell me you're just calling to pass the time of day."

I decided right then and there that Vergil did not sound as if he were talking to the grim reaper after all. If he'd been talking to the reaper, he would've, no doubt, sounded a *lot* more cheerful. "Tell me,"

Vergil went on, "please tell me you're just calling to say hi."

At *one* in the morning? And I'd thought *I* was blindly optimistic.

"Well, Vergil," I started to say, "I'm sorry to have to tell you this, but—"

He interrupted me. "Don't tell me there's been another one. *Don't* tell me!"

Vergil is real sensitive about crime in his jurisdiction. In fact, he seems to take any crime committed in Crayton County as a personal affront. I truly believe Vergil thinks that lawbreakers are just doing these things to get his goat.

I swallowed once before I spoke. "OK, Vergil, all I'll tell you is that you really ought to mosey on out to the Isom Puckett place, because his son Dwight needs you to take a look at him."

I thought I'd put that real diplomatic-like, but from the way Vergil reacted, I might just as well have simply blurted it all straight out.

"Oh, my God! He's not *dead*, is he?"

I really hated to answer. "Well, uh, yeah, Vergil, Dwight does seem to be—"

That's all I got out. "Oh, my Lordy, *Lordy, Lordy!* It's not a homicide, tell me it's *not* a homicide—"

"Well, uh, yeah, it looks like—"

Vergil interrupted me again. "Oh, God, this is awful. Oh, this is *terrible*. Lordy, Lordy, *Lordy*, this is the worst. Oh, God, oh, God, oh—"

I actually had to interrupt *him*. Vergil sounded as if he might be going on like this until, oh, say, dawn. "Vergil. Vergil! *Vergil!* I'm at Isom Puckett's place, and—"

Vergil cut me off. "Did they phone you *this* time, too?"

To somebody else, that might've sounded like a strange question, but unfortunately, I knew exactly what Vergil meant. I also couldn't mistake the accusation in his tone.

I gripped the Mickey Mouse phone a little tighter, feeling unbelievably weary. Vergil just can't seem to forget that, in one of the burglary incidents I mentioned earlier—in only *one,* mind you—the victim had called *me* to come investigate, instead of up and phoning Vergil.

I don't think this would've bothered Vergil all that much, except for one thing. Vergil actually seems to think that I'm after his job. Amazingly enough. I mean, I leave Louisville because I'm plenty burned out from doing police work, and I can't wait to get back home where I belong. Then, when I get here, for some reason I'll never understand, Vergil somehow manages to convince himself that I want to do that kind of work here. So that, apparently, instead of enjoying the pure pleasure of arresting total strangers back in Louisville, I could get a real kick out of hauling off to jail folks I'd known since I was a kid.

No, thanks, Verg. You can have my share of that kind of fun any day of the week.

"Vergil," I said, "nobody called me. I just happened to be here when Maedean found—"

Vergil interrupted me again. "Dwight Puckett wasn't a client, *too,* was he?"

Oh yes, this conversation had taken an ugly turn. It wasn't so much the way Vergil asked that last question, as how he emphasized that word—*too.* As if poor Dwight could now be added to the long, long, *long* list of folks who'd hired me and immediately met an untimely end.

In fact, here lately if you paid any attention at all to Vergil, you could get the impression that I was the private eye equivalent of Legionnaires' disease. Vergil actually acts as if all you have to do to put yourself in mortal danger is to put me on your payroll.

I have pointed out to Vergil several times that there are quite a few people for whom I've worked who are still walking around, actually breathing. Not on life support or anything. Vergil, however, seems to prefer to dwell on the significantly fewer who did happen to be murdered shortly after I came into their employ.

Which was, of course, a coincidence. Which Vergil knows very well. He knows it, and yet, he just loves getting in a dig or two.

In the past, I've tried to defend myself by naming off everybody in town for whom I've worked who are still among the living. Being as how I haven't had all that many clients, though, I've always run out of names pretty quick. The last time I actually ended up naming two librarians in town for whom I'd located missing books. That little scene was plenty humiliating, let me tell you.

I pretty much wanted to avoid putting myself through that again. That's why this time I decided to let Vergil's less-than-subtle insinuations go in one ear and out the other. "No, Vergil," I said through my teeth, "Dwight Puckett was *not* a client of mine."

I was stretching the truth a little, of course. While technically I had not actually been hired by Dwight, I *was* being paid with Dwight's money. So, arguably, Dwight could've been considered one of my clients. Sort of.

"If Dwight wasn't your client," Vergil said, "then who—?"

At this point, oddly enough, I up and decided this conversation had gone on long enough. "Vergil," I broke in, "do you want to get on out here and investigate this homicide? Or are we going to be yakking on this phone for the rest of the night?"

Vergil's answer was pretty clear. He hung up on me.

Mickey Mouse appeared to be snickering a little when I gave him back the receiver.

The sheriff, however, was doing anything but laughing when he showed up some twenty minutes later. Of course, by then I wasn't exactly a happy camper myself.

It wasn't enough that I'd had to spend twenty more minutes with poor Dwight for company, I'd also had to spend that same amount of time with the merry widow. In fact, the second I'd hung up, I'd turned around to find Maedean standing right next to me.

She must've come back into the living room while I was on the phone, because suddenly she was just there, looking up at me, batting the lashes of her too-small eyes. She'd shed her cashmere coat, and apparently, from the way she was standing, I was supposed to notice just how tight her yellow sweater happened to be.

Maedean still had Poopsie in her arms, however, so my own eyes, naturally, went straight to the dog. Old Poops may have missed biting me earlier, but I had faith in him. Next time I was sure he'd have better aim.

Poopsie, I believe, thought so, too. He was growling softly under his breath.

I took a quick step back, and goosed myself pretty

good with the corner of the phone table. While I was trying to get myself into a tad more comfortable position, Maedean was taking a quick step forward. "You know, Haskell," she said, her voice almost a purr, "it isn't too late. You could just go right over there to Dwight and get me that hanky. Quick as anything." She put out a forefinger and traced a circle on the front of my denim jacket. Poopsie, of course, growled a tad louder. "If you'd do that for me, I'd be *awfully grateful.*"

From the way Maedean emphasized those last two words, I was pretty sure that this time I was not jumping to unfounded conclusions. In fact, Maedean seemed to be trying to make it clear that her being *awfully grateful* meant that I might possibly expect something more from her than a thank-you note. Judging from the look on her face, I was also pretty sure she expected me to jump at the opportunity.

She *had* to be kidding.

For one thing, I believe I've mentioned I have a girlfriend named Imogene.

For another thing, I don't believe I've ever been the least bit partial to too-big noses, too-small eyes, *or* Jay Leno.

For still *another* thing, at that moment I believe Maedean's husband was lying not six feet away. While Dwight might not have been in any condition to object, the man *did* have his eyes open, for God's sake.

"Maedean," I said, "that hanky is staying right where it is."

She blinked at that, and immediately took a quick step backward. Then, squaring her shoulders, she said, "Haskell, leaving my hanky there will just muddy the waters. I mean, you and I both know that I couldn't possibly have done this. So why not just—"

"Maedean, I don't want to talk about it anymore—"

"But, Haskell—"

For a man who didn't want to talk about it, I did more talking about that handkerchief in the next few minutes than in all the minutes before put together. In fact, Maedean and I did nothing else *but* talk about her handkerchief until we heard Vergil and his entourage pulling up outside. I even tried to ask her a couple times if she had any idea who might've wished her husband harm, but Maedean's response was always, "All I know is that it wasn't me, and that my handkerchief being right there is just going to confuse things, that's all. Now, Haskell, if you would just ..." Just like that, we'd be back to discussing her hanky.

Once we heard the cars crunching on the gravel driveway, Maedean just had enough time to remind me all over again that I was a *private* detective before we heard car doors slamming outside.

I all but ran for the front door.

Vergil never looks any too cheerful, but when I opened the door and watched him getting out of his car, the sheriff looked about as happy as a stock broker in 1929.

Vergil was, as usual, wearing his crisply pressed tan uniform, but Vergil's hair—sticking up in salt-and-pepper wisps all over his head—gave it away that he'd just gotten out of bed. Vergil also looked as if he'd dressed in an awful hurry because he'd missed a button right over his beer belly. His shirt gaped there, revealing a white gash of undershirt.

I decided it probably would not be a good idea to point this out to him.

Following a few steps behind the sheriff was Horace Merryman, the Crayton County assistant coroner. Horace also happens to be the sole proprietor of Merryman's Funeral Home, the only funeral home in Pigeon Fork. I myself have always thought it a definite conflict of interest that the guy who pronounces you dead in this town is also the very same guy who immediately profits from your demise. This, however, has never seemed to bother anybody else but me.

Horace is a skinny little man with a pencil-thin mustache. One reason I believe old Horace stays so skinny is that he's always in motion. Right now, as he hurried after Vergil, he was fidgeting with the collar of his black undertaker's suit, fooling with the handle of his medical bag, and twisting the ends of his mustache. Horace was managing to do all this and still keep up with Vergil, who was moving at a pretty fast clip toward the house.

Following Horace, and indeed almost passing him a couple times, were Vergil's twin deputies, Jeb and Fred Gunterman. At six feet three and 250 pounds apiece, the Guntermans are definitely known more around these parts for their brawn than their brains. As a matter of fact, this last summer during the Crayton County Fair, when Lanky had been competing in that yodeling contest I mentioned earlier, the twins had been competing with each other in a how-high-can-you-lift-the-front-end-of-a-tractor contest. The tractor contest had ended like a lot of their contests do—in a tie.

Now as I stood in the Puckett doorway and watched the massive twins follow Vergil and Horace up the pebble sidewalk, it seemed as if the ground shook a little with the twins' every footstep. I'd seen the twins follow Vergil several times before, and each of those times whenever Vergil stopped, the twins had very nearly run smack into him. Once they'd even had to veer quickly to one side to keep from mowing him down.

On this particular occasion, however, they'd apparently solved this little problem. One of them, either Jeb or Fred—I can't tell the twins apart so I couldn't say for sure which one it was—was running in front of the other, more or less directing traffic. When Vergil stopped, the traffic twin dropped both beefy arms to his sides, signaling his brother behind him to come to an abrupt halt.

Vergil, I believe, had not yet been made aware of the twins' remarkable solution to the running-into-the-sheriff problem, but it was clear that the sheriff did know that something was going on in back of him. He just wasn't sure what.

Horace Merryman likewise seemed to be in the dark.

Twice on the way up the sidewalk Vergil and Horace both turned suddenly to look behind them, but each time the traffic twin immediately dropped his huge arms to his sides. At the same time the traffic twin gave both Vergil and Horace one of the ugliest grins I'd ever laid eyes on.

Vergil and Horace must've agreed with me with regard to the ugliness of that grin, because after seeing that grin twice, the sheriff and the coroner didn't look behind them again.

Even though the traffic controller was gesturing pretty wildly toward the last, making sure his brother came to a complete stop. No matter, Vergil and Horace just kept their eyes straight ahead. I did notice, however, that Vergil now looked even more morose.

A thing I wouldn't have thought possible.

Vergil's expression didn't change when he saw me at the door. "Haskell," he said.

Around these parts, just saying your name is the same as saying hello.

I tried to match Vergil's mournful tone. "Vergil," I said.

That was about all either one of us had time to say. At this point Maedean pushed past me and made a beeline for Vergil. "Oh-h-h, Sheriff," she said, "it—it's Dwight! It's my poor, darling Dwight!"

I stared at her. This was an about-face. Dwight had evidently made a remarkable transformation—from asshole to darling. Quite a feat for somebody in his present condition. What was possibly even more remarkable, considering that it had pretty much dominated the few conversations I'd had with her, was that Maedean had not yet even mentioned her hanky. It looked as if she needed one, too. Tears were spilling down both cheeks and dripping unceremoniously onto Poopsie's fluffy head.

I don't think there's a man in the world who really knows what to do when some woman starts crying. Vergil was no exception. The second Maedean turned on the waterworks, all the blood seemed to drain from Vergil's face. His eyes started showing the whites all around, and he took a few quick, stumbling steps backward.

Vergil must've realized right away that it was unseemly for an officer of the law to be backing away in terror from the grief-stricken next of kin, because almost immediately, he put on the brakes. Then he just stood there, stiff as a poker, wearing the sort of expression you'd expect to see on the face of somebody having matches inserted under his fingernails.

As it turned out, it didn't much matter whether Vergil had stopped backing up or not. Maedean, Poopsie in hand, was closing fast, anyway. Of course, maybe that's why Vergil had suddenly stopped; he'd realized he couldn't outrun her. Vergil's abrupt stop must've caught Maedean by surprise, because she—and Poopsie—didn't exactly quit moving when Vergil did. Instead, the two of them sort of bounced off Vergil's chest, accompanied by Poopsie's high-pitched squeal. Evidently, Maedean could've used a traffic twin herself.

Maedean recovered fast, though. She only reeled backward for a moment, and then she was moving forward again, grabbing Vergil's right forearm with the hand not holding Poopsie. "Oh, Sheriff," Maedean said, pulling Vergil past me into the foyer. Her voice was real close to a sob. "It's terrible! It's just terrible! My poor, poor, *poor* Dwight!" Maedean, apparently, was continuing to play the grieving widow to the hilt. Three *poor*s seemed a tad excessive to me, but Vergil didn't seem to notice.

Of course, at that moment virtually all the sheriff's attention seemed to be focused on Poopsie. After bouncing off Vergil's chest, Poopsie must've decided that Vergil was an enemy. All the time Maedean was holding onto Vergil, Poopsie was growling.

"I'm, uh, real sorry, Mrs. Puckett," Vergil said. He was obviously saying this to Maedean, but you couldn't tell by looking. Vergil's eyes remained on Poopsie.

For a small dog, Poopsie sure could make some noise. You could hear Poopsie's growls real clear even though Horace was now coming through the front door, followed by the Guntermans. Horace, of course, didn't make much noise, moving silently across the hardwood floor like the undertaker he was. The Guntermans, however, sounded like a herd of buffalo. A herd of buffalo that came to a stop a couple steps inside the front door.

Vergil's eyes were still on Poopsie when he said, "Jeb. Fred. Stand there."

The twins exchanged a glance, and then in unison, said, "Where?"

It seemed to me that their need for clarification was easy to understand, being as how Vergil wasn't even looking in their direction when he spoke. Vergil, however, didn't seem to see it that way. He heaved a deep sigh before he answered.

Vergil is real good at sighing. But then again, he gets a lot of practice.

"Stand there *at the door,*" Vergil said, enunciating every word, "so that nobody gets in. Understand?" This time it appeared to me that those directions were so straightforward that a person would have to *try* to misunderstand them. I reckon, however, that I didn't have a handle on how little effort it actually took for the twins to get confused.

The second Vergil stopped talking, both Guntermans cocked their heads to one side, their beefy faces taking on identical bewildered expressions. "Uh, Sheriff, do ya want that we should stand *next* to each other?" the twin closest to Vergil said.

"Or should we stand, with one in front, and the other in back?" the other twin asked.

Vergil was still a tad distracted, being as how Maedean's tears were now dripping pretty regularly on the arm she was clutching, and Poopsie's growls had become drooling snarls. The sheriff did look over at the twins this time, though. Fact is, he looked at them for a pretty long time. Vergil might've been mentally counting to ten, but I couldn't be sure. Eventually, the sheriff cleared his throat and said so quietly that you could barely hear him over Poopsie, "Side by side."

The twins brightened, and turned to head toward their post. They hadn't taken but one step, though, when they stopped again—in unison, of course—and turned back to Vergil. Vergil was even more distracted now, on account of Maedean having moved a whole lot closer to him. Apparently, when Maedean got closer, Poopsie decided that there was no doubt about it, Vergil *was* an enemy—an enemy shamelessly invading Poopsie's canine space. The dog immediately started lunging at Vergil, pretty much snapping his fluffy head off at the arm Maedean continued to cling to.

I stared at Vergil. I don't believe I'd ever seen Vergil's eyes get quite that round. They were beginning to resemble white Frisbees stuck to his face.

"Uh, Sheriff?" It was one of the twins, either Jeb or Fred. Fact is, it was a wonder that Vergil even heard the twin over Poopsie's snapping and Maedean's sobbing. But, then again, the twin that spoke fairly boomed his question. "Uh," he said, "do ya want that we should stand outside? Or inside?"

You kind of knew without asking which one the twins voted for—it being real close to two in the morning by now and having gotten fairly nippy outside.

Vergil didn't bother to give the twins a long-suffering

stare this time. Of course, the sheriff's attention was pretty much taken up with dodging dog teeth. *"Inside, OK?"* Vergil's voice was a snarl almost as loud as Poopsie's.

Apparently, the Guntermans had heard snarls from Vergil before. The huge twins actually looked a tad startled. "Uh, *yessir,"* the one in front said, backing away from Vergil.

"Yessir," echoed the one in back, backing away, too. They both turned and immediately headed toward their post. There, standing shoulder to shoulder in front of the door, they made a sort of deputy barricade.

Vergil may have gotten the twins under control, but Poopsie was another story. The dog was now lunging and snapping and growling, in a frenzy of furious motion. Maedean, for her part, was still intent on sobbing and holding onto Vergil's arm. That could've been why she didn't seem to much notice that Poopsie was doing his best to sink his tiny razor-sharp teeth into any part of Vergil that he could get ahold of.

Vergil, on the other hand, seemed to notice little else. He was trying to pull away from Maedean at the same time as she was trying to pull him into the living room. "Dwight's right in here, Sheriff. He—he—"

Whatever else Maedean had to say was pretty much drowned out by her additional sobbing. And, yes, to give Poopsie his due, by the dog's additional snarling and drooling. I believe, in fact, it was because the sheriff's Frisbee eyes were pretty much riveted on Poopsie that he himself didn't seem to notice that I, too, was now following him, Maedean, and Horace into the living room.

This was definitely a first. Up to now, the split second Vergil arrived at any crime scene where I happened to be, Vergil had made it a point to throw me out. In fact, in the short time I'd been back in town, I'd gotten the clear message that Vergil was of the opinion that crime solving was a game best played alone.

Maedean's sobs managed to get even louder as we got near where poor Dwight was lying. "See, Sheriff?" Maedean said, stopping about five feet from the body. *"See* what somebody else did to Dwight?"

When Maedean stopped, she'd finally let go of Vergil's arm, and he'd immediately taken advantage of the opportunity to put some distance between himself and Poopsie. Vergil had started making a beeline toward Dwight, but Maedean's last comment brought him up short. "Somebody *else?*" Vergil said, turning to look at her.

Maedean was wiping her eyes on her sleeve. Which, I suppose, was the best she could do. Being as how she didn't have a hanky. "That's right, Sheriff," she said, nodding her blond head. "Somebody *else.* I don't know who, of course. All I know is that it wasn't me."

Unfortunately—for Maedean, anyway—now that Vergil had moved away, Poopsie was no longer snarling. So that everybody in the room heard every word that Maedean had to say. She looked a little surprised to find me, Horace, and Vergil all looking straight at her. Vergil's eyes no longer resembled Frisbees, either. His eyes had gotten a whole lot narrower.

It must've occurred to Maedean a tad late that it probably wasn't the best idea in the world to say you hadn't done a thing before you were even asked. So, apparently, in an effort to correct any bad impression she might've left in anybody's mind, Maedean quickly added, "I admit, of course, that the hanky Dwight happens to be holding *is* mine. I do admit that. But," she said, looking first at Vergil, then over at Horace, "if I were guilty, would I have left it there? Now, really, I ask you—"

I couldn't help but notice that Maedean had not glanced in my direction. No doubt, because I knew that she was now neglecting to mention how, ever since she'd discovered Dwight's body, she'd been trying to talk me into letting her retrieve this particular item.

The upshot of Maedean's last little pronouncement was probably a real disappointment to her. The sheriff stood stock-still for about a half second, then he hurried to Dwight's side. Horace had beat him there, and the undertaker was already busily determining what everybody in the room knew just by looking—that when it came to vital signs, Dwight had come up empty.

For a man in his fifties with a gut on him, Vergil moved real quick around Horace. Getting as close as he could without actually touching the body, Vergil stooped heavily and craned his neck so that he could take a real close look at the white linen handkerchief in Dwight's hand. His back was to me, but you could tell when Vergil spotted the initials. His whole body stiffened. "It says, *M.P.*," he said. From his tone, he might've been talking to himself. Except that, once he'd said it, he turned to give Maedean an even longer look than he had before. It wasn't hard to figure out what Vergil was thinking.

I could hardly blame him. In the years I'd worked homicide, I'd found out that one thing almost always held true. The simplest explanation is the one that turns out to be so. Like, say, for instance, if you find a clue in a dead man's hand, and it points to the guy's wife, then she did it. It was as simple as that.

This particular case, though, wasn't that simple. I put a finger in the air, and said, "Uh, Vergil?"

His eyes still riveted on Maedean, the sheriff actually waved me away, the way you might a bothersome gnat.

"Uh, that's right, Sheriff," Maedean said, nodding her head, "I'm not denying it. That hanky says *M.P.* because it's mine, all right."

Vergil frowned as he said, "I see."

Vergil's frown must've made Maedean nervous. She began talking a whole lot faster. "Well, then, you see what's going on, don't you? Dwight's trying to make it look as if *I* had done this!"

Vergil continued to stare at her. "He's doing a terrific job," he said solemnly.

I, of course, was still trying to get a word in edgewise. "Uh, Vergil?" I said again.

Vergil waved me away again, his eyes still on Maedean. "Where were you all day today?"

"Where was I?" Maedean's voice went shrill. Indicating me with a wave of her hand, she said, "Why don't you ask Haskell? He was with me *all* day long!"

I swallowed uneasily. Thanks so much, Maedean. Vergil was no longer staring at Maedean suspiciously. He was now staring at *me* that way. "You spent the entire day with *Mrs.* Puckett?" Vergil put a little extra emphasis on the *Mrs.* in that last sentence. He can be such a blue nose. Vergil has always been like this, making no bones about disapproving of what he refers to as *hanky panky* among married folk. He's been complaining about the loose goings-on in movies and on television for as far back as I can remember. According to Vergil, that guy in the movie *Fatal Attraction* had deserved what he got.

I also noticed that Horace Merryman's head had jerked up and spun in my direction. Fidgeting with the lapels of his black undertaker's coat, Horace actually leaned a little in my direction, his eyes eager. I suppose I shouldn't have been surprised at Horace's interest. I reckon if you spend all your time with dead bodies, then hearing about what could possibly happen between live ones would, no doubt, be a real treat. I hated to bust Horace's balloon—not to mention Vergil's—but the truth was the truth. "Vergil, I had Maedean here under surveillance."

I was doing fine. I didn't think I needed Maedean to jump in at this point with, "Yeah, Sheriff, he was watching me all day long!"

Vergil now turned to look back at me. I may have been mistaken, but it seemed to me that the corners of Vergil's mouth were twitching a tad. As if, good heavens, the man might actually be close to cracking a smile. "She spotted you tailing her?" Apparently, the idea of my surveillance techniques being less than what they should be was cause for real amusement on Vergil's part.

I would've liked to have handled this particular question myself, but Maedean jumped in again. "Oh no," she said, scratching Poopsie between his ears, "I already knew Haskell was tailing me." Vergil looked confused. Unfortunately, however, Maedean once again cleared everything up. "After all," she went on, "*I* was the one who'd hired Haskell in the first place!"

The upside of all this was that Vergil was no longer looking at me as if he thought I was capable of murder. The downside was that he was now looking at me as if he thought I was crazy. "She hired you to tail herself?"

Even Maedean picked up on the derision in Vergil's tone. She must've been afraid that I was about to divulge not only that she had indeed done such a thing, but also the reason why. Before I could say a word, she said, "I hired Haskell to follow me around and kind of, uh, watch over me. Because I, uh, needed a bodyguard."

That got Vergil's attention. It also got mine. Maedean might've been a more accomplished liar than I thought. While I looked at her with some surprise, Vergil asked, "Bodyguard? Why did you need a body-guard? Had someone been threatening you? Or your husband?"

Maedean tilted her head to one side, as if she were trying to decide. "Uh no," she finally said. "Nothing like that." It seemed to occur to her a tad late that what she was saying didn't exactly make a whole lot of sense. She quickly added, "I, uh, just like to be careful."

That one went over big. The sheriff's narrowed eyes were fast becoming slits. It looked as if maybe I'd misjudged Maedean. She might not be all that great a liar, after all.

I was pretty sure the sheriff wasn't buying any of what Maedean was dishing out, and yet I sure didn't want to tell him the truth. The way I saw it, I didn't want to tell Vergil for his own good. Lord knows, Verg's heart might not be able to take the laughing fit he'd have if he knew.

"The important thing is," I said, "I had Maedean under surveillance all day long."

I believe I've mentioned that Vergil always looks a tad depressed, but at that moment he looked suicidal. He heaved a monumental sigh, and then said, "You mean—"

I hated to do it, but I nodded. "I don't think she was ever out of my sight for more than a couple minutes."

Vergil blinked, and gave me a look that said, *You mean to tell me that the one person incriminated by the hanky could not possibly have done it?* Vergil was now looking as if he might weep.

Maedean, however, beat him to it. Tears again streamed down both cheeks as Poopsie tried to flatten himself against her chest to get out of the downpour. "I just don't understand why Dwight would try to make me look guilty," Maedean wailed.

Vergil and I exchanged a glance. I believe it was crossing both our minds right about then that it might not have been Dwight who was trying to make Maedean look guilty.

Neither one of us had much time to think this over, though. Our attention was pretty much grabbed by something that sounded like thunder out in the foyer. Vergil pretty much summed up everybody's immediate reaction. "What the hell is that?" he said.

He turned and hurried in the direction the noise was coming from, with me and Maedean bringing up the rear.

CHAPTER 7

The thunder turned out to be the Guntermans. Standing side by side, they were blocking the front door, which now stood wide open. Both deputies were talking at once, their deep voices running together into one big rumbling roar.

As best as I could tell, one of the twins was saying: "Oh no you don't. Nobody goes in. Uhn-uh." And the other one was saying, "Nope. Nope. Nope. The sheriff *said.*"

Standing out on the porch, framed by the doorway, on the other side of the Gunterman twin wall, was a blond wearing a cashmere coat identical to the one Maedean had on earlier.

"But I'm family! Get it? I'm Maedean Puckett's sister, and I practically live here—" The blond broke off when she caught sight of Maedean. "Oh, Maedean," the blond yelled. She was now doing little jumps to see over the twins' beefy shoulders. "Oh, you poor, poor baby! I came as soon as I heard!"

This was an amazing statement, all by itself. It was two in the morning, and yet even at this hour, the Pigeon Fork grapevine apparently was still as efficient as ever. The 911 operator must've been on the phone, waking folks up all over Crayton County, spreading the word, right after she'd talked to me. Now I understood how come I'd been able to get Vergil on the phone *before* he'd heard from her. Hell, I should probably count myself lucky the operator had remembered to call the sheriff at all.

The blond continued to yell. "Maedean, honey," she said, "are you OK?"

Maedean's response was dramatic, to say the least. She immediately burst into tears all over again. Lord, that woman seemed to have an inexhaustible supply of moisture.

"Oh, Ginny Sue," Maedean wailed, "Dwight got himself killed, and he's trying to put the blame on me!"

Vergil had been opening his mouth, about to tell the twins something, but Maedean's last little comment caused Vergil to shut his mouth real quick. He turned around to stare openly at Maedean.

My own eyes were on the woman Maedean called Ginny Sue. You would've known, just by looking at this woman, that she had to be Maedean's sister. Ginny Sue had shoulder-length blond hair, too-small eyes, a too-big nose, and a chin quite a bit like— you guessed it—Jay Leno. Nearly the same height and weight as her sister, Ginny Sue would've looked a lot like Maedean even if she hadn't been wearing a cashmere coat exactly like Maedean's. The coat, though, helped.

"Wha-a-at?" Ginny Sue said. Turning back to the

Guntermans, she snapped, "Move out of the way, you
Neanderthals!"

Both Guntermans responded identically. They both
cocked their huge heads to one side, frowned, then
looked over at the other one, and soundlessly
mouthed, "Nee-and-derwhat?" It looked to me as if
the Guntermans had no idea what Ginny Sue had just
called them. I, for one, was glad of it. The twins have
been known to get downright scary when they think
somebody's calling them names.

"Move!" Ginny Sue was going on. "I need to get
inside!"

Staring at Ginny Sue, I swallowed uneasily. When
you saw the two women together, you could clearly
tell that Ginny Sue's nose was even bigger than
Maedean's, that her eyes were even smaller, and
that—unlike Maedean—Ginny Sue had two vertical
frown lines permanently etched between her brows.

From a distance, however, none of this would be
particularly noticeable. In fact, from not too many feet
away, this woman would probably look exactly like
Maedean. Which brought to mind a disturbing question: *During the time I'd been watching Maedean,
could there have been a switch?*

Let's face it. I hadn't taken Maedean's surveillance
job seriously enough to really pay all that close
attention.

Maedean was now poking Vergil with the hand not
holding Poopsie. "That's my sister, Ginny Sue, out
there. You tell your deputies to let her in!"

Standing there in the foyer, looking first at Ginny
Sue and then over at Maedean, something else flashed
through my mind. If Maedean had lied to Vergil earlier, she might also have lied to me, right from the

start. Instead of hiring me to reassure her husband, Maedean might've really been hiring me to establish an alibi. I took a deep breath, feeling more and more uneasy. Then something occurred to me that instantly made me feel better: From what I could tell, Maedean wasn't smart enough to have masterminded such a plot. Unfortunately, right after I started feeling better, something else also flashed through my mind. Could Maedean be so smart that she'd know to *act* really dumb?

All these things were not extremely cheery ideas to contemplate. The one thing, however, that took the cake—the one thing, in fact, that made my stomach knot up so bad, it felt as if a giant hand were twisting it—was this: If it were true that I had been hired to establish an alibi, what would've happened if Maedean hadn't been able to find some poor schmuck like me to follow her around all day with a camera? *Was it possible that if I hadn't agreed to go along with Maedean's idiotic surveillance scheme, poor Dwight might not have been murdered?* This particular idea was so disturbing that I didn't even want to think about it. I immediately shoved it right out of my mind, and instead turned my attention to the conversation still going on in the foyer.

"I have every right to be with my sister in her hour of need!" Ginny Sue was now saying.

"Nope. Nope. Nope." The twins backed up their statements by shaking their heads.

They kept on shaking their heads right up until Vergil said, "Jeb. Fred. Let the lady pass."

You could tell the Guntermans had been getting a kick out of being the twin wall, because when Vergil said this to them, their identical faces fell. "Aw, Sheriff," the one on the left said. "You *told* us that we oughtn't let anybody—" His voice was getting real close to a whine.

Vergil's voice, on the other hand, was getting real close to a snarl. *"Let the lady in!"*

The twins immediately reacted. In fact, watching the massive twins instantaneously split apart was, no doubt, similar to what it must've been like to watch the Red Sea part. Only I was pretty sure the Red Sea hadn't pouted.

Vergil ignored the twin pouts, and instead homed in on the new arrival. "And you are?" he said.

"I already said who I was," the blond snapped. "Ginny Sue Hester, Maedean's sister."

I believe Vergil might've been expecting Ginny Sue to stop and talk to him, but she sailed right by him, arms extended toward Maedean.

"Oh, Ginny Sue," Maedean said, "I'm so glad you're here!" Her voice quavered. "I'm so-o-o glad!"

Ginny Sue was at Maedean's side before Maedean had even finished. With her arms still extended and all, Ginny Sue seemed to be on the verge of giving Maedean a big hug. Until Poopsie, of course, began to growl. Ginny Sue must've been accustomed to Poopsie's less-than-cordial disposition, though, because she didn't jump back or look the least bit startled. In fact, she barely gave the dog a glance as she said, "Don't you worry, sweetie, I'm right here."

I did notice, however, that Ginny Sue lowered her arms. And maintained her distance.

"It—it's just been awful, Ginny Sue," Maedean said. "They've been *cross*-examining me!" Obviously, Maedean didn't know what the term "cross-examining" meant. From the way she put a little extra emphasis on the first syllable, though, she seemed to believe it meant that those who were asking you questions were in an exceptionally bad mood.

"Cross-examining you? Why, whatever for?" Those vertical lines between Ginny Sue's eyebrows deepened as she wheeled on the rest of us. "What on earth has been going on here? Don't you people know that this is a widow in mourning, for God's sake?"

I could've told Ginny Sue that, in my experience, I hadn't seen all that many widows in mourning who referred to the deceased as an asshole. I decided, however, that there was no use making Ginny Sue any angrier than she already seemed to be. She was now glaring first at me, and then over at Vergil.

Vergil was equal to the challenge. He immediately stepped forward. "Ma'am," he began solemnly, "we're just trying—"

Ginny Sue's Jay Leno chin went up. "That's *Ms.*," she said. "Not *ma'am.*"

Vergil shut his mouth all over again, and then just looked at her for what seemed like an interminable moment. I had a notion as to what Vergil was thinking, and take my word for it, it wasn't nice.

The fact was, just before Vergil's wife left him, she'd started reading *Ms.* magazine a lot, and quoting Betty Friedan and Gloria Steinem and just about anybody else who would've agreed with her that thirty-one years of marriage was thirty-one years too many. Vergil's divorce had been final over two years ago, but old Verg still doesn't have much patience with what he calls women-libbers.

"Look, *Miz*," he finally said, his voice still solemn but now with an unmistakable edge, "we're just trying

119

to do our job. We haven't been cross-examining anybody. All we've done is ask a few—"

"Ginny Sue actually cut Vergil off. "Why, that's police harassment! That's what it is! I won't have my sister treated this way. She's had a terrible shock, and I just won't have—"

Oddly enough, it was Maedean who interrupted Ginny Sue this time. "Now, Ginny Sue, it's not the sheriff's fault. It's Dwight's."

Ginny Sue turned to look at Maedean. *"Dwight's?"*

Maedean was tearing up again. "Dwight's the one who made it look as if I've killed him!"

The vertical lines between Ginny Sue's eyebrows deepened even more. Glancing around at the rest of us, she put her hands on her hips. "Now, isn't that just like a man?"

That little comment made Vergil give Ginny Sue another piercing stare.

Maedean seemed downright eager to tell Ginny Sue all about what she was sure Dwight had done to her. "Dwight is out in the living room right this minute, holding *my* handkerchief, just like he's trying to tell the world that I—"

Ginny Sue actually gasped. Interrupting Maedean, she said, *"Your* handkerchief? You mean to tell me that he—"

Vergil must've decided right then that this was a conversation he didn't want anybody having. Not before he talked to them separately, anyway. "Mrs. Puckett!" he all but shouted. He paused for a second and glanced at Ginny Sue, as if he was expecting her to correct him on his pronunciation of *Mrs.* "I'll be needing to talk to everybody here, one by one, out in the"—he paused here, scratching his bald spot, looking around for a suitable place—"out in the kitchen, I reckon."

Both Maedean and Ginny Sue looked a little alarmed at the prospect of sitting down and chatting with the police, but Vergil added, "It's just routine."

I could've assured the sisters that Vergil was indeed telling the truth. The routine, in this instance, was to isolate everybody involved and get separate statements from all of them. After that, the routine was to see if everything everybody said pretty much matched. Or if anybody had slipped up.

"I'll be wanting to talk to *you* first," Vergil hurried on, his eyes on Maedean.

Ginny Sue stepped forward. "Well, I won't have it. This is an outrage! I won't have my sister treated like a common—"

Maedean interrupted her again. "Now, Ginny Sue," she said, "you know I don't have anything to hide. I'll be *glad* to answer the sheriff's questions." She was saying all this with her eyes on Vergil, but when she finished, Maedean turned to give Ginny Sue what looked to me to be a significant look. The only trouble was, I wasn't all that sure what the significance could be.

Ginny Sue must've gotten the message, though, because right away she pressed her lips together in a thin line. "OK, Maedean," she sort of mumbled, "if you feel up to it."

Before Vergil went off with Maedean into the kitchen, he looked straight at Ginny Sue and said, "I'll be talking to you next—" After that he pinned me with a look. "And then you," he said.

I know it sounds paranoid, but I was pretty sure Vergil put me last on purpose. No doubt, trying to punish me for bringing yet another homicide into his jurisdiction. Legionnaire's detective that I was.

Vergil's punishment, though, backfired a little. While it did annoy me some that it was probably going to be dawn before I got some sleep, the order in which Vergil interviewed folks didn't turn out to be all that bad. It gave me a chance to talk to Ginny Sue alone.

Ginny Sue and I ended up in the dining room. Our choices, of course, were distinctly limited. With Horace still working on Dwight in the living room, that room was pretty much out. There were no chairs in the foyer, so the dining room was the closest room that had someplace to sit down. Ginny Sue immediately walked in and sat down at the head of the table. That left me with two choices, either sitting at the other end, like maybe I was playing dad to her mom, or taking one of the chairs in the middle.

I chose the middle. "So," I said, as I took my seat, "you're Maedean's sister."

I was just trying to start a conversation, for God's sake, but Ginny Sue fixed me with a look. "That's what I told the sheriff. What of it?"

I raised my hands. "Hey, I didn't mean anything—"

"I know who you are, too," Ginny Sue went on, tossing her blond hair in a gesture that reminded me uneasily of Maedean. "You're one of the ones trying to put my poor sister in jail."

I blinked at that one. Where on earth did she get that idea? Did she think I was working for Vergil? I shook my head. "Nope," I said, "you got that wrong. I'm a private detective, and I've been working for your sister."

Ginny Sue's eyes narrowed. "So you're the one."

"The one?"

"The idiot she hired to follow her around."

I just looked at her. I'd be damned if I was going to say, *Yep, I'm the idiot.* I cleared my throat. "Your sister hired me to document her activities so that—"

Ginny Sue interrupted me with a snort. *"Document* her activities? Oh, brother," she said, pulling a pack of cigarettes out of one of the front pockets of her jumper. She shook one out, stuck it in her mouth, and then looked at me. As if maybe she thought I'd light it for her.

I just stared right back at her. Not being a smoker, I didn't have any matches on me. I opened my mouth to tell her so, but she was already frowning at me. Like maybe she'd given me a little test, and I'd failed. She pushed back her chair, got to her feet, and stomped over to an antique sideboard standing against the wall across from me. There she reached for the small gold lighter lying in the middle of a large cut-glass ashtray. Lighting her cigarette, she blew a big cloud of smoke in my direction.

I resisted the urge to fan it out of my eyes. Instead, I just sat there, my eyes tearing up a little.

"You know," Ginny Sue said, pointing her cigarette at me, "men like you make me sick." I was looking at her, thinking, *Lord, she certainly judges harshly those men in the world who don't have matches,* when Ginny Sue hurried on. "Men like you just sail through life taking advantage of one vulnerable woman after another."

My response, of course, was the one I'd used earlier when talking to Maedean. "Huh?" I said.

Ginny Sue took another drag off her cigarette. "Poor Maedean was so anxious to save her marriage, she would've agreed to try anything—even your lame-brain scheme."

I hated to tell her, but the lamebrain that had come up with the surveillance scheme had not been me. I didn't have a chance to say anything, though, because Ginny Sue again hurried on. "Maedean would never have agreed to such a thing, except that she was so crazy in love with Dwight—"

OK, I'll admit it, Ginny Sue had me going for a moment there. I'd even started to feel a tad guilty, until she said this last. But she'd lost me with this one. If Maedean was in love with Dwight, I was the Easter Bunny. And, being as how I hadn't felt the least bit inclined to deliver any decorated eggs lately, I was pretty sure Maedean was no more in love with Dwight than she was with one of the Gunterman twins. Which, I might add, was a scary thought.

"Now wait a doggone minute—" I said, interrupting Ginny Sue.

She shook her head. "No, *you* wait a minute. You took my sister's money when you knew very well—"

I interrupted again. "Look, I tried to tell Maedean it wouldn't work, OK? She wouldn't listen."

Ginny Sue blew another cloud of smoke in my direction. It took real willpower not to cough. "Uh-huh. Right," Ginny Sue said. *"Sure* she wouldn't listen. Hell, you're just like Dwight."

I blinked. It seemed to me there were some distinct differences between us. Especially now. "How do you figure?"

"Always blaming everything on somebody else. I don't like talking ill of the dead, but the truth's the truth. Dwight was your typical male."

"Typical?"

"Just like you. Never taking responsibility for anything. Dwight blamed everything on Maedean and me. Complaining we spent too much money. Can you believe it? It never even occurred to him that maybe he just didn't make enough!"

That was one way to look at it.

Ginny Sue was on a roll. "Maedean and I couldn't help it if we had good taste, you know. We were brought up accustomed to the finer things in life, and we just couldn't be satisfied with anything but the best."

"I'm sure—"

I'd been intending to agree with her, saying, "I'm sure that's true." More or less, defusing her anger. Ginny Sue, though, didn't let me finish. *"You're* sure? That's the trouble with you men, all of you are sure about everything. Well, let me tell you, mister, you guys don't know everything!"

So much for defusing her anger.

"Dwight was sure that Maedean would be happy in this godforsaken nowheres-ville of a town! I mean, *really!"*

I took a deep breath. As a native of this godforsaken nowheres-ville, I could definitely take offense at that last remark. I swallowed a few rude replies, however, and quickly changed the subject. "Miss Hester, I'm determined to find out who killed your brother-in-law. And far from trying to put Maedean in jail, *I'm* the one who's giving her an alibi."

I decided it wasn't necessary to add that if it turned out there was a good reason to put Maedean in jail— like, for example, she really *had* been involved in

Dwight's death—I intended to do all I could to see that she got a very nice, very cozy jail cell on death row.

"Miss Hester," I went on, "I—"

Ginny Sue gave her hair another Maedean-like toss, and cut me off. "Didn't you hear me before? Is there something wrong with your ears? I told the sheriff it's *Ms.* Hester."

I cleared my throat. Lord. If I wasn't *miz*taken, Ginny Sue had one gigantic chip on her shoulder. *"Ms.* Hester, then," I said. "I was hoping you might be able to help—"

Ginny Sue took another long puff. "I'd gladly help Maedean, but to tell you the truth, I wouldn't help Dwight cross the street."

I decided not to mention that Dwight probably no longer required that kind of assistance. Instead, I said, "Oh? Why not?"

Ginny Sue just stared at me a second, as if she were trying to decide how much she should tell me. Finally, she shrugged and tapped her cigarette against the edge of the table, letting the ashes fall to the floor. "Well, I guess it's not exactly a secret," Ginny Sue said. "I didn't like Dwight because he treated my sister like dirt. I mean, just because you played basketball back in college, it doesn't mean you're some kind of celebrity, you know. I mean, it's a game, for crying out loud. A *game.*"

I didn't say a thing, one way or the other.

Ginny Sue didn't need encouragement, anyway. "The way Dwight acted, though, you'd have thought he was royalty or something. He got even worse once he came into his inheritance."

"What do you mean, he got worse?"

"Well, Dwight always was a jerk," Ginny Sue said. "He always acted as if he was doing Maedean some big favor letting her and me live under his roof."

I blinked at that one. *"You* lived with them?"

It was just a question, that's all. From Ginny Sue's reaction, you'd have thought I was making some kind of accusation.

"Yeah, I lived with them. Right up until they moved here. *So?* It wasn't like Dwight couldn't afford it. The guy had plenty of money, he wasn't exactly living hand to mouth, you know. He owned his own car lot, and he and Maedean had a real big house just outside of Nashville. They had *plenty* of room."

I nodded, and tried to look as if I thought having your sister-in-law live with you and your wife would, no doubt, be a wonderful arrangement. Particularly a sister-in-law who had the sort of cheery disposition as Ginny Sue here.

Lord. It could possibly be that Dwight's killer had done him a favor.

Ginny Sue was now demonstrating just how cheery her disposition could be. "That's the kind of person Dwight was," she said, frowning. "Here I'd lived with him and Maedean for the last ten years, for God's sake, and he actually tried to leave me behind when he came up here." Ginny Sue's voice shook with anger as she tapped her cigarette against the table edge again. "I mean," Ginny Sue was saying, "can you imagine?"

Actually, I could. Watching her ashes once again drift to the floor, I could also imagine at least one reason why Dwight might not have wanted this woman to continue living under his roof. Call me psychic.

"If it hadn't been for Maedean, he'd have left me behind without even thinking twice. He would've! And me, with no place to go. Maedean, though, took up for me." The creases between Ginny Sue's brows deepened even more as she remembered. "Maedean told him she wasn't about to go to some podunk town in the middle of the boonies without knowing anybody. She told Dwight, right to his face, that either we both go, or we both stay behind. For him to choose."

I tried to keep my face perfectly still, so Ginny Sue couldn't tell what I was thinking. My immediate reaction, though, was: *Good Lord, Dwight, you had a way out, and you didn't take it?* I was also thinking that the picture Ginny Sue was now painting of Maedean didn't exactly jibe with the picture she'd painted earlier. Did an adoring wife desperate to save her marriage threaten to leave her husband if he didn't include her sister in an upcoming move?

Ginny Sue was now taking another long drag, once again filling the room with secondhand smoke. Thanks so much, Ginny Sue. "In the end Maedean and Dwight compromised," she said. "He didn't want me living with them anymore, but he said he'd get me a place of my own, not too far from their house."

I continued to keep my face still. Because at this point I was thinking, *Dwight, Dwight, Dwight, were you out of your mind?*

Ginny Sue was actually smiling some now. "Maedean was great. She told Dwight he'd better get me a nice place, *real* close by, because she had no intention of moving here with nobody to talk to but a bunch of hicks!"

I just looked at her. Apparently, Ginny Sue didn't

realize that she was talking to a hick at that very moment. "What a woman," I said.

Ginny Sue shot me a look, as if checking to see if I was sincere, then hurried on. "You'd think, with him moving me up here and all, that Dwight was real free with his money, but he certainly wasn't." Leaning in my direction, Ginny Sue pointed her cigarette at me. "Can you believe, ever since he rented me this crappy little house down the road from here, Dwight has asked me every single day whether or not I'd found a job yet? Those days I didn't see him face-to-face, the jerk phoned me. I mean, *really*."

Ginny Sue tapped her cigarette on the table again. "And my rent isn't anything, either. Just three hundred dollars a month, for God's sake. But to hear Dwight talk, you'd have thought it was a fortune."

I didn't say a word. Several things were going through my mind, though. Like, have you ever noticed how folks who don't earn the money themselves always act as if money is inconsequential? I believe my daddy said it best: If you never float your own boat, you've got no respect for water.

"Not to be talking ill of the dead," Ginny Sue hurried on, "but it was obvious to me that Dwight was into that whole macho power trip that a lot of you men get into. You know, ruling the roost, expecting Maedean to account for her every move. She even had a curfew!"

"You don't mean it," I said. I hoped I sounded shocked. Actually, being shocked wasn't exactly a stretch. It always has shocked me what other men could get the woman in their lives to agree to. I could just imagine what would've happened if I'd ever tried to give either Claudzilla or Imogene a curfew. I'd have been picking up my teeth off the ground before the words were even out of my mouth.

"Oh yeah," Ginny Sue said, "you men are all alike. You're all just a bunch of babies." She pointed her cigarette at me. "Well, I for one am through with baby-sitting."

If she was expecting this baby to talk her out of her present frame of mind, she'd better think again. "Good for you," I said.

Talk about a mistake. Ginny Sue glared at me. "I don't need your approval," she said icily. "I'll do what I like."

I was about to say "Good for you" again, but I decided to quit while I was behind. Instead, I just looked at her.

That evidently wasn't a good idea, either. After a moment, Ginny Sue smirked. "You men just don't know what to say to an assertive woman, do you?"

Actually, I wouldn't have called Ginny Sue assertive. Argumentative, maybe. Aggressive, most definitely. But assertive, no. What's more, I did know what to say to her. *Good-bye* immediately sprang to mind.

Unfortunately I couldn't exactly say that yet. For one thing, I was pretty much a prisoner until Vergil called for me. For another thing, there were a few more questions I wanted to ask her. *"Ms.* Hester," I said, emphasizing that first word, "do you know if Dwight had any enemies?"

Ginny Sue blew another large puff of smoke. "Enemies? None that I can think of. He was a charmer, you know. Like a lot of you men. That's why Maedean was still so crazy about him—in spite of the abuse."

I just looked at her. Had she just said what I thought she'd said?

I leaned toward her. "What was that again?"

Ginny Sue looked irritated at having to repeat it. "*I said,* Maedean still loved Dwight in spite of the abuse."

I couldn't help myself. My mouth dropped open.

CHAPTER 8

Ginny Sue was nodding her blond head, looking downright pleased with my reaction. "Oh yeah," she said. "It was abuse of the worst sort. The *worst.*"

"You mean, Dwight actually *hit* Maedean?"

I knew, of course, that some men changed a lot as they got older. But still, I couldn't quite picture the big, happy-go-lucky guy I'd known back in high school ever laying a hand on a woman.

Ginny Sue let go with another huge cloud of secondhand smoke. "Dwight did something just as bad," she said. "He ordered Maedean around."

I blinked. "Dwight ordered—"

Ginny Sue nodded. "That's right," she said, interrupting me. "Dwight ordered poor Maedean around all the time. Like maybe he thought he owned her or something."

I found myself just staring at Ginny Sue. Apparently, she considered a man ordering his wife around to be a form of abuse. Granted, it probably wasn't the nicest thing in the world to do—and certainly no way to treat a lady—but still I was pretty sure that it wouldn't exactly warrant calling in the police to break it up.

Ginny Sue was hurrying on. "Dwight even told Maedean she couldn't drive his car! Can you imagine?" From Ginny Sue's tone, you might've thought she was giving an account of unspeakable cruelty. "Oh yeah," she said, "it was awful, all right. Dwight wouldn't let Maedean so much as touch his precious BMW—that's how selfish he was!"

I, of course, just looked at her. Because it did occur to me that Dwight had apparently gotten Maedean a brand-new silver Corvette, which Maedean seemed to be somehow managing to make do with. I mean, Lord, the woman was an inspiration to us all.

Ginny Sue seemed to be working herself up into a frenzy. "And, as if *that* wasn't bad enough, Dwight just flat out told poor Maedean that they were going to live the rest of their lives on this dumb farm of his. Can you believe it? *The rest of their lives!*"

I didn't say anything, but it did occur to me that, for Dwight, that had not turned out to be a terribly long time. Ginny Sue was nodding her blond head. "Oh yeah, practically the second his dad croaked—"

I blinked again. What a delicate way to put that.

"—and Dwight inherited this dumb farm, he started telling poor Maedean that they were moving. He told her that he was putting up his car lot for sale, and that from now on, he was going to be the farmer he'd always wanted to be."

I remembered the look on Dwight's face yesterday, when he'd stood in front of this very house and surveyed the landscape. Remembering how happy he'd looked made my throat tighten up.

Ginny Sue apparently was equally overcome with sympathy. "That damn jerk must've been having some kind of midlife crisis!" she was saying, shaking her head. "I mean, *really*. Dwight actually wanted Maedean and him to do a Ma and Pa Kettle routine." Ginny Sue rolled her eyes. "Can you imagine? If Dwight had lived, he'd have had Maedean walking behind a plow horse out in a field somewhere."

I just looked at her, not saying a word. The thing was, Dwight hadn't lived. It seemed to me that this turn of events was not exactly the worst thing to have happened for either sister.

Ginny Sue seemed to realize what she'd just said, because she hurried to add, "And, of course, Maedean would've agreed to it because she was so crazy in love with him!"

Uh-huh.

Ginny Sue gave her hair another Maedean-like toss. "Maedean never did have any sense when it came to men."

I was now watching Ginny Sue intently. She did seem considerably more intelligent than her sister. Which, of course, was not saying a lot. Could Ginny Sue have decided to take matters into her own hands, in order to help out Maedean? And yet if Ginny Sue had indeed made up her mind to do such a thing, did it make sense that she would've left behind a handkerchief incriminating the very person she was trying to help?

Ginny Sue must've been reading my mind. "That was a dirty trick, too," she said.

"Dirty trick?" I said.

"For Dwight to get hold of Maedean's handkerchief and all. I mean, what he was trying to do is obvious, isn't it? He was determined to get her in trouble, if it was the last thing he ever did."

If Dwight had done it, it *had* indeed been the last thing he ever did, just like Ginny Sue said. And yet how could Ginny Sue be so sure that it had been Dwight? "You know," I said, "it's not exactly been established that Dwight was the one who left the handkerchief behind. It could've been left by whoever killed him. Just to throw people off."

Ginny Sue took another drag off her cigarette, blew smoke once again in my direction, and said, "Oh, it was Dwight, all right. Maedean knows what she's talking about, believe me. Dwight could be so mean!" She shrugged, and added, "Fact is, it's such an obvious ploy to get Maedean in trouble that I find it hard to believe that hick sheriff is taking the damn thing seriously."

I rather hoped Vergil was not anywhere near enough to overhear what she'd just called him. I believe the word *hick* is about as popular with Vergil as *Ms*.

"I mean, *really*," Ginny Sue was saying, "do you think that Maedean could be so stupid as to shoot Dwight and then not notice that he had her handkerchief in his goddamned *hand?*"

Actually, now that she mentioned it, I did think that Maedean could be that stupid. But Ginny Sue apparently was under the impression that hers was one of those rhetorical-type questions. She didn't seem to be expecting an answer. It was a good thing, because I sure didn't have an answer for her. The way I saw it, since I'd followed Maedean all day long and her whereabouts were pretty much accounted for, the question was not whether Maedean could be that stupid. But whether Ginny Sue could be.

After all, it was Ginny Sue—not Maedean—who seemed to have had the opportunity to shoot Dwight.

"How could anybody even think Maedean could do such a thing?" Ginny Sue was now saying. "I mean, if Maedean didn't love Dwight, do you think she'd have given up her *career* to marry him?"

That one got my attention. "Career?"

Ginny Sue nodded. "Well, it was going to be a career. Maedean was in college, studying to be an elementary schoolteacher."

I just looked at Ginny Sue. Maedean was going to teach elementary school? My God. It would've definitely required that she make drastic changes in her wardrobe.

"She could've had a fine career," Ginny Sue went on, "but no, she met this dumb basketball player three years older than she was, and she dropped out of school to marry him. Just like that."

Considering that elementary schoolteachers generally don't make enough to purchase cashmere coats and brand-new Corvettes, it seemed to me that Maedean had not exactly made the sacrifice of the century.

Ginny Sue obviously saw it different. "Maedean gave everything up for the man she loved. *Everything.*" Ginny Sue shook her blond head sadly. "And for what? To end up here, all alone, in this godforsaken hellhole."

I might've taken exception to what Ginny Sue had just said, but I didn't get the chance. At that moment the sheriff of this godforsaken hellhole appeared in the dining room doorway, staring straight at Ginny Sue.

"You're next" was all Vergil said, but it was clear to me, that he'd heard what Ginny Sue had just said. If looks could kill, Horace Merryman would've had another customer.

Maedean had followed Vergil into the dining room, and was now standing right in back of him, clutching Poopsie tight to her chest, as usual. Old Poops looked a little worse for wear. The top of the dog's fluffy head was all slicked down and damp-looking. Staring at the dog, I suspected that Maedean had cried the entire time she was talking to Vergil.

I glanced over at Vergil, and he confirmed my suspicions by giving me a long-suffering look. A look that seemed to me to be undeniably accusing. Lord. Vergil actually seemed to be blaming me that he'd found it necessary to spend a significant part of his evening with a weeping woman. Like it was my fault that Maedean had apparently hooked her tear ducts up to a faucet.

To keep from looking at Vergil, I glanced past him only to find myself staring directly at Maedean. Interestingly enough, she and Ginny Sue seemed to be exchanging a look of their own. Once again I wasn't sure what it was they were trying to communicate to each other, but when Ginny Sue moved past her sister to follow Vergil down the hall into the kitchen, Maedean also had a few actual words to say to her. I suppose, in case the look they'd exchanged hadn't quite done the trick. "Now don't you worry, Ginny Sue," Maedean said, "I already told Sheriff Minrath that you and I spent the *entire* evening at that lovely party, playing cards."

Lovely party? I turned to stare at Ginny Sue. Had Ginny Sue been at the bunko party, too?

I tried to think back to all the women I'd seen there, but it was useless. The whole thing was pretty much a blur. As I said before, I hadn't taken the surveillance seriously, so I hadn't paid attention.

Now I could kick myself for it.

"It was a lovely affair, really it was, given by one of the most prominent hostesses in this area, Lucy Belle Haines." Maedean now seemed to be speaking to the room at large. "Lucy Belle's from one of the finest Southern families, you know. I actually felt lucky that Ginny Sue and I had been given an invite, because I'd only just met Lucy Belle a few weeks ago at church. And her party was such a lovely, elegant affair—"

I just looked at Maedean. It had been a bunko party, for God's sake. She was making it sound like a lawn party at Tara.

Vergil was now no longer just looking at Maedean. He was glaring at her. "Mrs. Puckett, I'd like to speak to your sister now. *Before* you tell her anything more, all right?"

I suppose Vergil could've been a tad more tactful. The way he'd put that, he'd all but spelled it out that he suspected Maedean was outright coaching Ginny Sue as to what she should say.

Maedean's Leno chin jerked up, and for a moment there, she actually looked hurt. As if somebody had just falsely accused her of cheating. "Well, of *course,* Sheriff, whatever you say. I didn't mean to be talking out of turn, but I guess I'm just so upset about my poor Dwight that I simply don't know what I'm doing anymore."

Poopsie evidently picked up on his mistress's tone, because he immediately started whimpering, and looking around frantically for cover.

It was too late, however. Tears once again began coursing down Maedean's cheeks, dripping onto Poopsie's head. I had to kind of admire Maedean. She seemed to be able to turn on her waterworks more or less at will. That took real skill. Poopsie, of course, seemed to have an entirely different view. When the tears began to dampen the top of his head this time, he howled.

Vergil looked as if he might be inclined to do a little howling himself. In fact, he looked downright anxious to get away from Maedean before she turned on her water valve full tilt. Not to mention, before she gave her sister any additional hints. Turning quickly toward Ginny Sue, Vergil said solemnly, "Miss Hester? If you'll follow me—"

They disappeared down the hall, but on the way, Ginny Sue's voice floated back to us clear as a bell. "Look, Sheriff," she said, "I believe I told you that it's *Ms.* Hester, not *Miss.*"

I was starting to feel good that I was missing this particular interview.

I did not feel good, however, about spending any more time with Maedean. Particularly since the moment the sheriff was out of sight, she wheeled on me, her eyes blazing. "Now, see what you've done?" she hissed at me. Poopsie, of course, backed up Maedean's comments by cutting out the whimpering. And going straight into the growling.

I took a quick step backward, staring at Maedean. In less than a second, the woman had apparently turned her water valve to OFF. The only way you'd even guess that she'd been boo-hooing up a storm a split second earlier was that her cheeks were still wet. What control.

"If you'd taken that stupid handkerchief out of Dwight's hand like I told you to," Maedean was now saying, "that idiot sheriff wouldn't be grilling me and my sister the way he is." She gave her blond hair another toss. "I don't believe I have ever been so humiliated in my entire life—"

"Maedean," I broke in, "the sheriff would've talked to you, regardless."

"He wouldn't have talked to me like *that!*" she said. "Why, you ought to see the way that man looks at me. As if I were some kind of cold-blooded—"

I cut her off. "Maedean, the sheriff looks at everybody that way. He looks at his barber that way, he looks at *me* that—"

Maedean wasn't listening. "Well, it's insulting, I tell you! And it's all your fault!"

Now wait a second. This was the woman who referred to her deceased spouse as an asshole, who turned off tears a little faster than I turned off the faucet in my tub, and who wore clothes that a hooker would probably find too revealing. And she thought it was *my* fault that she was a suspect in her husband's murder? Was she kidding?

"Look, the person you should blame for implicating you is whoever left your handkerchief in the first place, not me."

Maedean drew an irritated breath. "I *told* you it was Dwight. He got himself shot, and then he—"

This was where I'd come in. I cleared my throat, and changed the subject. "You know, Maedean, I don't remember seeing Ginny Sue at that party earlier."

Maedean gave her blond head yet another toss. "Some detective you are! Ginny Sue was there, big as life. If you don't believe me, you can ask our hostess. A lovely, elegant woman—"

Yeah, yeah, I'd heard already. A lovely, elegant woman from one of the finest Southern families, who wore aprons with the words *Bunko Squad* written across the front. Hell, you couldn't get any more elegant than that.

I had every intention of speaking with Lucy Belle Haines—in fact, you could take that one to the bank. I saw no reason, however, to tell Maedean my intentions. I waved my hand in the air as if what she was saying was ridiculous. "I believe you, Maedean. OK? If you say Ginny Sue was there, I'm sure she was."

I may have been wrong, but I thought I saw a look of relief sweep across Maedean's face. It was gone as quickly as it had come, though, so I couldn't be sure. "Well, then," Maedean said.

Whatever that meant.

Since she'd calmed down a little, it seemed like a good time to ask her a few more questions. "Maedean, do you know of anybody who might've wanted your husband dead?"

I must've caught her off guard. She hesitated for just a moment, and then said, "Well, uh, no, of course not." She scratched the top of Poopsie's head, but her movements seemed suddenly nervous.

I just looked at her. Maedean *had* thought of somebody. I was sure of that. "You don't know of *anybody* who might've held a grudge against Dwight? Anybody he might've argued with?"

Maedean immediately started shaking her head, even before I'd finished asking my questions. She opened her mouth, already forming the word *no,* and then apparently thought better of it. "Well," she said, "Dwight *was* a used-car salesman."

I blinked at that one. Was Maedean implying that all used-car salesmen were in danger of being shot?

Maedean was still scratching Poopsie's damp head. "I imagine," she said, "that some of Dwight's customers might not have been real happy with the deals he gave them."

The woman lifted her small eyes to mine, and actually said this as if she believed it. As if she were really entertaining the notion that Dwight had met a tragic end at the hand of some guy who'd discovered that he could've bought his automobile cheaper at another car lot.

I ran my hand through my hair. "Maedean," I said, and I believe I was showing remarkable patience at this point, "can you think of anybody else?"

"Nope," she said without the least bit of hesitation this time. "Not really." She tapped her chin speculatively. "Unless, of course, you count Nolan, Dwight's brother. Nolan *said* he didn't mind the least bit that Dwight inherited all this land and all, but maybe he was just saying that." She shifted her weight from one foot to the other, and cocked her blond head in my direction. "I mean, you'd have to be a half-wit not to care that your brother got a whole bunch of stuff when your dad died, but you didn't get anything, I mean, wouldn't you?"

How well put. And yet, I had to admit Maedean could be right. At any rate, this seemed a tad more promising than the irate customer theory. I still had the feeling that Maedean was not telling me everything, but now I also had two other folks on my list that I wanted to have a little chat with—the bunko hostess, Lucy Belle Haines, and Dwight's younger brother, Nolan.

Unfortunately, before I talked to anybody, I had to talk to Vergil. He took his time, too, showing up again. It must've been well past three before I finally heard Vergil's footsteps outside in the foyer.

Following right in back of Vergil when he walked into the dining room was, of course, Ginny Sue. From the way Maedean greeted her, you'd have thought Vergil had been torturing the woman the entire time they'd been gone. "Oh, Ginny Sue, you poor thing, are you OK?" Maedean seemed once again—no surprise—to be tearing up. "Oh, sweetie," she said, her voice quavering, "was it awful?"

Vergil apparently didn't want to wait around to hear the rest of this emotional conversation. He gave me a pointed look, and hooked his thumb toward the kitchen, as if he were hitchhiking a ride to that room for the both of us. I reckon I knew when I was being summoned. I followed Vergil to the kitchen without a word.

Of course, once Vergil and I started talking, it went pretty fast. I didn't have all that much to tell him. The only bad part in the entire conversation was right after I'd told him everything I could think of, and we were both just sitting there at the Pucketts' kitchen table, staring at each other. It was at this point that Vergil laid down his Bic, closed his notebook, and heaved one of his world-beating sighs. "So," he drawled, "you're sticking with that story, then. That you were *bodyguarding* Maedean Puckett."

143

I was real tired by then. Maybe that's why I couldn't quite meet Vergil's eyes. I found myself staring instead at the cover of his notebook. Like some idiot. "Look," I told the notebook. "I followed Maedean around all day long, and I watched her. That's exactly what I did. Honest to God."

Vergil didn't say a word for what seemed like an awful long time. He just sat there, and just like me, he started staring at the cover of his notebook.

He was so quiet I could hear him breathing. That and his staring, I think, made me feel real fidgety. "Vergil," I finally said, "if you don't believe me, I can show you the pictures I took." I definitely should've thought that one over, before I said it out loud. Vergil blinked, and if anything, he looked sadder than he'd looked all night long. And that was going some. "Your bodyguarding involves taking pictures?"

I swallowed once before I answered. "Yes, Vergil," I said, lifting my head and looking him straight in the eyes, "it does."

Vergil's response was to sigh. Longer and louder even than before. Pushing back his chair, he said, "Haskell, if I find out that you're covering up for somebody, I won't let family feelings get in the way. I'll put your ass in a jail cell, just as sure as the sun's coming up tomorrow."

The way I saw it, the sun was coming up in about three hours, but I knew Vergil would not appreciate this little update. Besides, I got his meaning.

"Vergil, I'm not covering up for anybody." Except maybe for myself, I thought. I sure didn't want to tell him all about the job I'd been doing for Maedean. I'd rather have him looking at me as if I were a criminal than looking at me as if I were a fool. I gave Vergil a tight smile and got to my feet.

Vergil did not return my smile.

I was so tired walking down the hall to the front door, that when I passed the dining room where Maedean and Ginny Sue were still sitting, I didn't pause. The two of them seemed to be pretty deep in a whispered conversation, too, but I didn't even try to eavesdrop.

When I passed the living room, I could see out of the corner of my eye that Horace was still in there, doing whatever to poor Dwight. I didn't pause this time, either. I went right past the Guntermans, straight out the front door, and headed across the road to my truck. It took me ten minutes to get home, and I almost fell asleep twice on the way. Even Rip's wild hysteria at seeing me again was not enough to wake me up. I got into bed and fell asleep just as if a light had been turned off.

The next morning I can't say I felt a whole lot better. Of course, I'd only had four hours of shut-eye. I filled Rip's dog bowls, carried that dumb dog outside and then back inside, and fixed me a large glass of Coke so that the cold and the caffeine might pop my eyes open. It didn't work.

Neither did the shower I took right after I drained the entire glass of Coke. I drank another glass of Coke on the way into my office, but by the time I was parking my truck, as usual, in the alley by Elmo's Drugs, I was still blinking pretty bad. I was still so groggy, I almost forgot to check in with Melba. Just before I headed up the stairs to my office, however, I happened to notice Melba standing in the candy aisle. She was apparently trying to decide between a Milky Way or a large box of M&M's. This is the kind of decision that occupies a goodly portion of Melba's workday.

The candy aisle is real close to the front windows, it being Elmo's thinking that, in order to pick up most anything—from a prescription to an antacid—you'll have to walk right by all those enticing candies. As it turned out, Elmo's thinking was right on the money. Ever since Elmo moved his candy aisle, his candy sales have more than doubled.

I also believe Elmo's plan was, what you call, two-pronged. In addition to improving sales, he wanted to get the candy as far away from Melba as he could. This last part of his plan hasn't worked anywhere near as well as the first part. It's just kept Melba away from her desk even more than she'd been before.

I headed into the drugstore, made my way around the Maybelline display and the comic book racks to where Melba was still looking over the candy. "Melba," I said, "any messages?"

Melba looked up at me, but, oddly enough, she didn't answer right away. Her attention seemed caught almost immediately by something she saw over my left shoulder. Judging from the direction her eyes seemed to be focusing, I guessed it had to be something out on the sidewalk right in front of Elmo's picture windows.

I started to turn to look myself, but Melba grabbed my arm. "Haskell!" she said.

Her tone was so urgent, it startled me. "What?" I said, immediately turning back toward Melba.

Once I was looking straight at her, Melba seemed suddenly at a loss as to what to say next. She looked first at me, then down at the floor, and then up at the ceiling. Finally, her eyes went back to where they'd been in the first place. To the candy shelf. "Uh, Has-

kell," Melba said, "did you know that, uh, these Cara-
mello bars are real good?" She reached over, picked
one up, and held it right in front of my face.

I just stared at her.

"You yelled at me to tell me that?"

Melba shrugged. "Well, I thought you'd like to
know."

Her tone implied that *I* was the one at fault here.
For not being all that interested in her unsolicited testimonial on the quality of Caramellos.

"Well, gosh, *thanks*, Melba," I said, "I'll sure keep
that in mind." I'll admit, I was now looking at her as
if maybe her five kids had finally done what almost
everybody in town had always thought they'd eventually do. Those five hellions had finally driven Melba
stark staring crazy.

She had the staring part down pat, too, because
even now she was once again looking right past me,
her eyes fixed on something directly over my left
shoulder. I was getting tired of playing whatever game
Melba had going now. Not to mention, while she was
still coherent, I decided I'd better get an answer out
of her real quick. "Melba, as I was saying, do I have
any messages?"

Melba's eyes slid back to mine, and she started talking real fast. "Uh, Haskell, uh, why don't we talk back
at my desk?"

"You left my messages back there?"

"Well, uh, *yes*," Melba said, her plump face growing
stranger by the minute, "uh, that's it, all right. I got
your messages back there, uh, yeah, that's where—"
The whole time she was talking, her eyes kept dart-
ing back to whatever it was she'd been looking at in
the first place. Something just outside, something she

147

could obviously see over my shoulder, something that made her small blue eyes quite a bit larger.

I was determined to see what it was this time. As I started to wheel around, I knew Melba would reach out again to grab my arm. So, as fast as I could, I stepped away from her, dodging her hand. I turned. And I looked. At first all I saw was a dark-haired woman in a tailored blue suit standing awfully close to a guy dressed head to toe in black. Then, in a split second, I realized who it was. And what they were doing. Oh, my God, it was Imogene. You know, my girlfriend? And Randy Harned. You know, the blooming idiot? The moment it hit me exactly what they were up to out there, my entire body went rigid, as if an electric shock had just gone through me.

Either Randy was giving Imogene mouth-to-mouth resuscitation *standing up*. Or he was kissing her, right out on Main Street, in front of the entire town.

CHAPTER 9

The first time I'd ever seen my ex-wife, Claudzilla, in the arms of another man, I'd made a complete fool of myself. It had been at one of the parties that our neighbors always seemed to be giving around Christmas, and around midnight it had dawned on me that I hadn't seen Claudzilla in a while. So, dumb me, I started looking for her. Going from room to room in this big, sprawling, brick ranch.

I'd finally found Claudzilla and the husband of one of Claudzilla's best friends, wrapped up in each other, in the laundry room, of all things. I'd actually walked up to Claudzilla, tapped her on the shoulder, and said, "What the hell do you think you're doing?" As if maybe it had been so long since she'd let me kiss her that I needed reminding what it looked like. After I'd asked Claudzilla what had to be one of the dumbest questions ever to come out of my mouth, I did an even dumber thing. I grabbed the guy who'd been kissing her, flung him away from her, and when he

149

bounced off the side of the washing machine, I punched him right in the mouth.

For the next week or so that guy had not been in any condition to kiss anybody. In fact, I'd heard that all you had to do to get the guy to run out of the room, holding his mouth, was to point toward any mistletoe hanging overhead.

Oh yes, I'd been a macho asshole, all right. I'd put the guy's kisser out of commission for a few days, and I'd worried for the next year whether he was going to bring me up on charges. During that same time I'd also had to listen to Claudzilla, trying to make me believe that I had not really seen what she and I both knew I had.

Now, staring at Randy and Imogene out in front of Elmo's, I didn't feel the least bit inclined to go out there. I didn't feel like listening to whatever Imogene might have to say. And I didn't feel like punching Randy. What I felt like doing was heading straight back home. I wanted real bad to get right back into bed, pull the covers over my head, and pretend I'd never gotten up. I also wanted to pretend that right this minute I wasn't really feeling as if somebody had just kicked me in the gut.

Melba was staring at me with the sort of expression on her round face that I believe she'd wear if my doctor had just phoned to say my illness was terminal. I cleared my throat. "Melba," I said. I was surprised. My voice sounded just as calm as anything. "I'm asking you one more time. Do I have any messages?"

Melba's small blue eyes were very round as she shook her head. "Nope," she said. Her eyes traveled once again to the scene out front.

"OK," I said, without taking my eyes from her face,

"I'm going to be out of the office for a little while. If anybody calls, please take a message."

Melba's eyes now returned to mine. "Sure thing," she said. I may have been imagining it, but Melba's eyes seemed filled with pity.

"Hey, don't look so worried, Melba," I said. "I'm fine, OK?" I tried for a light tone, but I reckon I didn't quite make it. Melba, if anything, looked even more worried.

I turned to go—to head back out to the alley where I'd left my truck. I intended to go out the back door and walk around the back of the drugstore to the alley. It was not the shortest route to take to get to my truck—not by a long shot—but it suddenly seemed real important that I avoid Elmo's front door. It also seemed real important that I avoid my office for the next few hours, in case anybody—like, for example, Imogene—got a notion to drop by.

Wouldn't you know it, Melba wouldn't let me just leave. I hadn't taken two steps away from her when she said, "Haskell?"

I was still too close to pretend I hadn't heard her. I stopped and turned around to face her.

"For what it's worth," Melba said, "I was watching them two all along. And I think he sort of surprised her."

I swallowed once before I spoke. "Take my messages, OK?" I said.

I turned back around, but once again Melba stopped me. "Haskell?" she said.

I took a deep breath, and again turned to face her.

"I don't think Randy Harned's all that good-looking, after all," Melba said.

I just stared at her. I knew, in her own way, Melba

was trying to make me feel better. She was, however, failing miserably.

"Melba," I said, "I'll talk to you later." Then I turned and walked very quickly toward the back of the drugstore.

On the way, I didn't let myself think once about what I'd just seen out front. It was as if I'd put it away somewhere, and later, when I could stand to look at it, I'd take it out. I went out Elmo's back door, walked around to the alley, got into my truck, and started the engine. The whole time I was doing this, I deliberately made myself concentrate just on the task at hand. Nothing more. It wasn't until I'd already started the engine that I even thought about where I was headed. Let me see, last night I'd decided that I was going to have a little chat with the hostess of the bunko party. Because if Maedean and Ginny Sue had indeed worked out a switch sometime during the evening, it had to have been noticed. This sure seemed like a good time to check this out.

The quickest way to the Lincoln Log cabin where the party had been held was straight down Main Street. Straight past Elmo's. I took instead what had to be one of the longest routes to the cabin, down one of the side roads running parallel to Main. Usually, this route wouldn't have been so bad. In the last month or so, though, a significant portion of Crayton County has been getting city water.

This significant portion, unfortunately, does not include my house, but I'd heard it included some of the side roads parallel to Main. The road I traveled to get to the bunko party log cabin had to be, without a doubt, one of these roads. There was a freshly dug trench lining one side, and long sections of pipe were lying next to the trench, all ready to be buried. There was also more mud, piled up on the side of the road and sliding into the middle of the road, than I had ever seen in my entire life.

I'd heard that the folks owning property along the new water pipe, who wanted their houses hooked up to the thing, were being charged three thousand dollars for the privilege. Now, looking at all that mud, it occurred to me that the entire water project could probably be financed by just roping off a few of the affected roads and holding mud wrestling tournaments in the middle of them. I do believe folks from all over the county would pay big money to attend such an event. Particularly if some of the participants—both male and female—were scantily clad.

Unfortunately, with Pigeon Fork being right smack dab in the middle of what some call the Bible Belt, I had a feeling it would not be wise to suggest my mud wrestling idea at the next town meeting. Or else I might find out real quick what the term "mudslinging" really meant. Speaking of which, all the way to the log cabin, I heard the steady slap, slap, slap of mud slinging all over the underside of my truck. The sound continued even when I pulled onto Highway 11 and headed out of town. Highway 11 is a two-lane blacktop, and there weren't any trenches lining either side, but the slap of mud under my truck didn't slow down a bit. I figured the sound was from mud dropping off as I went, or it was mud being thrown under my truck off my well-coated tires.

Ten mud-slinging minutes later, I was knocking on the front door of the Lincoln Log cabin. The woman who answered my knock I immediately recognized. She was, no doubt about it, the tall lady who'd carried the tray of can-apes into the living room. Up close, I realized she was at least ten years older than I'd thought yesterday when I was looking at her through my telephoto. Lucy Belle Haines had to be at least fifty. I'd also guess, looking at the deep rich brown of her hair, that Lucy Belle would answer "Yes," to "Does she, or doesn't she?"

Today her brown hair was no longer in a bun. It had been pulled back into a ponytail. And, instead of the apron with *Bunko Squad* printed across the front, she was wearing navy blue sweats, rubber gloves, and carrying a spray bottle of carpet shampoo. This was the woman that Maedean had described as lovely and elegant.

Lucy Belle demonstrated just how lovely and elegant she could be right after she opened the door. *"What?"* she snapped.

Her tone was so outright hostile, for a second it threw me. Lord. Had she been taking nasty lessons from Ginny Sue? I took a deep breath, and gave her one of my best winning smiles. "Mrs. Haines? I'm Haskell Blevins, and—"

The winning smile didn't work. "Look," Lucy Belle said, pointing a rubber-gloved finger in my direction, "if you're selling something, I don't want it. And I'm real busy here—" She was already shutting her door.

Having a door shut in my face was not an entirely new experience. Back in the sixth grade, trying to get a new bicycle, I'd sold seeds door to door. I'd responded to an ad in the back of a comic book, and in no time at all, I'd been in the seed business. It had been a hopeless effort right from the start. The number of seed packets I would've had to sell in order to qualify for a bike was roughly equivalent to what it would've taken to supply food to an entire Latin American country. What's more, a good portion of the seeds I was given to sell were not exactly the sort folks in a small town bought on a regular basis. Things like kohlrabi and eggplant. In fact, the only thing I got out of the entire seed-selling venture was learning how to stick my foot, very quickly, into a doorway to keep the door from shutting in my face.

That sort of thing must be like learning to swim— you never forget it. I had my foot in Lucy Belle's door before I even thought about what I was doing. "I'm not selling anything," I told her. "I'm investigating a murder."

Funny thing, you mention the word *murder*, and right away you've got a person's attention. Lucy Belle not only stopped shutting her door, she opened it a little wider and stared at me. "The Puckett murder?"

Now it was my turn to stare at her. The thing had happened too late for it to appear in this morning's *Pigeon Fork Gazette*, and yet, already Lucy Belle had heard about it. Once again I found myself marveling at the efficiency of the grapevine in this part of the country. "You know about that?" I said.

Lucy Belle waved her carpet shampoo in the air, and said, *"Everybody* knows about it by now." Her tone implied that she was telling me something I myself should've already known.

I nodded. Of course. It had been more than nine hours since Dwight's body had been found. No doubt folks as far away as Louisville knew every detail by now. Sometimes, I wonder why Pigeon Fork even bothers with a paper.

"Well, then, I guess you know I want to talk to you," I said.

Lucy Belle was nodding. "On account of Maedean coming to my bunko party last night. Ever since I heard what happened, I've been kind of expecting the law to come by." She opened her door all the way, and motioned me inside with the carpet shampoo bottle she was holding. "I knew you all would be wanting my statement."

I didn't hesitate to step inside, but to tell you the truth, what Lucy Belle had just said put me into a quandary of sorts. I wasn't exactly the *law*, as she so quaintly put it. And I really ought to tell her that I wasn't. There *was* such a thing as impersonating an officer, and the last time I checked, it was a thing you could get arrested for. I couldn't help recalling what Vergil had said early this morning about putting my butt in a jail cell. I'd sure hate to test him on that.

As I followed Lucy Belle into her living room, though, she said over her shoulder, "I'm not one to gossip, anybody will tell you that, but since this is official, I guess I don't have a choice. I'll have to give you a statement. Even though I sure don't hold with minding other folks' business."

I took a deep breath. From the way she sounded, it looked like Lucy Belle might not be inclined to tell me a thing unless I let her continue to think what she seemed already to want to think.

"I should've recognized you when I first opened the door," Lucy Belle was going on. "Because your picture was in the paper, wasn't it? It was right after you caught some criminal or another, as I recall."

This is one of the disadvantages about living in a small town. Folks have all heard of you. Sort of. Only between hearing about you and actually meeting you, they sometimes get a tad confused. So that they end up remembering things about you that's only dimly connected to the truth.

Lucy Belle here was apparently remembering the write-up the *Pigeon Fork Gazette* had done on me right after the last case I worked on. It being awhile ago and all, the thing that obviously stuck in her mind was that I had something to do with law enforcement.

I made up my mind. If she asked, I'd tell her I was a private eye, not a cop. And if she didn't, I didn't see any reason to volunteer anything.

"I must say," Lucy Belle was now saying, "it's good to see that the law has brought in their top man on this one."

"Yes ma'am," I said. Lord. I may have been wrong, but it seemed to me as if I suddenly sounded a whole lot like Joe Friday on that old series, *Dragnet.* In another minute, I'd be saying, *Just the facts, ma'am, nothing but the facts.*

I reckon, without even thinking about it, I'd slipped right back into cop mode. Of course, after eight years on the force, I reckon cop mode is practically second nature to me.

As I followed Lucy Belle, I found myself taking out a Bic and my 3×5 spiral notebook, just like I used to do when I was back on the Louisville police force. I flipped to a clean page as Lucy Belle watched.

She apparently was waiting until I was all ready to take notes, because she didn't say another word until I'd settled myself into one of a pair of beige-striped Queen Anne chairs positioned on either side of the large stone fireplace in her living room.

Then, taking a seat in the other Queen Anne chair and putting her carpet shampoo bottle on the floor next to her chair, Lucy Belle said, "She did it, you know. I can't tell you how, but she did it."

I was taking the top off my Bic, so what she said caught me pretty much off guard. For a second, I wasn't even sure she'd said it. "Excuse me?"

"Maedean murdered Dwight," Lucy Belle said. "You wanted a statement. Well, that's mine. *She did it.*"

One thing about it, this little turn of the conversation certainly took my mind off the should-I-tell-her-I'm-not-a-cop issue. I leaned toward Lucy Belle and tried not to look eager. "What makes you think that Maedean did it?"

Lucy Belle tucked one foot under her, and leaned toward me. "Well, I don't like to gossip, anybody that knows me will tell you that—"

I might've believed her if her large gray eyes had not been sparkling so much with excitement. I didn't say anything, though. I just looked at her as she continued, "—but that Maedean Puckett, well, it's as plain as the nose on your face that she doesn't care about anything except that damn dog of hers!"

"No kidding," I said.

"Can you believe she brought that mangy thing to my party? Can you?"

Actually, I could.

"If I'd had any idea she was going to bring her dog, I'd never have invited her! I was just trying to be neighborly, you know, her being relatively new in town and all."

I gave Lucy Belle a quick smile, opened my mouth to begin my questions, but I didn't get the chance.

"And this morning, guess what I found in a corner of my upstairs bathroom?" Lucy Belle was going right on. "It's carpeted, too. And guess—just guess—what I found?"

It seemed to me this was yet another one of those problems you didn't need to be a detective to solve. Judging from the rubber gloves, the carpet shampoo, and the faint smell I'd picked up on as I walked in the front door, I really didn't have to guess.

I hoped I looked sympathetic.

"Dog crap!" Lucy Belle said. *"That's* what I found! Maedean excused herself to go to the little girl's room two or three times during the night. So that damn mutt must've done it one of those times!" Lucy Belle pointed at me with a rubber-gloved finger again. "There's no way Maedean could not have known what that mutt was doing! All I can say is that she'd better be glad I didn't find her dog's mess until this morning, or else she'd have had two deaths to deal with! That's all I can say!"

We appeared to have strayed off the subject. "Uh, Mrs. Haines," I said, "you said that you thought Maedean had mur—"

That was all I got out before Lucy interrupted me.

"Goodness yes, she murdered him! No doubt about it. I mean, anybody will tell you how much I hate to gossip, but *everybody* had heard the rumors, you know. Not just me."

"The rumors?"

"Everybody knew Maedean was running around on Dwight."

I blinked at that one. Wait a second now. The woman who'd hired me to convince her husband that she was not being unfaithful really *was* being unfaithful? "You don't say!" I said. I've never known exactly what this particular phrase means, but you hear it around these parts all the time. Oddly enough, instead of encouraging folks not to say any more, it always seems to make them say a whole lot more stuff almost immediately.

Lucy Belle was no exception. She nodded her dark head eagerly. "I do say! Everybody in town has been talking about it. It's a scandal, a real scandal, I don't mind telling you. That woman was carrying on right under poor Dwight's nose. And now look what's happened!" She gave me a pointed look. "I mean, Maedean had herself a motive, sure as shooting."

I sort of wished Lucy Belle hadn't used that particular phrase. "Do you know who the other man was?"

Lucy Belle waved her rubber-gloved hand in the air again. "Well, now, that's the sixty-four-thousand-dollar question right there. Nobody seems to know for sure. I mean, I bet I've talked to nearly everybody who knew Maedean, or Dwight, or any of their friends."

I didn't say a word, but it did occur to me that this seemed to be a lot of talking for a woman who didn't gossip.

"Wouldn't you know it, nobody seems to know." Lucy Belle pointed her rubber-gloved finger at me again. "Or else," she said, lifting an eyebrow, "they're just not telling."

At this point Lucy Belle seemed to have realized that the image of her dialing up everybody in town who was familiar with the Pucketts, searching for Maedean's mystery man, didn't exactly set real well with what she'd been telling me earlier. Her cheeks pinked up some, and she got real busy pulling off her rubber gloves. "Not that I like to gossip, mind you," she said. "Anybody will tell you how I hate to gossip.

I'm not some busybody, minding other folks' business, that's for sure." She put one rubber glove in her lap, and started working on the other one. "Anybody'll tell you, I've got enough to do around here, I certainly don't have the time—"

OK. OK. I didn't care whether she gossiped or not. As a matter of fact, given both options—to gossip, or not to gossip—I definitely hoped that she'd gone with the former. That meant she'd have more to tell me.

And that I could get it out of her easier.

"—Oh no, I can't sit around on the phone all day, talking my head off about things that are none of my business. I'm just not one—"

I'd heard enough. I interrupted her. "Then, you don't have any idea who this other guy could be?"

Lucy Belle seemed sort of relieved to be on another topic. She shook her head. "Well, I do know it was somebody. That's for sure. Oh my, yes, Maedean was seeing somebody, no doubt about it."

I stared at her. *Somebody?* This was the best she could do? What Lucy Belle was telling me, then, was that I could pretty much cross off animals and birds? And narrow the field down to just humans? Was that what she was telling me?

I moved restlessly in the Queen Anne chair. "You're absolutely certain that Maedean was seeing somebody, but you can't even guess—"

Lucy Belle interrupted me by waving a limp rubber glove in my direction. "Well, now, I didn't say I couldn't *guess*. Because I do have a guess. I just hate to say, on account of my not being one to gossip and all."

I leaned toward her. "What's your guess?"

Lucy Belle hesitated for about two seconds max.

Then, in a sudden rush of words, she said, "Nolan! That's my guess. *Nolan Puckett.*" She emphasized what she was saying by nodding her head up and down.

As my daddy used to say, my flabber was gasted. "Nolan, Dwight's younger *brother,* was having an affair with Dwight's *wife?*"

Lucy Belle waved her limp rubber gloves at me, as if trying to shush me. "You wanted my guess. Well, that's it." She shrugged and added, "I know I'm right, though. I know it. Because if you ever really look at Nolan when he's talking about Maedean, well, all I can say is, it's obvious that boy's in love."

I swallowed. Surely, this wasn't all she was basing her suspicions on. "Do you know if anybody ever saw Nolan and Maedean together?"

Lucy Belle shook her dark head. "I don't believe so."

I was getting a little impatient here. So far, it seemed as if Lucy Belle was heavy on speculation, but a quart low on facts.

I cleared my throat. "Well, then, did you or anybody you know ever see Maedean with *any* man other than her husband?"

Lucy Belle gave me an indulgent smile. "Well, *of course,* nobody ever saw Maedean with anybody! She was running around on her husband! You don't do that sort of thing out in public."

What could I say? Her point *was* well taken. I did, however, have a slight problem with her logic. "If nobody has ever seen Maedean with another man, then how do you know she was running around on Dwight?"

Lucy Belle now gave me the sort of look you'd give somebody questioning the existence of the moon.

"Have you ever taken a good look at Maedean?" she asked.

I wasn't sure where she was going with this, but I nodded, anyway. Yes, I believe I could say without fear of contradiction that I'd taken several very long looks at Maedean.

Lucy Belle pinched her mouth together in an expression of prim disapproval. "No woman dresses like that for her husband."

I stared at Lucy Belle, beginning to get a real bad feeling. Had I just been wasting my time, listening to what amounted to just a lot of gossip? From a woman who said she never indulged in such a thing?

Lucy Belle leaned toward me this time. "Oh my, yes, you can tell the sort of woman Maedean is, just by looking at the way she dresses. She's a trollop, sure as I'm sitting here."

Oh yeah, this was a waste of time, all right. I gave Lucy Belle the briefest of nods. What I was thinking, of course, was: *trollop?* That was a word I hadn't heard in a while.

Oddly enough, I decided spending any more time on this particular topic was pointless. Clearing my throat, I said, "Mrs. Haines, we've had a report that Mrs. Puckett was not here all night long. That, in fact, she left for quite some time."

If Lucy Belle here could indulge in a little unfounded rumormongering, I could, too.

Lucy Belle's big eyes got even bigger. "I don't know where you heard that, but somebody's lying to you."

"How do you figure, ma'am?" Lord. In my effort to get back to the facts, ma'am, nothing but the facts, I was once again sounding like Jack Webb.

Lucy Belle was shrugging again. "Maedean was here

from about six to after midnight. She never even left the living room. Except those times I mentioned before when, you know, she went to the little girl's room." Lucy colored a little when she said this, and dropped her voice to a whisper. Apparently, she felt that mentioning bodily functions to a cop might be something you could be given a ticket for. She hurriedly added, "But she wasn't out of the room for very long."

"You're sure about that?" I asked.

Lucy nodded even more emphatically. "Just as sure as I am that Maedean and Dwight were not getting along."

I didn't blink. "Not getting along, ma'am?" Really, all I needed was a partner named Frank.

Lucy Belle nodded, her eyes sparkling again. "It was on account of the inheritance, you know. Evidently, Dwight wanted to keep working his father's farm, just like his dad had done before him. You know, to sort of continue the family tradition?"

"Yes, ma'am?"

Lucy Belle nodded again. "Dwight wanted to raise a few head of beef cattle, and grow tobacco, and be, you know, what he called a real farmer. Maedean didn't want to."

"Yes, ma'am?"

Lucy Belle nodded. "Maedean wanted to sell all the property off to some land developer who was interested in turning all that land fronting the road into a subdivision."

I had been scribbling along, taking notes on what Lucy Belle was saying, but now I lifted my head to stare at her. This last was news.

It was news, oddly enough, that neither sister had thought to mention.

"A land developer had contacted Maedean?" I said.

Lucy shifted position in the Queen Anne chair. Leaning toward me, she dropped her voice to a whisper. "From what I'd heard, this big company contacted Maedean and Dwight right after Isom Puckett died." Arching an eyebrow again, Lucy Belle added, still whispering, "I also heard that Maedean and Dwight had some real big fights over this."

I stared at her again. There didn't seem to be anyone but us in the entire log cabin, so why exactly was she whispering? Still, I supposed I ought to follow suit. "You heard this from Maedean?" I whispered back, feeling like a fool.

Lucy nodded. "Everybody at the party did," she whispered again. She actually looked around as if to check that the walls around us weren't listening, and then added, in a stage whisper loud enough to be heard outside in my truck, "Maedean had herself a little too much to drink, if you get my meaning, and by the time the party was over, she'd told just about everybody in the entire room how mad she was at her husband." Lucy Belle leaned forward at this point and waved her limp rubber gloves at me again. For emphasis, apparently. "That right there is how come I know she killed him. Sure as shooting."

Have I mentioned that I wished she'd stop saying that? Even when the words were stage-whispered, they made me cringe.

Lucy Belle was hurrying on, her stage whisper getting louder and louder. "Even Maedean's own sister, Ginny Sue, heard her saying how mad she was."

That one got my attention. "So Ginny Sue *was* here?"

Lucy was nodding. "She sure was. She left early, though."

I blinked. Yet another bit of news the sisters had not told me.

"Early, ma'am?"

"About eleven."

I was so surprised to hear this that for a moment I stopped whispering, and outright blurted, "What? I don't remember—"

It was only Lucy's wide eyes on my face that kept me from finishing my sentence. "You don't remember?" she said.

I stared at her, thinking fast. "I don't remember anybody else reporting this, ma'am," I said. God. Am I good, or am I good?

Lucy Belle shrugged. "Well, probably not all that many even noticed that Ginny Sue had left. Ginny Sue *was* parked out back, you know, so nobody had to move their car to let her out. She left by the back door, and there's a road leading out of here that winds straight back through the woods. Once you get real deep in those woods, you know, you can't even see a car's headlights."

I stared at Lucy some more. Ginny Sue had parked her car in back of the cabin, gone out the back door, and traveled through the woods. If you didn't know better, you could actually believe that Ginny Sue had known that I was across the street. And that she'd deliberately left in such a way that I wouldn't see her go.

I was beginning to feel real uneasy. Could I have confused the two sisters at a distance? Could they

have actually worked out a switch? Hell, it wouldn't
have been too hard. I hadn't even watched Maedean
the entire time through my telephoto. In fact, as I
recalled, I'd been so bored, it had been hard to keep
my eyes open. I wondered. Could I have dozed off
some, and not even realized it? I sure didn't remember
seeing anybody leave the party early.

I was feeling more and more uneasy. Until I suddenly recalled that Maedean had been carrying Poopsie around with her the entire time she was at the
bunko party. I couldn't remember even a minute that
she'd put Poopsie down. So the woman I'd been
watching through my telephoto lens had to have been
Maedean, didn't it? Lord knows, Poopsie snapped at
everybody else. I'd even seen him snap today at Ginny
Sue. I sat there in that Queen Anne chair, opposite
Lucy Belle, trying to look as if I were still just taking
notes, while all this was flashing through my mind.
What also was flashing through my mind was this: Can
you believe, in this particular case, it looked as if
Poopsie was a more credible witness than I was?

This was not a particularly comforting thought.

Of course, even if I knew for a fact that the two
sisters could not possibly have switched places, it still
didn't necessarily mean that the two of them were
not involved in Dwight's death. It was possible that
Maedean could've gotten Ginny Sue to shoot Dwight,
all the while Maedean herself stayed right in front of
me. So that I, of course, could be Maedean's personal
alibi. My head was beginning to ache.

It turned out to be a little harder to get away from
Lucy Belle than I expected, too. When I got up to
leave, saying, "Well, thanks so much, I sure appreciate

your taking the time to answer my questions," Lucy remained seated.

"So what do you think?" she said.

"Excuse me?" I said.

"Do you think it was Maedean? That she really did do it? I heard, you know, that Dwight had written her initials—you know, *M.P.*—in his own *blood,* on the floor," Lucy Belle said. "That's what I heard anyway."

The woman who didn't gossip was clearly pumping me for details. Gory details at that. "Ma'am," I said, "I'm not at liberty to give out any information on—"

Lucy Belle interrupted me. Leaning forward, her big eyes once again sparkling with excitement, she said, "I also heard poor Dwight was shot many times." She lowered her voice once again to a whisper. "Many, *many* times."

All told, it took me another ten minutes to finally make my way to the door. During those ten minutes Lucy Belle let me know that she'd heard that Dwight had been stabbed, shot, and strangled, that he'd left a note naming his killer, that Maedean had tried to kill herself, and that Maedean and Ginny Sue had had a fistfight right after discovering Dwight's body. For a non-gossiper, it was hard to believe how much Lucy Belle had managed to hear.

Even after I was out her front door and heading at a pretty fast clip toward my truck, Lucy Belle had still another question for me. Standing on her front porch, she waved her rubber gloves at me one more time and shouted, "Oh, by the way, do you think O.J. really did it?"

I laid rubber, getting out of there. The only bad thing about heading away from Lucy Belle that fast was that it brought me back that much quicker to downtown Pigeon Fork. It seemed as if I had time to only take one deep breath, and then I was driving down Main Street again, with Elmo's Drugs just two blocks up ahead.

I knew, of course, that I was being stupid, but my throat actually went dry when I first looked toward Elmo's. As if maybe I actually expected that Imogene would still be out in front. With Randy. Neither one of them, of course, was there. I found myself, though, looking all around as I pulled into the alley next to the drugstore and parked my truck. That's how much I dreaded running into Imogene.

Lord. You'd have thought Imogene had caught *me* with somebody, instead of the other way around. I knew I was being a coward, no doubt about it, but as I made my way up the stairs to my office, I was still looking from side to side, and back over my shoulder.

What I should've been doing was looking straight up as I climbed. I was halfway up the stairs before I noticed up above me on the landing, obviously waiting for me, a tall, dark-haired guy wearing a brown corduroy coat thrown carelessly over faded overalls. Up until that very moment I hadn't been able to get a face when I'd thought of this guy. And yet, now, looking at him as I climbed the stairs, I knew who he was even before I got close enough to read the name stitched above the left pocket of his jacket: *Nolan Puckett*. The guy who, according to Lucy Belle Haines, had been carrying on a torrid affair with his own brother's wife.

CHAPTER 10

I'd barely set foot on the landing outside my office door when Nolan took a quick step forward and stuck out a huge, calloused hand. "Hi there, I'm Nolan Puckett, Dwight Puckett's brother," he said.

I took his hand to shake it, and for a moment, my own hand completely disappeared in his. I stood there and watched this happen with some amazement. It was a whole lot like watching a large fish swallow a minnow.

I was kind of relieved when Nolan finally let go, and my hand showed up again. "Glad to meet you," I said, a tad uncertainly.

Nolan, however, was not a bit uncertain. "I am real glad to meet you, sir," he said. "*Real* glad. I seen you around town, you know, and I been hearing folks talk about you. I even read about you in the paper a while back. I don't mind telling you, sir, that this here is a *real* honor."

I was opening my office door, getting ready to step

aside so that he could go in before me, but after hearing all this, I turned around and just looked at him. Did he have me confused with somebody else? Like maybe some war hero, or something? Not to mention, what was this *sir* stuff? The way I figured it, Nolan was, at most, only six years younger than me, so that would make him twenty-eight to my thirty-four. So why was he talking to me as if I were a couple generations ahead of him?

I suppose, if pressed, I would have to admit Nolan did look quite a bit younger than twenty-eight. He wore his light brown hair cut real short, parted on one side and combed neatly across, like a little boy's. He had a cowlick, too, right at the back of his part, and he'd obviously tried to slick it down with something. Whatever he'd used hadn't worked. All it had done was make his hair look a tad greasy at that particular spot. The cowlick was still sticking up big as life.

With brown eyes a size too large for the rest of his features, a nose that tilted up at the end, and dimples in both cheeks, Nolan Puckett had a little boy's face on top of a big man's body.

The whole time I was looking him over, Nolan was doing the same to me, his large brown eyes as eager as a puppy's. He was a good inch taller than Dwight had been, and judging from the way his hand had totally engulfed mine, I'd say he could palm a basketball easy. So why was it that Nolan had never played basketball like his older brother? I wondered this right up until Nolan walked into my office. As he went on past me, right through my front door, he stumbled over the doorjamb and pitched headfirst into my floor lamp, knocking it over.

"Oops," Nolan said.

As Nolan was picking up my lamp and checking to make sure the bulb wasn't broken, his elbow somehow connected with a stack of magazines on the edge of my desk. The magazines tumbled to the floor.

"Oops," Nolan said again.

While Nolan was picking up the magazines, his other elbow connected with the electric pencil sharpener sitting on one of my wall shelves. The sharpener hit the floor and bounced.

"Oops," Nolan said one more time.

While he was trying to grab the sharpener on the bounce, Nolan up and dropped every one of the magazines he'd just picked up.

"Uh-oh," Nolan said this time. No doubt, he'd worn *oops* out.

All in all, it must've taken Nolan a good ten minutes to finally sit down. Mind you, I did not spend those ten minutes wondering anymore why he hadn't played basketball. I pretty much spent them wondering how in hell Nolan had ever managed to climb the stairs to my office without falling and breaking his neck.

I was also wondering, was it really possible that this bumbling kid was Maedean's lover? You'd think, having a torrid affair would require *some* coordination, wouldn't it? That, of course, was not a picture I particularly wanted to dwell on, so I turned my attention back to Nolan himself.

He was still bending over, picking up my magazines off the floor and very deliberately stacking them one by one on the edge of my desk. Twice he knocked them off again, and had to begin all over. Both times, he said—you guessed it—"Oops." I couldn't be absolutely positive, but I was beginning to strongly suspect

that Lucy Belle Haines, with her affair theory, was—
to put it kindly—out of her tree.

When Nolan was finally seated in the wooden chair
opposite my desk, and the magazines and everything
else were back to where they'd been before he came
in, he gave me a sheepish grin. "Sorry," he said.
"Dwight always did say I didn't belong indoors."

I shrugged. "No problem," I said. What I was thinking was: *I'm not real sure you belong outdoors, either.*

Now that I had a good look at him, I could see that
there were dark circles under Nolan's eyes. His face
was real close to the color of ashes, and although he
was smiling at me, big as anything, the smile didn't
quite reach his eyes. I felt a quick rush of sympathy.
This poor guy had first lost his dad, and now he'd lost
his brother, both within three months of each other.
That had to be hard.

Assuming, of course, that he himself had not had a
hand in his brother's death. Although, now that I
thought of it, shooting somebody would require some
coordination, too, wouldn't it? It could very well be
that Nolan here could be eliminated as physically incapable of committing the crime.

Sitting there behind my desk, looking at Nolan's
grief-stricken face, I felt almost guilty for even considering him as a possibility.

I cleared my throat. "Nolan," I said, "I want you
to know how very sorry I am about—uh—about
everything."

Lord. Am I terrible in situations like this, or what?
I never do know what to say. I wanted to add something kind of upbeat, like I was sure that Dwight and
their dad were together now, both no doubt in a better
place, something like that. The only trouble with say-

ing that, though, was that it pretty much ignored the particularly cruel way Dwight had been sent to that better place. It also pretty much overlooked the fact that, if given a choice, Dwight probably would not have chosen to go, better place or not.

While I was scrambling in my mind for something more appropriate to say, Nolan was just sitting here, his big eyes pinned on my face. I thought for a moment that he was just waiting for me to go on, but then I realized the guy was actually fighting tears. That is, I realized it just about the time Nolan broke into loud, racking sobs. That was pretty much the tip-off.

I sat there, watching Nolan cry, all but squirming in my chair. I don't mind admitting that I was now at a total loss as to what to do. For one thing, this had never happened to me before. What I mean to say is, by now, after Maedean, I was getting downright accustomed to having a woman burst into tears right in front of me. In all my born days, however, I'd never had a guy do it.

Generally, when a woman starts crying right in front of me, I take her in my arms and let her, more or less, cry on my shoulder. That is, if the aforementioned woman doesn't happen to be holding a fluffy golden-haired dog with sharp, tiny teeth.

I was not, however, the least bit inclined to take Nolan here into my arms. Even though in this day and age I realize I'll probably be accused of being sexist, I'm sorry, but I might as well confess right here that my shoulders are pretty much exclusively reserved for those of the female persuasion. I know. I know. It's the nineties, for God's sake, and these days men are supposed to be able to express their emotions just as freely as women. Hell, it's not even supposed to be embarrassing or anything for a man to cry in public any more. In fact, men getting in touch with their emotions seems to be outright encouraged.

Uh-huh.

Right.

The problem with this whole men-getting-in-touch-with-their-feelings concept, however, is that nobody has exactly said what one guy is supposed to do when some other guy starts getting in touch right in front of him. Given my total lack of preparation, I just sat there behind my desk, like a bump on a pickle, waiting for poor Nolan to get a grip. It took him a while. In fact, I was seriously considering picking up the latest *Home Mechanix* magazine, which was lying on top of my desk, and leafing through the thing, when Nolan finally dried up.

"Hey, man, I'm sorry," Nolan said, wiping his eyes—and, not incidentally, his nose—on his sleeve. "It's just that I can't believe Dwight is really gone."

Now, what was I supposed to say to that? *Oh, he's gone, all right, you can take my word for it?* I decided saying nothing was better than saying that.

"One thing I can believe," Nolan went on, "I can sure believe that idiot Sheriff Minrath hasn't caught who did this yet. I can sure believe *that.*"

I moved uneasily in my chair. This was fast turning into a conversation I not only didn't want to have, I also didn't want Vergil to find out about. "Now, Nolan," I said, holding up my hand, "I'm sure the sheriff is doing his level best to—"

Nolan interrupted me with a snort. "Only his best just ain't good enough, is it? That's why I've come to you," Nolan said. "You, sir, are the only person in this whole damn town with any real crime-solving experience."

Oh, my Lord, this was most definitely a conversation I never in my wildest nightmares wanted Vergil to find out about. I was beginning to wish they'd never written that article about me in the *Gazette*. "Nolan," I said, "I appreciate the vote of confidence, I really do. But, I'm telling you, the sheriff is real competent, and—"

"You think so, huh?" Nolan said, interrupting me. "You really think so? Well, answer me this—wasn't the sheriff the one who hired the Guntermans?"

I just looked at him. What could I say? He did have quite a compelling argument there.

Nolan knew it, too. He pointed his finger at me and said, "You know damn well that them Guntermans couldn't detect their way out of a paper sack."

I had to agree that a paper sack probably would severely challenge the twins' detecting skills, but I wasn't about to tell Nolan that.

Nolan was hurrying on anyway. "Mr. Blevins, I'm counting on you to find out who killed my brother—"

I interrupted *him* this time. "It's Haskell," I said, "not Mr. Blevins."

Nolan gave me a quick nod, as if to say, *OK, I heard you,* and went on, "I'll pay whatever your going rate is, and I don't care what it costs. I want you to find out whoever done this terrible thing to my brother. And I want him *punished!*"

While Nolan was saying this last, he was looking at his lap, twisting his huge hands together. When he said that last word, though, he glanced up at me.

Looking into Nolan's eyes at that moment, I actually felt a chill. Because, for a split second, you could see the raw rage there. Nolan looked like a man angry enough to kill. Lord. Had his brother's death made him this furious? Or had it been something else? When you come right down to it, it didn't necessarily have to be Dwight's death that made Nolan so angry. In fact, there could be an entirely different reason for his fury. Like, oh, say, him being left out in the cold, as far as the family farm was concerned.

I pulled out my middle desk drawer, and took out one of the spiral-bound notebooks I keep in there. Then I scrambled around for a minute or so until I found a pencil. "If I'm going to help you, I'll need some information," I said.

Nolan was still wiping his moist eyes with the back of his hand, but his head went up at that. He scooted his chair a little closer to my desk, and said, "Yessir. Whatever you need to know."

I chewed on the end of my pencil, and then said, as casually as I could, "So, who inherits the Puckett farm now ... ?" I'd been intending to finish with ... *now that your brother is gone,* but I thought better of it. I'd already sat through one flash flood, and I sure didn't see any reason to risk starting another one.

Nolan immediately sat up a little straighter and started nodding. Like maybe he was some eager schoolkid who wanted the teacher to know that he had the right answer. "Um, that would be Maedean. She inherits everything."

I was watching Nolan real close for any sign that he objected to this turn of events, but if he did, he hid it well. He even leaned forward a little more, watching me write her name on my notebook, soundlessly spelling it as I wrote. *M-A-E-D-E-A-N.*

"She gets it all?" I said.

177

Nolan nodded again. Evidently, he had the right answer this time, too. "All three hundred acres. Dwight made a will right after he and Maedean got hitched, you know, and um, that's what it said."

I made my voice real calm. "It says she inherits it all from Dwight?"

Nolan cocked his head to one side, pondering this one. "Well," he finally drawled, "I think it said something like she gets everything if she lives thirty days longer than Dwight. Or something like that."

I nodded. What Nolan was talking about was a pretty much standard phrase in wills: *If so-and-on survives the deceased by 30 days.* I'd been told by an attorney once that the reason this phrase is used is that it generally takes about thirty days for a will to be probated.

What was interesting to me, however, was that Nolan here knew so much about his brother's will. Did he just happen to know, or had he made it his business to find out?

I cleared my throat. "Well, now, it hardly seems right that the wife would end up with all the property, does it? I mean, you'd think that it would only be fair that *you'd* get some of it." I let my voice trail off, watching Nolan intently.

If I'd been expecting to see even a hint of discontent, I was disappointed. Nolan just shrugged. "Naw, it's fair. Dwight was the oldest, and with us Pucketts, the oldest always gets the land." Nolan looked up at me and actually smiled a little. "I grew up knowing that's the way it was, and I ain't never had a problem with it."

I couldn't help wondering if Nolan was telling the

truth. The story of Cain and Abel did come to mind. "You really don't mind that you don't get any of it?"

Nolan's response was to look bewildered. "Why should I mind? I got me a good job, you know, at the McAfee Brothers Garage, and I ain't got no special hankering to be a farmer."

I just stared at him. Was it possible he really felt this way?

Nolan was smiling again. "Matter of fact," he went on, "I can't think of anybody I'd rather have the land than Maedean." He sat back in his chair, and his boyish face took on a look of unabashed admiration. "Yep, she's one fine lady."

I just looked at him. Lucy Belle was right about one thing. Nolan did sort of glow when he talked about Maedean. Lord. Could Lucy Belle have been right about the affair, after all?

"Maedean is a special person, all right," I said, still studying Nolan's reactions. It took some doing, but I managed to say this without cracking a smile.

Nolan immediately nodded. "She's special, all right," he said. "Why, I musta told Dwight a million times how lucky he was to have her."

Uh-oh. As Nolan said the words, it seemed to occur to him that Dwight could no longer be called lucky by any stretch of the imagination. Nolan's big brown eyes were once again swimming with tears.

I, of course, jumped in real quick, trying to head off the downpour. "You and Maedean were real close, then?"

Nolan was swallowing hard and blinking up a storm, but he shook his head. "Well, I wouldn't say we was *real* close. Fact is, I wish I knew her better."

I was watching him intently, but Nolan said this last

as casually as if he were talking about some woman he admired on television. "I've been down to Nashville a few times, visiting and such," he went on, "and, well, I knew, after visiting with Dwight and Maedean just once, that Maedean had class. Why, she had real flowers in a vase in the middle of her dining room table. *Real* ones, mind you, not plastic."

"No kidding," I said. It would appear that Nolan here was not all that hard to impress.

Nolan was nodding again. "Maedean's a real classy lady, all right. You can take my word for it. And, if you ever hear anything else about her, well, I'm here to tell you that whoever's saying it is just jealous."

"Jealous?"

Nolan looked uncomfortable. "Well, yeah, I've heard talk around town, you know, but I know them that's saying stuff about Maedean is just saying it on account of out-and-out jealousy." He looked straight at me, his eyes as guileless as a child's. "Everybody's jealous of Maedean being so gorgeous and all."

I just looked at him. It was on the tip of my tongue to ask Nolan what he thought of tiny eyes, big noses, and Jay Leno chins, but I thought better of it. Nolan was obviously, along with everybody else in town, it seemed, listening to money talk.

Nolan was going on. "Maedean's a real classy dresser, too. That's another reason folks around town are jealous of her. Because she's got such great taste. She always looks like she just stepped out of a Sears catalog."

Apparently, the news that Sears was no longer producing a catalog had not reached Nolan yet. Not to mention, the catalog I would've thought that Maedean had just stepped out of was Frederick's.

I nodded. "Maedean *is* something else, all right," I said.

Nolan scooted his chair closer to my desk. "It's partly on account of Maedean, you know, that I decided to come up here and talk to you."

"Oh?" I said.

"Maedean is just so broke up about Dwight," he said. "Every time I've talked to her, she's been crying her eyes out." Nolan ran his hand through his hair, making his cowlick stand up even worse. "I tell you, it's pitiful. Just *pitiful.*"

At last, Nolan was saying something I could agree with. It *was* pitiful, without a doubt.

"Poor Maedean can't sleep, she can't eat, she can't do nothing except cry. She was so much in love with my brother, she doesn't know how she's going to live without him."

I just looked at him, beginning to feel uneasy for the first time. It sure sounded to me as if Nolan had spent an awful lot of time with Maedean just lately. "How do you know all this?" I looked down at my spiral notebook, as if I wasn't really all that interested in Nolan's answer.

"She told me," Nolan said. "Over the phone." He shook his head again. "I tell you, I can't hardly stand listening to that poor woman cry."

Hey, I felt the same way.

Nolan's voice was choking up again. Sitting on the edge of my wooden chair, as straight as if a yardstick had been stuck down the back of his shirt, he wiped his eyes again with the back of his hand. I couldn't help feeling sorry for him. I also couldn't help thinking: Lord. If Nolan had really been fooling around with Maedean, he was a world-class con artist.

Nolan had evidently gotten himself under control again. He cleared his throat a couple times, and then said, "That's why I need you to solve this thing right away. It ain't good for Maedean to be this upset in her condition."

I hadn't wanted to be staring at Nolan while he was obviously trying not to cry. So I was looking back down at my notebook when he first started speaking. My head went up when he said that last part, though. "Condition? What do you mean, condition?"

Nolan smiled through his tears. In fact, he smiled so wide, it revealed a gold side tooth. "Why, I thought you knew. Maedean's expecting. She done told Dwight just before they moved back here."

I was back to chewing on my pencil. Maedean may have done told Dwight, but she certainly had not done told me. I also couldn't help getting a quick mental picture of Maedean in her black bodysuit and skintight leopard pants. For a pregnant woman, she did not look the least bit plump. Of course, the Pucketts had only been back in town for three months. Maybe she wasn't that far along.

"Do you know when the baby's due?" I asked.

This time apparently Nolan didn't have the right answer. Or for that matter any answer at all. He ducked his head and said, "Uh, no, I can't rightly say." He blinked his big eyes a couple times, and then added, "I don't believe I was ever told."

Right away I wished I hadn't said anything, because Nolan's eyes started filling up again. "If only Dwight could've lived to see his child born," he mumbled. He looked so upset, once again I was at a loss for words. Nolan was looking straight at me, too, obviously waiting for my reply.

"Yeah." That was all I said, but evidently, even that was not all that great an idea. The second I spoke, Nolan's face sort of crumpled.

"Yeah," he repeated, and then once again, he was sobbing. He must've cried solid for at least five minutes. He cried for so long, in fact, that after a while I was reminded of Maedean, and her inexhaustible supply of moisture. Which, of course, had all been an act.

That little thought made me give Nolan a long stare. Was it possible that Nolan, too, was acting? Was he really this brokenhearted over his brother's death? Or was he just sobbing up a storm so that no one would even think that he might've been the one who'd ended poor Dwight's life? I didn't have a whole lot of time to think this one over, however, because just as Nolan was winding down his tears, my office door suddenly opened.

I'd been pretty much concentrating on Nolan and his flash flood, so it came as a complete surprise to suddenly be sitting there, staring at the one person in the world I wanted least to see. Right then, anyway.

"Haskell," Imogene said as she walked in. She was still wearing the tailored blue suit I'd seen her in earlier. Her voice sounded as cheerful as ever. She was even smiling, just like always.

Then, seeing Nolan sitting there, still sniffling and wiping his eyes with the back of his hand, Imogene stopped dead in her tracks. Looking first at Nolan and then over at me, she said, "What's going on?"

It was a question I could have easily asked *her*.

CHAPTER 11

Imogene stood just inside the door to my office, obviously waiting for me to answer her question. I had every intention of telling her what indeed was going on, and why Nolan was sniffling—I even opened my mouth to do it—but I got waylaid by Nolan himself.

Somebody must've drilled it into Nolan's head that when a female comes into a room, a gentleman gets to his feet. What with his eyes being blinded by tears and all, it must've taken Nolan a moment to realize that Imogene did indeed belong in the female category. I believe this was, no doubt, the reason Nolan was still seated, wiping his eyes on the sleeves of his corduroy jacket, when she spoke.

The minute Imogene spoke, though, Nolan evidently realized that this was most definitely a female-type voice. He sprang to his feet so fast, he knocked over the chair he'd been sitting on. Imogene jumped back just in time, or the chair would've fallen right on her toes.

While Imogene was jumping backward, Nolan was saying his usual, "Oops"—a word that has got to be one of his favorites, considering how much use he gets out of it.

That said, Nolan immediately bent over to pick up his chair. No surprise, as he bent over, he backed right into the magazines he'd stacked on the edge of my desk, sending them tumbling once again to the floor. Along with my prized Garfield coffee mug filled with pencils and pens. Thank goodness the mug didn't break. Its contents, however, scattered from one end of my office to the other.

Nolan just stood there for a moment, watching the pencils and pens bouncing all over the floor, and then, once again he used his favorite word: "Oops."

That said *again,* Nolan immediately stooped and began picking things up.

I immediately stooped and began to help him.

So did Imogene.

Of course, by that time I'd pretty much forgotten whatever the question was that Imogene had asked. She didn't seem intent on repeating it, so I moved right on to the introductions. I know there's some etiquette rule or another about the order you're supposed to introduce folks to each other, but I never can remember exactly what it is. So I just sort of mumbled, as I scrambled around on my hands and knees, reaching under my furniture for Bics and No. 2 pencils, "Nolan, this is Imogene Mayhew."

I was almost glad I was busy looking for pens and such, because it gave me a reason not to be looking at Imogene when I said her name. Somehow, when I looked at Imogene, all I could see was her and Randy all over again.

"And Imogene," I went on, "this is Nolan Puckett."

As soon as I said Nolan's last name, Imogene did this quick intake of breath. Evidently she, too, had been tuned into the ever-efficient Pigeon Fork grapevine. I gave her a quick glance, but she was looking over at Nolan, her face filled with sympathy.

Imogene waited, however, until my magazines and my mug were back on my desk, and the three of us were all standing upright again, before she turned to Nolan. Reaching out to touch his arm, she said, "I was real sorry to hear about Dwight."

Nolan was dropping the last pencil into my mug. He sounded completely under control as he said, "Yeah."

I, however, had already witnessed exactly what Nolan could do with a *yeah,* so I immediately started bracing myself for another flash flood.

Imogene, on the other hand, did not have the benefit of my experience. "It's a real tragedy," she said, giving her dark curls a little shake.

"Yeah," Nolan said again, but this time his voice quavered.

I knew it. A heartbeat later Nolan was bawling all over again.

Unlike myself earlier, Imogene seemed to know exactly what to do. She walked right over to Nolan and wrapped her arms around him.

"There, there," she said, "you poor thing. Now, you just cry all you want to. Just let it loose."

I could have told Imogene that Nolan needed no such encouragement, but I decided that would not sound any too kind. Instead, I just stood there, watching Imogene with her arms around Nolan. And Nolan with his arms now around her. They made an odd picture, Nolan being so much taller than Imogene and all. Nolan actually had to hunker down a little, so that Imogene could hold him. I know that all I should've been feeling right then was a whole lot of sympathy for Nolan. I know that.

Unfortunately, what I was feeling was something entirely different. In fact, it occurred to me, as I stood there, that this was the second time today that I'd seen my girlfriend in the arms of another man. I didn't feel angry or anything, I really didn't, as this flashed through my mind. But right after that, I did something so idiotic that I'd like to blame it on temporary insanity. No doubt, seeing Imogene with Randy earlier had unhinged my mind. That had to be it. Besides, if cold-blooded murderers can get off with an insanity defense, then I certainly ought to be allowed to use it here, to more or less excuse my totally deranged behavior from this point forward.

Can you believe, one minute I was just standing there, watching Imogene comfort Nolan, and the next, I was reaching out and tapping Nolan on the shoulder? I'm not sure what I was thinking. Maybe I figured it was like cutting in on a dance floor. Nolan's sobbing must've been taking up all his attention, though, because he didn't even seem to notice. Imogene noticed, though. The second I touched Nolan, her dark head sort of jerked in my direction.

I barely gave Imogene a glance. Instead, I tapped Nolan again. With a tad more force. I also cleared my throat—evidently so that I could say, loud and clear, "Nolan? Imogene here is *my* girlfriend. Understand?"

I don't think I really meant to, but I put a little extra emphasis on that one word: *my*. I guess my tone wasn't all that kind, either, because right away Nolan's head came up and swiveled in my direction. Fast.

"Oh," Nolan said, reddening. Then, looking back down at Imogene, he uttered his favorite word. "Oops."

Imogene started to say, "No—" I think she was intending to say "Nolan," but she never did finish. Mainly because Nolan was letting go of her so fast, she actually stumbled forward a little. While Imogene regained her balance, Nolan backed away from her, holding his hands out to me in a gesture of innocence. His cheeks still wet with tears, he said, "Hey, man, I didn't mean nothing. Really. I was just, uh, I was just—" Nolan's voice trailed off.

Imogene had not yet said a word, but her eyes were speaking volumes. Volumes, it looked to me, containing page after page of an extremely loud vocabulary. Of course, in order to hear the volumes Imogene's eyes happened to be speaking, I had to be looking straight at her. So naturally, under the circumstances, I did the gutsy thing. I looked away.

Nolan was now frowning as he swiped at his cheeks with the back of his hands. "You're still going to work for me, aren't you?" he said to me. His little-boy face looked as if he thought he'd been bad, and he was afraid he was going to be punished. "I mean, I ain't made you mad or nothing, have I, Haskell? You'll still find out who done this awful thing to Dwight, won't you?"

I just looked at him. He'd finished swiping at his cheeks, and was now running one hand nervously over his cowlick. Apparently, I had not gone completely crazy. Although I certainly could see how just about anybody might get that idea.

By the time Nolan was asking me this, I was already feeling pretty guilty about how I'd just treated him. I reckon even the insane can figure out that they've been way out of line. *Way* out of line. "Nolan," I said, and my tone this time was as kind as I could make it, "I'll find out all I can about what happened to Dwight. You can count on it."

Nolan then did a thing that made me feel like a total jerk. He actually looked relieved that I was being so understanding. "Well, uh, I'll just get out of your way so's you can do your, uh, job." He gave Imogene a quick, sheepish look, ducked his head, and then all but ran out my door.

I halfway expected to hear Nolan fall headfirst down my stairs, but amazingly enough, his footsteps appeared to make it all the way to the bottom. When I heard his footsteps fading away, I actually had a wild impulse to run after him to get him to come back. Because, of course, his departure left me and Imogene alone.

Imogene wheeled on me the second Nolan's footsteps faded. She was, no surprise, wearing the Claudzilla Look. Her hazel eyes had gone dark gold, like they always do when Imogene is angry, and her mouth was pinched into such a thin line, it could've been drawn on her face with a ruler.

"Well," Imogene said, crossing her arms in front of her chest, "I hope you're satisfied." Oddly enough, she sounded as if she fervently hoped I was anything but.

I, of course, responded the way I believe a lot of men do when the women in their lives go on the warpath. I played stupid. "Why, what are you talking about?"

Imogene's dark gold eyes flashed fire. "Don't play stupid with me."

I blinked and tried my best to look shocked that she'd even accuse me of such a thing. I don't want to brag, but I'm pretty good at looking shocked. Of course, I've had a lot of experience. In fact, during the years I'd been married to Claudzilla, I'd played this shocked-indignation scene so many times, I probably qualified to join the Actor's Guild.

Imogene's voice was working itself into a crescendo. "You know damn well what you did. You made that poor kid feel like—"

I interrupted her. "He's no kid, Imogene. He's twenty-eight, if he's a—"

Imogene interrupted me, her eyes flashing again. "I don't care if he's a hundred, Haskell, you embarrassed the hell out of him. You made him feel awful, and the poor guy was already feeling pretty terrible about what had happened to Dwight."

Imogene said all of this without stopping to get a breath. Now she took a long, deep one and just looked at me. "For God's sake, Haskell, what an unbelievably cruel thing to do!" Imogene was now staring at me as if she'd just caught me pulling the wings off butterflies. "What on earth did you think you were doing?"

I've always thought a strong offense was the best defense.

"What did I think *I* was doing? What were *you* doing?"

I may have been wrong about a strong offense. Imogene was looking at me as if I were plenty offensive, all right. "I was *comforting* the poor guy, of course! What did you think?" she said. "I mean, his brother's been murdered, for God's sake, and I think I just might have a pretty good handle on how he feels."

Having lost a sibling under similar circumstances

just six months ago, she probably did have a valid point. The insane, however, never let a little thing like facts bother them.

"Oh?" I said. "Well, while you were thinking that you were comforting him, it looked to me as if Nolan was thinking that you were making a pass at him. I was trying to help you out, Imogene, before you found yourself in a real uncomfortable situation." I actually sounded self-righteous. Not to mention, outright indignant that Imogene obviously didn't appreciate my going to all this trouble on her behalf.

Obviously, I needed shock treatment. Bad.

Imogene seemed happy to oblige.

"Bullshit," she snapped.

In all the time I'd known her, I'd never heard that particular word out of her mouth. I was so surprised, it was all I could do to keep my own mouth from dropping open. I mean, I realized, of course, that Imogene no doubt knew what this word meant and all. I reckon, though, up to that moment, I'd been under the impression—since I'd never actually heard her curse—that she might not know how to use it in a sentence.

"Bullshit, bullshit, bullshit," Imogene went on.

That sounded like a sentence to me. Not a particularly complicated sentence, but a sentence, nevertheless. Obviously, I'd misjudged her.

Imogene wasn't finished, either. Uncrossing her arms and pointing her finger at me, she said, "You weren't helping me out. You were just being an asshole."

Unfortunately, being called an asshole was not a new experience. Lord knows, I've had Melba call me this quite a few times. Not to mention, Claudzilla virtually wore the word out. Still, hearing it from Imogene, the woman who'd actually told me that she loved me not even a week ago, was pretty startling. In fact, for a second there, it wiped my mind clean. All I could do was just stand there in the middle of my office and stare at Imogene. It seemed to take forever, but I finally came up with a clever comeback.

"Oh yeah?" I said.

Imogene did not look impressed. She looked disgusted. *"Yeah,"* she said. "Nolan didn't think I was making a pass at him. That was all in your head. You were just being a jealous, macho asshole!"

OK, she'd done it. She'd finally made me zoom right past *mad,* and go all the way to *furious.* I mean, how dare she tell me the truth. I took a deep breath. "OK, Imogene," I said, my voice unnaturally calm, "just tell me this. What am I supposed to do when I see some guy pawing you? Exactly what am I supposed to do?"

As I spoke, I could see a subtle change in Imogene's face. It was almost as if I could see in her eyes what she was thinking. Standing there, staring at me, unblinking, she was wondering, *Did Haskell see me earlier today? With Randy? Or had somebody told Haskell about it?*

It was obvious watching Imogene's expressive face, she couldn't quite make up her mind if I knew about the Randy incident or not. Finally, after an interminable moment, Imogene said, her voice now every bit as calm as mine, "Are we still talking about Nolan, or are we talking about somebody else?"

I blinked. There it was. My chance to bring up the entire thing with Randy, and have it out, once and for all. I could find out exactly how Imogene felt about Randy. I could even ask her what the hell she was doing, kissing him out on the street. I opened my mouth, pretty much intending to bring all this right out in the open. What came out of my mouth, though, even surprised me a little. "We're talking about *Nolan*, of course. Who else would we be talking about?"

I could've kicked myself the second the words were out of my mouth. I mean, in my line of work, I've had some pretty tough conversations. I've talked with confessed murderers. I've listened as folks told me exactly how they intended to murder me. Hell, I've even chatted with some guy who actually seemed to enjoy letting me know how he'd tried to murder my dog. And yet, when it came right down to having a nice little chat with Imogene about Randy Harned, apparently I turned into an abject coward.

Imogene looked about as disgusted with me as I felt. "Haskell," she said, her voice now unnaturally calm, "if you've got a problem with me—if you think I've been a little too friendly with other men—then I want to hear about it."

She was giving me another chance. Imogene stood there, in fact, for a long, long moment letting me think it over. I could tell she still wasn't sure I'd seen her and Randy, but just in case I had, she was making it real easy for me to bring it up. And yet, I couldn't bring myself to do it.

Even today I'm not real sure why. I reckon it was just that this whole scene seemed, all of a sudden, far too much like similar scenes I'd played with Claudzilla. In fact, if I had a penny for every time I'd talked to Claudzilla about what was going on with her and some guy, I'd be a rich man today. Hell, I'd never have to worry about Imogene and her Dutch treats ever again.

Now that I think about it, every time I confronted her, Claudzilla always had a great explanation. Even the Christmas I caught her in the laundry with that guy I punched, she'd told me, "It wasn't my fault. We were just standing there, talking one minute, and the next, he was all over me!"

Uh-huh.

Now, standing in the middle of my office, looking straight at Imogene, I suddenly felt real tired. It just seemed like too much effort to do a rerun of a conversation I'd already had with Claudzilla far too many times.

I shrugged. "I don't know what you're talking about," I lied. "I don't have a problem."

Imogene now not only looked disgusted, she looked furious all over again. "Haskell," she said, "believe me, you've got a problem. The way you treated poor Nolan was—was—" Her voice now started shaking a little, and abruptly she broke off in midsentence.

She swallowed once, blinked a couple times, and then abruptly changed the subject. "Look, the reason I came up here in the first place was to ask you if you'd like to go to lunch, but now—"

I wasn't about to give her the chance to uninvite me. I interrupted her. "I'm real busy, Imogene. You just heard me promise Nolan that I'd get right to work, so I—"

Imogene didn't wait around to hear what else I had to say. She turned on her heel and moved at a pretty fast clip toward my door. She did have one final word for me as she went out, though.

"Idiot," she said. She said it under her breath, but I was pretty sure she meant me to hear it.

Idiot, to my way of thinking, was a definite improvement over *asshole,* but somehow, I didn't feel I should be all that encouraged about the direction our relationship was headed.

Once Imogene left, there didn't seem to be anything else for me to do except what I'd promised Nolan. Hell, I might not be able to bring myself to discuss uncomfortable matters with Imogene, but I certainly had no such problem with Maedean. It only took me about fifteen minutes to get down to the alley, get in my truck, and drive to the Puckett residence. It seemed a lot longer, though. I reckon because I spent the whole time I was driving there, kicking myself pretty good.

Insane or not, I was playing right into Randy's hands. In fact, if I'd planned to drive Imogene away, I couldn't have done it better. I mean, which would any woman choose—a man so jealous and possessive that he ended up abusing the recently bereaved, or a guy who looked like a TV star and sent her flowers? Lord. It wasn't even a contest.

By the time I turned off the state road and into the Puckett driveway, I was feeling downright depressed. Seeing Dwight's black BMW up ahead, parked in practically the same place it had been when I'd followed Maedean home from the bunko party, didn't help my mood any.

Neither did seeing Maedean, bending over and pulling a large carton out of the BMW's backseat. It was a box that to my mind looked awful heavy to be toted by a woman in the condition Nolan said Maedean was in. Maedean didn't hesitate, though. She balanced the box against one knee and then hefted it. I stared at her. This was probably the first time I'd ever seen Maedean without Poopsie in her arms. Unless, of course, Poopsie was in the box.

I was pulling in back of the BMW about then, and Maedean didn't even put the box down when she saw me. She just turned, still gripping the carton, and stared at me. Oddly enough, she didn't look all that delighted to see me. I didn't waste time trying to out-stare Maedean. Instead, I turned my attention to the BMW. Its backseat looked crammed with cardboard boxes and piles of clothes, some on hangers, some not. So what was going on here? Had Maedean just gotten back from a shopping trip?

Maedean was wearing skintight brown leather pants and a brown leather jacket, unzipped halfway, so that I could see that underneath she had on a bright red bodysuit cut so low it revealed at least an inch of cleavage. If it had been anybody else, I'd have said she was hardly dressed for shopping. In Maedean's case—since this was how she always seemed to dress— she could've been doing anything, from shopping to going to church.

I got my answer a second later when Ginny Sue walked out of the front door of the old farmhouse. Unlike her sister, she was wearing a ski jacket over a navy blue sweatsuit. Her hands were empty, but Ginny Sue had left the front door standing wide open. I could see quite a few cartons stacked in the foyer. Evidently, Ginny Sue had just carried inside a carton similar to Maedean's, and now she was on her way back out to the BMW for another load.

I looked from Ginny Sue, to Maedean, and finally, back at the BMW. This wasn't the end of a shopping trip. This was moving day. When Ginny Sue saw me, she looked even less delighted than Maedean. *Great,* I thought, turning off my ignition. Talking to two sisters who looked as if my showing up had ruined their day ought to be just the thing to snap me out of my depression.

CHAPTER 12

I could be wrong, but it certainly looked to me as if Ginny Sue was not letting any grass grow under her feet. She was moving back in with her sister before Dwight was even in his grave.

I also couldn't help but notice that Maedean and Ginny Sue were unloading Dwight's BMW—not Maedean's Corvette. In fact, the Corvette was parked only a few feet in front of the BMW, and from where I sat in my truck, I could plainly see that there were no cartons or clothes crammed inside. Maedean, then, was not letting any grass grow under her feet, either. With Dwight no longer around to tell her she couldn't touch his car, Maedean had apparently begun to touch it to the max.

I took a deep breath, fighting a quick surge of anger. I knew I was being silly, of course, but it did seem downright unkind for Ginny Sue to be moving into his house and Maedean to be driving his car before Dwight was even buried.

Like I said, I knew I was being silly. I mean, what did I expect? Did I actually think Maedean would have Dwight's BMW buried with him? Not to mention, the house and the car now clearly belonged to Maedean. She could do whatever she wanted with them. Still, all this could actually make you think that these two women were not all that unhappy to have Dwight out of the picture permanently.

I took a deep breath, pasted a smile on my face, and got out of my truck. Walking toward the two women, I said as brightly as I could, "Hi there. You two look as if you could use a helping hand." I turned to look directly at Ginny Sue. "You moving in?"

Ginny Sue was her usual cheerful self. "So what if I am?"

I forced myself to continue to smile.

"Well," I said, "I think—"

I'd been about to lie and say how great I thought all this was, but Ginny Sue cut me off. "I don't care what you think. We don't need your—"

Maedean interrupted. "What brings you out this way?" she said to me. Her tone was impatient.

Of course, one reason she might've been getting a tad impatient was that the carton she was holding must've been getting kind of heavy by then. Abruptly, she turned and heaved the thing on top of the BMW's hood with a loud thunk. I could imagine Dwight wincing somewhere. I purposely did not look to see if that thunk had done any damage.

"Well, I just talked to Nolan," I said, "and I've got a few questions I need answered."

Ginny Sue made a sound real close to a snort. *"Nolan?* Dwight's idiot brother?"

I just looked at her. What a truly caring human

being she was. Mother Theresa had nothing on Ginny Sue. Of course, as soon as all this went through my mind, something else occurred to me: *Who was I to talk?* I'd just humiliated Nolan and all but accused the poor guy of making a pass at my girlfriend. I wasn't exactly giving Mother Theresa a run for her money, either.

Maedean was continuing to sound impatient. "Look, Haskell, we're kind of busy right now, and, uh, I'm still pretty upset over Dwight and all."

For a woman still pretty upset, she looked remarkably dry-eyed. Of course, maybe Maedean had simply forgotten to turn her waterworks valve back to ON.

"After we get done here," Maedean was going on, "we've got to go over to Merryman's and, you know, pick out the casket and stuff—"

I just stared at her. She was moving in Ginny Sue even before she planned Dwight's funeral? Lord. She *really* wasn't wasting any time.

"—So this isn't a good time to talk." As Maedean finished saying this, she began to ease the carton off the hood of the BMW, preparing to pick it up all over again. That box did look awfully heavy.

I took a few steps forward, until I was standing right next to Maedean. "Why don't you let me help you with that?"

Although I'd asked the question of Maedean, it was Ginny Sue who immediately answered. "Oh, for God's sake." She ran her hand through her blond hair, and rolled her eyes. "Look, Haskell, we women aren't the weaklings you men seem to think we are. We can handle things perfectly well on our own without depending on one of you to help little old us with—"

Ginny Sue's argument probably would've been

more effective if Maedean had not interrupted her again, saying, "I'd *love* you to help me, Haskell. That would be *great.*" With that, Maedean practically heaved the box into my arms.

Lord. It didn't just *look* heavy. It *was* heavy. It felt as if it were filled with rocks. Or, maybe, boulders. On the way into the house, with Maedean trotting along beside me, I decided I must be more out of shape than I thought. I was actually breathing hard by the time I got that damn carton inside. Hell, if I'd known the box was this heavy, I might not have offered. Still, this little maneuver had gotten me into the house. Not to mention, if Maedean really was pregnant like Nolan said she was, she shouldn't be trying to pick up a box of boulders. I all but dropped the carton in the foyer.

Ginny Sue came through the front door right behind me and Maedean. When she saw me drop the carton, Ginny Sue smirked and said, "Uh, Haskell? That one goes upstairs."

I acted as if I hadn't heard her.

Instead, I turned to Maedean. "Should you be lifting things this heavy in your condition?"

Maedean frowned at me. "What do you mean, my condition? I'll have you know I've never been in better condition in my life." She gave her blond hair a toss. "I work out, you know, every day to an exercise video. I do thirty minutes every single—"

I interrupted. "Maedean, what I'm talking about," I said, "is your *condition.*"

I know I probably sounded like a prude or something, but these last few months I reckon I've gotten used to the way things are in Pigeon Fork. Here things have moved a tad slower than in the rest of the country. Around these parts there are still a whole lot of folks who don't think that pregnancy is something you should talk about in mixed company. In fact, Pigeon Fork is, no doubt, one of the few places left where you can still hear folks whisper about somebody "being in the family way," or "having a bun in the oven." I found myself lowering my voice to a whisper when I said the word *condition,* before I'd even thought about it.

Maybe I'd lowered my voice a tad too much. Maedean blinked her tiny eyes at me, and cocked her blond head to one side. She was looking more like my dog Rip every day.

I tried again. "Nolan told me that congratulations were in order."

Maedean continued to blink. "Why, whatever for?"

I gave up. Evidently, I was going to have to be blunt. "The baby," I said. Maedean was still staring at me blankly, so I repeated myself. "The *baby?*"

The last time I said the word *baby,* my voice was pretty loud. Almost immediately, Poopsie showed up, running into the foyer from wherever he'd been, looking around with his bright little beady eyes, as if he thought somebody had just called him.

Maedean immediately walked right over to Poopsie and lifted her dog into her arms. "Why, here's my widdle baby," she said. "My widdle Poopsie woopsie."

Really. That's what she said. I realize it's hard to believe that an adult would actually talk like this, particularly in front of witnesses, but this is most definitely what she said, word for word.

I raised my voice even louder. "Maedean, what I'm trying to say is that Nolan told me you were expecting!"

Maedean actually gasped. She looked first at me,

then down at Poopsie, and then over at Ginny Sue. "Oh, for crying out loud," Maedean finally said. Her tone was irritated. "I don't believe it! I asked Dwight not to tell a soul. And he promised me—he crossed his heart and hoped to die—that he wouldn't!"

I swallowed. Evidently, the irony of what she'd just said totally escaped her.

Ginny Sue's response was predictable. "That's a man for you. You can't believe a word they say."

I ignored Ginny Sue, and once again turned to Maedean. "Then you *are* expecting?"

Maedean didn't seem to hear me. She was still looking over at Ginny Sue, her tiny eyes getting rounder and rounder. "You don't suppose that stupid fool Nolan is telling this all over town, do you? You don't think Nolan's blabbing it to *everybody,* do you?"

Ginny Sue's response was a shrug.

Maedean now started pacing, still holding Poopsie. The dog's head bobbed up and down with every step she took. "Because, damn it, if that idiot Nolan has spread this all over town, I'm going to have his nuts in a paper sack!"

Now this last was a phrase I'd heard before. In fact, you could even get the idea that this little phrase might be as much a favorite of Maedean's as Nolan's *oops.*

"That damn idiot will be sorry he ever learned to talk!" Maedean said.

I didn't say a word myself, but I was doing a lot of thinking. For one thing, the possibility of Lucy Belle being right about Maedean and Nolan was looking real dim. After all, would a woman call the man she loved an idiot? The second this thought crossed my mind, I almost choked. Recalling the last thing Imogene had said to me, I certainly hoped that the answer to that last question was a resounding *yes*. I peered at Maedean even more closely, as another idea hit me. Could she be getting this upset because the baby was not Dwight's?

Maedean certainly looked as if she were getting more rattled by the minute. Yet another thing she probably shouldn't be doing in her condition. I held up my hand. "Look, Maedean, everybody's going to know anyway once you start showing, so what does it matter if—"

Maedean lifted her Jay Leno chin, and glared at me. "I'm not going to be showing, you moron!"

I blinked at that one. Apparently, this was my day to have women call me names.

"What do you mean, you won't be showing?" Good Lord. Was she actually considering getting rid of the baby now that Dwight was gone?

"Look," Maedean said, pointing Poopsie at me, "get this clear. *I'm not pregnant!*"

It was my turn to blink and cock my head to one side. "You're not—"

Maedean shrugged and went right on as if I hadn't spoken. "I just told Dwight that I was pregnant so he'd let Ginny Sue move up here with us."

I stared at her. The woman actually said this almost offhand, as if it were a course of action anybody would take under similar circumstances.

Maedean was now scratching the top of Poopsie's head as casually as anything. "I told Dwight that I'd be needing somebody to help me real soon, and that I'd feel so much better if it was somebody who was family." She actually sounded proud of herself. "It worked like a charm. Pretty smart, huh?"

Smart was not the word I would've used. *Under-handed. Devious. Slimy.* All those words came to mind, but not *smart.*

Ginny Sue answered Maedean for me. "It wasn't just smart," she said. "It was brilliant."

I reckon I didn't look quite as admiring as Ginny Sue thought I should, because she immediately jumped on me. "Oh, don't stand there looking so holier-than-thou, Haskell," Ginny Sue said. "If it wasn't for you men being so damn controlling, women wouldn't have to do things like this. If you guys were a little more reasonable, we could be up-front with you. But, no, you make it so damn difficult, for God's sake, we women are forced to be sneaky in order to get our way. It's not our fault!"

I stared at Ginny Sue, struck by how much she sounded like all the men I'd arrested in spouse abuse cases during my years on the force. These guys never said, *I lost my temper, and I hit her.* Nope, they always said, *Look what she made me do.*

No matter which sex was saying it, it still ended up being just one more excuse to avoid taking responsibility for your own actions. I took a deep breath. It was, however, beginning to be real clear why Maedean might've thought she needed pictures and a neutral witness such as myself to convince Dwight that what she was telling him was so. Evidently, Maedean lied on a regular basis. A thing like this could possibly make a person not believe a word she said. It could also make a person want to sever all ties with her.

I turned back toward Maedean, and at the same time I reached into the inside pocket of my denim jacket for my checkbook. "Maedean," I said, "the way I see it, I didn't work for you long enough to earn the retainer you gave me. So now I want to refund the money that I didn't—"

Can you believe Maedean actually looked alarmed? I mean, here I was, getting ready to write her a check, and she was looking as if I were pointing a gun at her.

"Oh no," she said, shaking her head and backing away. "You can't do that."

I blinked at that one. "Maedean, maybe you misunderstood me. I want to refund you the money I didn't earn. That's all. No big deal."

I was actually talking real slow, the way you might to a preschooler.

Maedean was still shaking her head. "I'm not taking any damn check, understand? I've paid you, and you're still working for me. You're my *private* detective, and that's all there is to it."

The way she emphasized the word *private* gave me a real uneasy feeling. As if maybe what Maedean wanted me to keep was some kind of hush money.

"Like you said when I first hired you," Maedean said, "you're confidential. That's what you said, and that's what I expect."

"Maedean," I said, "I'm writing you this check—"

Maedean shook her blond head. "If you do, you're wasting your time, because I'm not cashing it."

For a long moment we just stared at each other without saying a word. Then I let out a long sigh, and put my checkbook back into my inside pocket. Maedean looked triumphant.

I gave her a quick, tight smile. "Well," I said, "since I'm your *private* detective, and you can confide in me and all, there *is* something I need to ask you."

Maedean's eyes narrowed some, but she tried to maintain a casual attitude. She glanced over at Ginny

Sue, who seemed to be looking a tad apprehensive all of a sudden, and then back over at me. "What do you want to know?" Maedean said. "I've got nothing to hide."

From the way she always dressed, I already had a pretty good idea that Maedean had nothing to hide. At least, not to the world at large.

I indicated Ginny Sue with a nod of my head, then looked directly at Maedean. "Is it all right to speak freely?"

If I had not asked her, Maedean would've probably once again threatened me with that charming phrase I liked so much. You know, the one that mentions the paper sack? I was just being careful, for God's sake, but you might've thought I'd accused Ginny Sue of being a double agent.

Maedean looked irritated. "Well, of course, you can speak freely in front of my sister!"

Ginny Sue looked insulted. Waving her arms, she said, "That's just like a man. *Just* like a man! Thinking that we women are always conniving against each other, so that you've got to be real careful what—"

Once Ginny Sue got going, Maedean started looking impatient again. Evidently, Maedean had already heard everything Ginny Sue was now saying. Perhaps, oh, say, a million times. "My sister and I don't have any secrets!" Maedean said, loud enough to drown Ginny Sue out.

I took Maedean at her word, and plunged right in. "Well, Maedean, I've heard some rumors around town, and I've been wondering if they were just rumors, or if—"

Maedean's too-tiny eyes squinted at me. "Rumors?"

My eyes never left hers. "What I heard was that you were having an affair."

Maedean's eyes looked like an explosion went off behind them.

"Right under Dwight's nose," I added.

"What?" Maedean's voice went so shrill that Poopsie, beginning to doze in her arms, gave a little start. "Did Nolan tell you this? Is that where you heard this? Did that damn—"

Ginny Sue's voice was almost as shrill as Maedean's. "Is that stupid moron going around town, spreading vicious—"

I interrupted both of them. "Hey, I didn't hear it from Nolan, OK? I just heard it around town, that's all." I paused at this point and looked straight at Maedean. "What I wanted to know is this: is it true?"

Maedean actually sputtered. "Well, uh, well, uh, of *course,* it isn't true!" She had started scratching the top of Poopsie's head so vigorously, the dog let out a yelp. Maedean immediately stopped. "Oh, I'm sorry, sweetie cakes," she told Poopsie. Then taking a deep breath, she seemed to get herself under control. "Haskell, I ask you," she said, "does it make any sense that I'd have hired you to follow me around if I really *was* running around on Dwight?"

She did seem to have a point. But if this was so, and she was innocent, why was she acting so rattled all of a sudden?

"I mean," Maedean went on, "what do you take me for?"

I knew instinctively that she really didn't want to hear my answer to that question, so I just shrugged.

Maedean's too-tiny eyes seemed to be getting even tinier as she took a step toward me and lowered her voice. "Did you happen to, uh, hear *who* I was supposed to be having this affair with?"

Ginny Sue took a step closer to me, obviously waiting for my answer, but I reckon I disappointed them both. "Nobody seems to know." As I spoke, I kept my eyes glued on Maedean's face.

"Well, then," Maedean said. *"See?"*

I did see, that was for sure. In fact, it appeared to me that the moment I told Maedean that nobody knew who her mysterious lover was, a look of relief passed quickly over her face.

A quick glance over at Ginny Sue told me that she, too, was looking a tad more relaxed.

"If they don't even know who I'm supposed to be running around with, then it's pretty obvious, isn't it—that they're just making the whole thing up?" Maedean went on.

I nodded my head, but I wasn't real sure Maedean's logic was all that logical. "While we're at it, I've got something else to ask you," I said. "It's about Dwight's will."

Maedean gave her blond hair another toss. "What about it?"

"Well, what exactly does his will say?"

Actually, what I really wanted to know was if Maedean knew what it said.

As it turned out, not only Maedean knew, but Ginny Sue did, too.

"Dwight left everything to me," Maedean said, her tone challenging me to find fault with that. "That's what he wanted."

Ginny Sue was nodding. "That's pretty standard," she put in. "I mean, husbands generally leave all their stuff to their wives. It's not exactly news."

By now I was getting used to ignoring Ginny Sue. Without so much as a glance in Ginny Sue's direction, I asked Maedean, "What happens if something should happen to you?"

Maedean was now beginning to look a tad anxious. She exchanged a look with Ginny Sue—a look that seemed to be saying, *What in the world is Haskell driving at?* Then, looking back over at me, Maedean shrugged and said, "Well, if something happens to me within thirty days of Dwight's death, everything goes to Nolan." The moment she said his name, her eyes widened a little. "Why are you asking about Dwight's will?"

It was my turn to shrug. "Just curious," I said.

Maedean didn't believe that for a moment. "Do you think it could've been *Nolan* who killed Dwight?"

Ginny Sue piped up with, "She's right, isn't she? You do think it was Nolan, don't you? You think it was Dwight's idiotic moron bro—"

I cut her off. "Look, I don't think anything, understand?" I looked from Ginny Sue to Maedean and back again. "I'm just trying to get an idea of how the land lays, that's all."

I now turned back toward the door, intending to get out of there before the sisters started making the Inquisition look like nothing more than a casual chat.

Apparently, however, I didn't move fast enough. Maedean followed me right through the door and on out to her porch. "Well, if you don't think Nolan did it, then who do you think did?" Still clutching Poopsie in one hand, Maedean reached out with the other and grabbed my arm. "Look, I want to know, Haskell," she said. "You're still working for me, you know, and I want you to tell me right now—who do you suspect?"

I was about to take a step off the porch, but when she grabbed my arm, I had to either stop or drag her down the stairs with me. I stopped. "Maedean," I said, "at this point, I really don't—"

It was then that a lot of things seemed to happen all at once.

I felt an odd rush of air, right past my left ear. It was so sudden, for a split second I didn't know what it was.

Then, spinning to my left, I saw the wood molding around the living room door splinter. Before I could even form the thought, *What the hell,* I heard the rifle report. Oh, God. Somebody was shooting at us. Maedean must've reached that little conclusion at the exact moment I did, because she let out a scream that seemed to echo off hills in the distance. I reached out to grab her, and as usual, Poopsie immediately began to snarl and snap at my hand. Dropping to the floor of the porch, I pulled Maedean and the dog down with me. On the way down, Poopsie expressed his gratitude by growling and snapping at my hands. Also on the way down, I heard another report. Beside me, Maedean screamed again.

CHAPTER 13

Maedean was pretty amazing. She managed to continue to scream from the moment I pulled her down until she landed with a smack on the floor of the porch. She screamed even while making sure that she was holding Poopsie out and away from her body so that she wouldn't fall on him.

Unfortunately, however, Maedean didn't seem to have any problem at all with falling on *me*. She fell across my legs, landing on both my shins like a sack of doorknobs. I was considering screaming myself when Ginny Sue came running out the front door.

"What—? Who—? What—?" Ginny Sue yelled, apparently unable to make up her mind exactly what she wanted to ask first. Her eyes were wild, looking first at me and Maedean, and then over in the direction of the shooter.

"Get down!" I shouted.

One thing about Ginny Sue. You didn't have to tell

her twice. She dropped like a rock, screaming, like her sister, all the way.

Ginny Sue's screaming set off Maedean again. Lying there, as flat as pancakes, on the floor of the porch, both of them screamed in unison. Apparently, just in case the shooter had gotten the idea that he'd killed us, the sisters wanted him to know that they were still very much alive. And in good voice.

"Shut up!" I hissed through my teeth.

In the sudden silence that followed, I could hear Poopsie. The dog was whining a little. Evidently, Poopsie didn't like screaming any more than I did.

I could also hear footsteps moving rapidly away from us, and the noise of snapping twigs. It sounded as if somebody was running through the woods directly across from us, on the other side of the driveway. I sprang up and ran toward the sound.

In back of me, I could hear Maedean. "Poopsie love, are you OK, sweetie pie? Is my sweetums . . ."

I picked up speed. Once I'd run several yards into the woods, brushing aside branches, two things occurred to me. The first was that my legs were pretty sore. Evidently, when Maedean landed on my shins, she'd left some major bruises. The second thing that occurred to me was that this little chase through the woods might be further evidence supporting my insanity defense. I mean, what was I going to do if I caught the guy? He obviously had a rifle, and what did I have? A checkbook.

While writing checks had definitely caused *me* quite a bit of pain in the past, I was pretty sure that my checkbook would not be all that great a weapon against anybody else. I'd been running lickety-split through the trees, but after briefly weighing the effectiveness of checkbook versus rifle, I came to an abrupt halt, turned, and started walking back toward the Puckett house. It was just as well. My legs were killing me. And whoever the shooter had been, he was long gone. I would've had to have been an antelope to catch him.

When I got back to the farmhouse, I was limping a little. Maedean and Ginny Sue were still on the front porch. They were now on their feet, however. "Where the hell did you go?" Ginny Sue asked.

I just looked at her. "I thought I'd go for a little jog in the woods. I needed the exercise," I said.

Ginny Sue apparently did not appreciate sarcasm. Her tiny eyes flashed. "Well," she said, "after *you* ran off, leaving me and Maedean totally unprotected, we discover that Maedean here's been shot!"

"Wha-a-at?" It was only then that I noticed that Maedean was holding a compress of some sort against the top of her right forearm. I suppose I hadn't noticed it immediately because Maedean was also still holding Poopsie. The dog was sitting in the curve of her arms, blinking its little beady eyes at me. Now, I realize I'm not exactly a doctor or anything, but it appeared to me that Maedean couldn't possibly be wounded too bad, or else she wouldn't be able to hold Poopsie.

Maedean was now nodding her head vigorously. Yet another thing I don't believe she'd be able to do if she'd sustained a massive injury. "That's right," Maedean said indignantly. "Right after you *abandoned* us, I realized that"—here she searched for a moment for the right word—"that *assassin* had shot me!" She paused here to glare at me. "Some bodyguard you turned out to be!"

I took a deep breath. Apparently, it had slipped Maedean's mind that I had not actually been hired to be her bodyguard. As I recalled, the entire bodyguard story was a ruse she'd come up with to explain to Vergil why I'd been following her in the first place.

"Let me take a look," I said, moving toward Maedean.

Poopsie, however, had other ideas. The second I moved closer, that damn dog bared his teeth, growling.

I, of course, took the hint. I backed up.

Maedean was getting close to whining. "It's a huge, huge, *huge,* gaping wound!"

Ginny Sue wasn't getting close to whining. She'd made it. "Don't you worry, Haskell. *I* did your job for you. I went inside and got Maedean a towel to hold against her gunshot wound. *And* I called an ambulance. And *then* I called the cops. I did all this right after *you* ran away."

I just stared at her. Was I being overly sensitive, or did Ginny Sue seem to be implying that, once bullets started flying, I'd taken off like a scared rabbit? "Look," I said, my tone clipped, "I ran after the gunman. Understand? *That's* what I was doing. The gunman took off into the—"

"Gun*man?*" Ginny Sue said. "What makes you think it was a man? Did you get a good look at him?"

I took still another deep breath. Both my shins were hurting where Maedean had fallen on them, the palms of both my hands were scraped, and I had evidently run through a mess of thorns when I was hightailing it through the woods. Thorns were sticking all over my denim jacket, jeans, and socks, and not incidentally, right through my jeans in places I could not exactly get my hands on in mixed company.

I believe, considering the leg situation and the thorn situation, I was outdoing Job in the patience department. "No," I said through my teeth, "I did not actually see the gun*person*." I punched up the *person* part of that word, giving Ginny Sue a pointed look. "There were too many trees in the way to get a good look at the gun*person*."

Maedean looked disgusted. "You let whoever it was get away, and now we've got no idea who it could've been." She rolled *her* tiny eyes. "What the hell kind of detective are you?"

My answer to that was *unarmed*, but I didn't say it. "The guy had a pretty good head start."

"The *guy?*" Ginny Sue said.

"Whoever!" I said right back, glaring at her.

"Damn it, Haskell," Maedean said, "it could've been *anybody*."

I couldn't have put it better myself. In fact, if I were positive that the gunman had been aiming directly at Maedean, or for that matter, had mistaken her at a distance for Ginny Sue, I'd say the possibilities included anybody who'd ever talked to either one of them for more than five minutes. Hell, right this minute I felt like pumping a few bullets into both of them myself.

"My arm stings," Maedean said, pouting. "When is that old ambulance going to get here, anyway?"

The compress now had a dark red circle in the middle of it. Unfortunately, Maedean noticed this circle about the same time as I did. She stared at the thing, her eyes suddenly getting very round and very dark. Her face rapidly drained of color. Uh-oh. It looked to me as if in another minute I was going to have an unconscious woman on my hands. And a really pissed-off dog.

"Maedean, you need to sit down, OK?" I said. I would've taken her arm, but when I made a move toward her, Poopsie growled once again under his breath.

I stayed where I was. "Sit down right this minute, Maedean."

Can you believe, Maedean actually shook her head. She was swaying a little on her feet, but she said, "I'm not sitting down. It's dirty down there. The porch hasn't been swept—"

I blinked at that one. The woman had been lying flat out on the porch, but she drew the line at *sitting?*

"Then let's go inside, OK? You can sit down in—"

Ginny Sue spoke at the same time that I did. "Look, Haskell, Maedean is not some hothouse flower, OK? She is perfectly—"

It was Maedean who interrupted us both.

She sank to the porch floor like an inflatable doll with a fast leak.

Poopsie apparently felt Maedean go. Before they both made contact with the porch, the dog had the good sense to jump out of the way.

Poopsie didn't seem any too eager to return, either. Instead, he squatted on his haunches a good three feet away and stared at the unconscious Maedean accusingly.

Evidently, this hitting the deck while she was holding him was getting old. It was kind of a good thing that Poopsie was keeping his distance. At least I could actually touch Maedean without having to dodge dog teeth. Moving to her side, I dropped to my knees and lifted the compress off her forearm. Contrary to popular belief, her wound was not a huge gaping one. It was pretty deep, though, and it was still bleeding some.

I pressed the compress against the wound. "Hey, Maedean? *Maedean? Hey, Maedean!*"

Ginny Sue moved to sit on the other side of her sister. I thought she was going to join me in calling to Maedean, but evidently, she thought other methods would be more effective. She reached out and slapped Maedean right in the face. I immediately glanced over at Ginny Sue. If I hadn't known better, I'd have thought she enjoyed doing that. Whether Ginny Sue enjoyed it or not, it didn't work. Maedean's eyes remained closed, and her head lolled to one side.

Ginny Sue drew back her hand again, but I stopped her. "Why don't you go inside and get a cold cloth, OK?"

Ginny Sue might've looked a tad disappointed at missing out on yet another opportunity to belt Maedean one, but she headed inside, anyway.

Fortunately for Maedean, she'd opened her eyes before Ginny Sue returned.

It took another ten minutes for the ambulance to arrive. This is, of course, one of the down sides to living out the country. Nobody knows where the hell you are. We've had ambulances wander through these woods out here for hours, ending up at folks' houses long after the injured person's family finally got in their truck and drove whoever it was to the hospital.

By the time the ambulance pulled up, Maedean was, unfortunately, talking. "Didn't I say I didn't want to sit? Didn't I?"

I tried to tell her she'd fainted, but it apparently went right over her head. "And what's Poopsie doing all the way over there? Did you do something to him?"

Maedean, of course, insisted that Poopsie be taken to the hospital, too. "I'm not going unless my baby goes." Naturally, the minute she said that, one of the ambulance guys who didn't know better headed straight over to Poopsie to pick him up.

Poopsie, of course, reacted the way he always did. By letting go a snarl that a dog twice his size would've been proud of. Lord. I don't believe I have ever seen a human being jump backward that far, or that quick. After that little display, nobody made any motion toward the dog, at all. Unless, of course, you counted Maedean waggling her good hand at the animal, and cooing, "Come here, you brave, brave little sweetheart. Come to Mama, Poopsie sweetie."

Poopsie, no doubt sensing hostility from virtually every other human present, immediately trotted over to Maedean and jumped into her lap. Maedean did not insist on Ginny Sue accompanying her, but Ginny Sue got into the ambulance with her anyway. As the ambulance went roaring off down the road, I stood there in the driveway, watching after it. If Maedean had been killed, the person who would've immediately benefited was Nolan. No doubt about it.

So, the question was: Could Nolan have been the shooter? Could he actually be trying to systematically eliminate everybody ahead of him in the inheritance line? First, his brother Dwight? And now, Maedean? I ran my hand through my hair. Nolan had seemed incapable of doing such a thing. Had I misjudged him that badly? The wind had picked up, and it was getting real cold standing in the driveway. Vergil apparently was taking his time. I decided I'd rather wait for him inside.

I moved into the foyer, and walked right past the living room without even glancing in that direction. I didn't need reminding what I'd seen in there less than twenty-four hours ago. Instead, I moved quickly into the dining room. I sat down in the same chair at the dining room table that I'd sat in the night before. And that's when I noticed it. There was a large bouquet of flowers now standing in the middle of the antique sideboard.

For a long moment I just stared at them. A large arrangement of orange, red, and yellow mums in a wicker basket, the bouquet certainly added a lot of color to the room. It was downright cheerful, in fact. Which was kind of odd. I mean, after somebody dies, don't folks usually send things like white roses, or lilies, or something like that? This loud splash of autumn colors seemed almost disrespectful.

I scooted back my chair. Another thing also struck me as odd. Weren't flowers usually sent to the funeral home? Not to the home of the deceased? At least that's the way it had been done when my dad had died. I'd ended up with flowers at my house only after the funeral was over. And, yes, as I recalled, the flowers had generally been real subdued.

I kind of wanted to know who it was in town who seemed to know even less about etiquette than I did. I got up, and after taking a quick looksee out the front window—just to make sure Vergil wasn't sneaking up on me—I went over to the huge bouquet. It took me awhile to find the card. It wasn't on one of them little, plastic prong things, like it usually was. The bouquet did actually have one of those prong things, sticking into the green foam holding the flowers in place, but the prongs were empty. After getting the ends of my fingers dirty, digging around among the flowers, it finally occurred to me to lift the vase. And there it was.

A tiny white card with handwriting in red ink scrawled across it.

Even as I picked the card up, the handwriting already looked vaguely familiar. Where had I seen this before? Then I read the message, and it came to me.

"Dear Maedean: You are the flower in the garden of my life."

It was signed with a little red heart.

CHAPTER 14

I stared at the note.

Talk about déjà vu.

The message on Maedean's card was word for word the exact message that Randy Harned had written Imogene when he'd sent her one of his obnoxious bouquets. So how could this be?

Could this message have been sent by Harned, too? I turned to stare at the colorful mums. Could this bouquet actually be from him? It seemed unbelievably farfetched. And yet, Maedean's message was written in red ink and signed with a little heart, just like Imogene's. The only difference was, Harned had actually signed his name to Imogene's card.

Of course, it was real easy to understand why Harned would not have signed his name in this particular instance. If you were sending flowers and a note like this to a widow whose husband was not even in the grave yet, you might not want folks to know it was you. What's more, it was pretty plain Maedean didn't want folks to know who'd sent it because she'd hidden the card. She'd hidden it badly, but she *had* hidden it.

In fact, it was the secrecy of the thing that really made me wonder. It could actually make you think that something might've been going on between whoever had sent this bouquet and the merry widow. Like, oh, say, an affair, maybe?

I swallowed and studied the card all over again. Was it really possible that Randy Harned could be Maedean's mystery lover? And yet, if he was carrying on with Maedean, why would he also be making a move on Imogene?

It didn't make sense. Unless Harned was one of those men who tried to score with as many women as possible. Was Imogene just another conquest to him? The very idea made me so angry, I couldn't stand still. I started pacing Maedean's dining room.

When you came right down to it, it *had* to have been Harned who'd sent these flowers to Maedean, didn't it? I mean, that was certainly a lot more likely explanation than there were now two blooming idiots in town, penning the exact same message on the bouquets they were sending.

Or was I leaping to conclusions here? Because, let's face it, this could very well be exactly what I wanted to believe. It would certainly not break my heart if it turned out that Harned was having an affair with Maedean—and because of that, the guy had a motive for murder. I'd be the first one to admit it. The opportunity to put Randy Harned in jail would not be the worst thing that ever happened to me.

I stopped pacing and looked at the note yet again. On the other hand, it *was* possible that two different people could've sent the same note. Somebody else could've seen Harned's note on Imogene's flowers, been struck, no doubt, by its eloquence, and immediately decided to copy it. Or maybe this mystery person had gotten his note from the same book that Harned himself had copied it out of. That was possible, wasn't it?

I cleared my throat. I had to admit it, all of this was possible. But was it probable? As I mentioned before, in most cases it's the simplest explanation that turns out to be true. In this case, no doubt about it, the simplest explanation was that Harned had written both notes in red ink. And signed each of them with little hearts.

I'd be lying if I said that the way my logic was going didn't make me happy. Hell, it did more than that. Standing there in Maedean's dining room, holding that card, my heart started pounding. I reckon my heart pounding like that must've reduced the blood supply to my brain, causing me not to think all that clearly. I'm hoping that was what happened. Otherwise, I'd have to say that the reason I did what I did next was that I had once more come down with a bad case of insanity.

I still had Maedean's card in my hand when I heard a knock on the front door. I immediately headed into the foyer, and opened the door.

Vergil, no surprise, was standing there. The Gunterman twins were right behind him. "Haskell," Vergil said.

What I should've said was, "Vergil." Just that, nothing more. Instead, I said, as Vergil walked in, "Look what I just found. Just look!" I handed him the note with a little flourish.

Vergil, I have to say, was pretty much unimpressed. He stood there in the foyer, slowly reading the thing, and then handed the card back to me. "What's this got to do with Maedean Puckett getting herself shot?"

So I explained it to him. All about Imogene's note. All about Maedean's. And all about how Harned was probably Maedean's mystery lover, and how that would certainly give the guy a terrific motive for doing away with Dwight.

By the time I'd finished, Vergil was looking at me even more mournfully than usual. "Haskell, Haskell, Haskell" was all Vergil said for a long moment.

I was tempted to answer, "Yes, yes, yes," but I figured if I started acting smart, all it was going to do was make Vergil mad. So all I did was just look at Vergil, real patient-like, waiting for him to go on.

Vergil, of course, had to sigh first before he said anything. It took him awhile, his being a world-champion sigher and all. Finally, though, Vergil said, "Like I said before, what does all this have to do with Maedean getting herself shot?"

I just stared back at him. "What do you mean?"

Vergil sighed again. "What I mean is," he said, his tone infinitely patient, "if Randy Harned was having himself an affair with Maedean, then why on earth would he try to kill her?"

That did seem to be an excellent point. "Well, uh," I stammered, "maybe Randy was, uh, shooting at me, and he, uh, got Maedean by mistake?"

Vergil sighed again. This time was the longest sigh of all. "You know," he finally said, "I already heard about Randy and Imogene." He made it sound like tragic news.

In back of Vergil, I noticed the Guntermans exchange a look, and then sadly shake their massive heads.

I swallowed. I should've expected this, of course. Vergil and the Guntermans and God knows who else would've most certainly already have heard. After all, Harned had kissed Imogene right out in broad daylight. Hell, the Pigeon Fork grapevine had, no doubt, been having a field day.

I held up my hands. "Vergil," I said, "all that is beside the point. The notes are the same! Can't you see that—"

Vergil held up his own hands as if to tell me to stop. "Look, Haskell," he said, "don't you think it's odd that, of all the folks in town who could've done this, you just happen to think it's Randy Harned?" He scratched his bald spot for a moment, and noisily cleared his throat. "I mean, really, Haskell, it's awful convenient, isn't it?"

I just looked at Vergil. And at that moment, a truly horrible thought occurred to me. What if Harned had planned this all along? What if he'd been romancing Imogene, knowing all along that she was my girlfriend? So that if I ever did try to accuse him of anything, everybody would say just what Vergil was saying now? Lord. Was this possible? Could Harned have just been using Imogene? This possibility was enough to make me so angry, I could hardly breathe.

Vergil, of course, was continuing to look at me with pity in his eyes. I cleared my throat. "You're right, Vergil," I said. "Maybe I am jumping to conclusions here."

The pity in Vergil's eyes did not go away. "Yep," he said. He seemed almost relieved to move on to safer topics—like how Maedean got herself shot, and what, if anything, I'd seen when I was chasing the gunman through the woods.

While I gave Vergil all the particulars, the Guntermans went stomping off into the woods to look for clues. No surprise, they didn't find any. Actually, it sort of surprised me that they found the woods.

When Vergil finally called it a day, I closed up the Puckett farmhouse and headed straight to my office to make a phone call. A long distance phone call, as a matter of fact, all the way into Louisville to one of my old cop buddies who shall remain nameless. This particular nameless cop buddy owes me one. Actually, since I'd covered his butt a blue million times over the course of my illustrious eight-year career, Nameless owes me a lot more than one.

Nameless knows it, too. He must've dropped everything else he was working on just to do the favor I asked of him, because in no time at all, he was calling me back.

"Haskell," Nameless said, "Randy Harned is not exactly the most upstanding character in the world."

I tried not to sound delighted when I said, "Oh, really?"

"Let's put it this way," Nameless went on. "Snakes would look down on the guy."

Nameless went on to tell me that all the money Harned had been flashing all over Pigeon Fork had been an insurance settlement for what looked like a real suspicious fire.

"Harned's house in Carrollton, Kentucky, burned right to the ground," Nameless said. "One of his neighbors said she thought she saw fire in one of the kitchen windows a good half hour before Harned called the fire department. What's more, there was almost nothing in the house that was of any real value."

"Why wasn't Harned arrested?"

"Well, according to the computer file, there wasn't any concrete evidence that the fire had been started," Nameless said. "It really did appear that the fire had started in the kitchen, from grease left on the stove too long."

I thanked Nameless, got off the phone, and started to go straight to Vergil's office with what I'd find out. Thank God I stopped myself before I'd even gotten halfway down the stairs. Because, when you came right down to it, what did I really have? The house Randy had owned before he moved here had burned down. So?

Nobody was even sure he'd done it, for God's sake. And, even if he had, what did that have to do with the death of Dwight Puckett? Even if I could prove, beyond a shadow of a doubt, that Harned was a low-life, that still didn't necessarily mean that he was also a murderer. What I needed was concrete evidence.

I picked up the phone and started dialing: 733-WATR.

The phone was picked up on the third ring. "Harned Water Service, Randy Harned speaking."

I had to hand it to him. Randy sounded downright businesslike. "Randy, this is Haskell Blevins. You and I need to talk."

Randy's voice immediately went from downright businesslike to downright wary. "What about?"

"I've found out about you and a certain lady and what you did to her husband, and I'm going to be needing a reason to keep my mouth shut."

"Look, if you're all hot under the collar about me

and Imogene, it's Imogene you need to talk to. Not me."

I actually had to swallow once before I could speak. "Randy, I'm not talking about Imogene. I'm talking about a certain widow lady. With a dog."

I was gambling big time here, and I knew it. For a long, long moment I couldn't hear anything on the line except static. And then, finally, Randy said, "Where do you want to meet?"

"Well, I don't think it would be a good idea to meet in public, so why don't you just come by my house, OK? Around seven?"

I could tell Randy wasn't thrilled with the idea, but he agreed anyway. I made our little appointment at seven so that I'd have enough time to drive all the way into Louisville and back.

Nameless once again came through. He let me borrow all the surveillance stuff I needed, and before I knew it, I was on the road again. Hightailing it back home.

I got back to my place with plenty of time to spare. Which, of course, was a good thing. Since I had some preparations to make before Harned showed up. Carrying in the stuff Nameless had given me, I headed upstairs to my bedroom so that I could do what I had to do in front of a mirror. Rip, of course, followed right behind me, watching my every move. Sometimes I think that dog doesn't trust me out of his sight.

For the next few minutes, while Rip eyed me suspiciously, I busied myself setting up the surveillance equipment just the way I'd been shown. Just before I went downstairs, I checked myself a couple times in the mirror on the back of my bedroom door.

The wire I now had on was fastened to my chest

with adhesive tape. I turned this way and that, but you couldn't see it under my heavy flannel shirt. I swear you couldn't.

Naturally, Rip began carrying on something awful the second Randy's burgundy Jeep Cherokee came rumbling up my hill. I immediately turned on my front lights so that the driveway in front of my A-frame was lit up like a baseball stadium.

Rip was doing such a great Cujo routine up on my deck that Randy wouldn't even get out of his Jeep. "Tie that damn mutt up, or I'm leaving," he said.

I'd been expecting this little turn of events. In fact, I already had Rip's leash in my hand. Of course, I should also have been expecting one more thing. Rip's reaction once he noticed what I had in my hand. Have I mentioned how much Rip hates being tied up? If I hadn't known it before that particular moment, Rip's behavior would've most certainly convinced me. The moment Rip's startled brown eyes fell on the leash, he let out a yelp and then took off at a full gallop.

I immediately shouted down to Randy. "Just a sec." Then, of course, I also took off at a full gallop after Rip.

Rip's being afraid to go downstairs was a help, because there was only so many places he could run on top of my deck. What wasn't a help, however, was just how fast that damn dog could move. A couple of times I almost grabbed him, but he immediately did a little twist of his body and jumped away from me. After a while I was sure old Rip was enjoying the chase. He seemed to be grinning at me as he ran by.

It took me a while, but I did finally catch him. It was real embarrassing, though. In my opinion, it kind of spoils the mood if you're trying to come off as a ruthless blackmailer, when you spend the first few minutes of the initial meeting with your blackmail victim, running up and down your deck yelling, "Here, Rip, here, boy! *No,* Rip! *No, no!* Not there! *Here!* Here, boy!"

The whole time I was scrambling all over my deck, making wild grabs for Rip, Randy was sitting out in my driveway, watching me. It was pretty dark by then, so even with the lights on, I couldn't see him real clear. I don't think he was outright laughing, but he did appear to be downright cheerful, what times I had the chance to glance over at him. Having finally grabbed Rip as he tried to leap past me, I clipped the leash to his collar and the other end I fastened to the top rail of my deck.

Once I'd done all this, Rip did what he always does when I tie him up. He let out a loud, plaintive howl just to let me know that this whole leash thing was sheer torture. When Plan A—howling—didn't immediately get me to let him loose, Rip went straight to Plan B—choking and coughing. He always does this. He thinks I'll be convinced that the leash is making his collar too tight, and that since he's obviously near strangulation, I'll release him. When neither Plan A nor Plan B worked, Rip sat down heavily on the deck and eyed me accusingly. That little maneuver didn't work, either.

Ignoring Rip, I turned instead to Randy, who was now coming up the stairs. As usual, Randy was dressed all in black—a black leather jacket, black jeans, and black cowboy boots. I just looked at him. Who did he think he was? Zorro?

"Great dog you've got there. *Real* obedient," Randy said with a smirk.

I gave him a tight smile. First, he kisses my girlfriend. Then he insults my dog. If Randy was trying to get on my good side, this wasn't the way.

"I don't think you came all the way out here to talk about my dog, did you?"

Randy's smirk turned into an outright grin. "Nope, I guess I didn't. So what is it you seem to think you know?"

"I know everything," I said.

"Yeah?" he said. He ran his hand real casual-like through his shaggy blond hair. Let's face it. The man needed a haircut. "What specifically do you know?"

I looked him straight in the eye. "I know you killed Dwight Puckett. How about that for starters?"

Randy's grin didn't change in the least. "So what am I supposed to do now? Confess?"

I shook my head. "Nope, you're supposed to pay me ten thousand dollars to keep my mouth shut."

Randy just looked at me. "Now, Haskell, why on earth would I do that?" As he was saying this, he was moving closer to me.

I, of course, wasn't about to start backing up. Like maybe he was intimidating me or something.

I held my ground even when he said, "I'm not paying you a red cent." He punctuated what he said by tapping me on the chest.

Of course, now I realize he set up the whole scene on purpose. Just to give him an excuse to touch me. The second his hand touched my chest, he looked up at me and grinned even wider. "What's this, Haskell?" he said. "What the hell is this?" He reached out and laid his hand right against my chest. "You wouldn't be trying to record our conversation, would you?"

I just stared at him, my mouth suddenly going so

dry, I would've had trouble saying a word. Fortunately, there really wasn't anything for me to say. I shrugged. I unbuttoned my shirt. And, what else could I do, I pulled off the wire. Since Randy was staring at me, I tried not to wince when I ripped off the adhesive tape. I was going to drop it on the floor, but Randy held out his hand for the whole contraption.

"You're not dealing with some fool, Haskell."

I shrugged again and dropped it in his outstretched hand. At least, I thought I was dropping it in his hand. The second I dropped it, Harned jerked his hand away.

So that everything fell right on the floor.

Looking straight at me with a big grin on his face, Harned stomped the little mike gizmo with the heel of his boot.

Once again I tried not to wince. But to tell you the truth, I was thinking, *Lord, I'm going to be paying Nameless a good portion of the retainer Maedean had given me.*

After Harned had done his boot stomping, he looked back over at me and winked. "Hey, I'm not dumb like all those other folks you've caught. Did you really think I'd just sit down and have a little chat with you? All about how I killed Dwight?"

I shrugged. "OK," I said, "I admit it. You're pretty damn smart."

Randy gave a quick nod of his head, as if to say, *I know.*

"But," I went on, "you've already made a big mistake."

Randy's grin faltered for just a second. "What do you mean, a big mistake?"

"You made a mistake when you shot at Maedean.

233

Because now she's going to start putting it all together."

Randy gave me a look that was almost pitying. "Don't you get it? That right there is exactly why I shot at Maedean in the first place. Because she *was* getting suspicious."

I just looked at him. Not saying a word.

Randy apparently needed no further encouragement. "I shot at her so that Maedean would think that it had to be somebody else who'd killed Dwight. Somebody like that idiot Nolan, for instance."

I cocked my head to one side. "I don't understand."

Randy was actually looking a little impatient at how slow I was on the uptake. "Don't you see?" he said. "Maedean would never believe that I would try to kill *her*. She knows I wouldn't get anything unless she stays alive."

Well, what do you know. The man really was damn clever.

Randy was shrugging now. "Besides, I wasn't really trying to kill Maedean. I was trying to kill that damn dog of hers. In fact, I hadn't meant to hit Maedean at all." He took a deep breath. "It was her fault, you know. If she hadn't moved at the last minute, I'd have gotten that damn Poopsie with a clean shot."

I could understand his disappointment.

Randy grinned at me again. "My intentions where Maedean is concerned are strictly honorable, Haskell. I plan on marrying her as soon as we can. After an appropriate time of mourning, of course." He leaned toward me and said, "How else will I get all that land of hers?"

"You did all this for the land?"

Randy was looking at me as if I were a moron again.

"No, I did it for all the money I'm going to get when I sell the land to a real estate developer."

"Oh," I said.

"I hate to admit it, but money's getting kind of tight for me lately. Ever since Crayton County has been getting city water, my water delivery business has been going downhill." He smiled and shook his shaggy head, the expression on his face rueful. "I should've known when that guy was so anxious to sell the damn water company that he knew something I didn't know."

Rip now moved so that his head was right under my hand. He does this a lot. It's his way of letting me know that I'm missing out on a petting opportunity.

I scratched Rip's head idly, staring at Randy. "Then, you planned everything right from the beginning?"

Randy actually looked proud. "I sure did," he said. "It was even my idea to have you follow Maedean."

This one was a surprise. It was all I could do to keep my mouth from dropping open.

I must've looked shocked anyway because Randy looked positively delighted. "Yep," he said, "I told Maedean she ought to have you follow her so Dwight wouldn't be suspicious when she started divorce proceedings against him. That way things wouldn't get messy in court." Randy slapped his knee. "Can you believe she actually bought it?"

In all honesty, I could.

Randy hurried on. "Of course, what I really intended to do all along was get rid of Dwight. I wanted Maedean followed so that when I left her handkerchief at the scene, there'd be no way she'd get charged in the crime." Randy was grinning again. It was real annoying. "Pretty smart, huh?"

I had to agree. "Pretty smart," I said.

Randy actually laughed out loud. "I left Maedean's handkerchief there to confuse things, you know. So that the one person incriminated would be the one person who could not have done it!" Randy's eyes were sparkling, and he was waving his arms around. He was obviously enjoying himself. He could've been recalling some harmless practical joke he'd played. Only it had not been harmless.

"And, of course," Randy went on, "I left the handkerchief so Maedean wouldn't think it was me who'd done her husband. See? Maedean would never, ever believe I'd try to incriminate *her*. For one thing, if she were convicted of murdering her husband, she couldn't inherit the land." Randy paused here, and then added, "And, oh yeah, she thinks I'm crazy about her." His tone now was mocking.

I just looked at him. This guy was a real prince.

Randy winked at me again. "But then again, your girlfriend thinks I'm crazy about her, too."

I could feel the anger building. It was all I could do to just keep standing there, scratching old Rip's head.

"I knew," Randy went on, "that the only guy in town who has a reputation for solving murder mysteries was one Haskell Blevins. Right? So I figured out a way to discredit anything you might have to say against me. Smart again, huh?"

I was breathing hard, but I nodded again. "Smart again," I said through my teeth.

Randy shrugged. "Of course, I told Maedean I was just romancing this other woman to provide a cover for us until she got her divorce."

I took a deep breath. "You know, Randy," I said,

"aren't you afraid I'm going to tell it all over town exactly what you've just told me?"

Randy's grin got the widest yet. "If you do, I'll deny it. And what proof do you have? Nothing but your word. And everybody in town knows I've been romancing your girlfriend. They'll think just what I planned for them to think. That you're just making things up, trying to get your rival in trouble."

Randy actually reached over and tapped me on the shoulder. "You know, the worst thing about committing the perfect murder is that nobody ever knows that you did it."

I just looked at him. *Bummer,* I thought.

"So—I appreciate your listening, Haskell," Randy said as he stepped off my deck and headed toward his truck. "Really."

What could I say? *Glad to help out?*

I stood there, motionless, watching Randy's truck disappear down my driveway. I'd never felt so bone-tired.

CHAPTER 15

As soon as Randy was out of sight, I reached over to grab ahold of Rip's collar. Rip, of course, immediately started doing his choking act, coughing and trying to pull away. I ignored him, and reached underneath his collar to pull out what I knew was hidden there.

I reckon even Rip must've known that what I was doing was kind of important, because he calmed down pretty quick, sat down on his haunches, and solemnly watched as I pulled out the second wire I'd hidden in his collar.

I, on the other hand, was anything but solemn. In fact, the grin on my face felt like it could possibly wrap around my entire head a couple times. "Good boy," I told Rip. "Good boy."

I went inside to check the recorder Nameless had loaned me just to make sure that everything had worked just like it was supposed to. It had. Every single thing that Randy had said had been recorded real clear. Ain't technology grand?

Vergil, I must say, was real impressed with it. He was also real impressed with everything I had to tell him about Randy. Once Vergil heard all this, what do you know, he wasted no time in putting old Randy behind bars.

I, on the other hand, wasted no time in giving Imogene a phone call. I started the conversation with something I knew she and I would immediately agree on. "Imogene," I said, "I am an asshole."

This must have been the sort of person that Imogene preferred to hang out with, because in no time at all, she was accepting my invitation to dinner.

We met at Frank's Bar and Grill the very next night. Of course, by that time the Pigeon Fork grapevine had been pretty much buzzing with the news of what had happened to Randy and all. I knew the second I saw Imogene's face that she'd heard the whole story.

She didn't say anything right away, though. In fact, it wasn't until they brought our order—fried chicken, served family style—that she leaned toward me and said, "You know, Haskell, I never was swayed a bit by Randy's attention."

At first I thought she was just telling me that, but then she hurried on. "I thought he was a nuisance. I mean, every time I turned around, there he was." She leaned even closer to me, and her cheeks grew real pink. "You know, once he just out and out grabbed me. Right in front of your brother's drugstore."

I just looked at her. "No kidding," I said.

Imogene gave me one of her soft smiles. "No kidding," she said. "I think I knew all along he was just a—a wolf!"

I couldn't help smiling at her. Imogene was probably one of the last women in America who still used that term. Coming from her, it sounded real cute.

"I wasn't the least bit surprised to find out that he's just one of those men who are always on the make."

I nodded, listening. I had no intention of ever telling her Randy's real motive behind his sudden attention.

"Why," Imogene went on, "I think he just went after every woman he saw."

"I think he mainly concentrated on the real attractive ones," I said.

I was rewarded with another one of Imogene's smiles.

We ate in a companionable silence, and then a little later, Imogene leaned across the table again to whisper, "To tell you the truth, the only thing I enjoyed about having Randy hitting on me all the time was seeing how jealous it made you."

I immediately started to protest. To lie, in fact, and say that I hadn't been jealous a minute, but I thought better of it. "I was real jealous," I whispered back.

Imogene rested her hand briefly on mine. "I know," she said.

We both ate in silence some more, and then Imogene said something that really surprised me. She said, "You know, Haskell, I feel so sorry for Maedean."

I just looked at her. "Maedean?" I said. I didn't add it, but I thought, *The woman who ran around on poor Dwight and got him killed?*

"Why do you feel sorry for her?"

Imogene shrugged, and speared a green bean with her fork. "Because she fell in love with Randy—I mean, she really did—and he never really cared two cents about her."

Two cents, I thought. Now that was an apt phrase if I'd ever heard one.

"Randy was just interested in poor Maedean for her money," Imogene said. "That was all." Imogene shrugged again. "How on earth," she added, "can anybody be that shallow?"

All the time Imogene had been talking, I'd been chewing a mouthful of green beans, but after she said this last part, I had some difficulty swallowing. I realized, sitting there across from Imogene, that I myself had actually thought that *Imogene* might leave me because I wasn't making enough money.

I felt suddenly so guilty, that for a moment I couldn't meet her eyes. Lord. How insulting it had been for me to even think such a thing about her. I swallowed my mouthful, and looking away, I took a long, long drink of my Coke.

When I could look at Imogene again, I said, "You know, if you wanted to pay for this here dinner, it would be OK with me."

Imogene's dark head went up at that. For a second she just looked at me, and then, like sunshine breaking through clouds, she gave me a real big grin.

What could I do? I grinned right back at her.

While Imogene and I just sat there, grinning at each other like two fools, I couldn't help remembering the last time I'd seen a woman look that happy to spend money. It had been, of course, when I'd been married to Claudzilla.

Back then, the money in question had been mine.

You know, things could definitely be looking up.

241

ABOUT THE AUTHOR

An identical twin, Taylor McCafferty decided she was going to be a writer in the third grade, and it took her a mere thirty-three years to achieve that dream. During those years, she graduated magna cum laude with a degree in fine art from the University of Louisville, and worked as an art director/advertising copywriter for a Louisville ad agency. She now lives in the small town of Lebanon Junction, Kentucky. *Hanky Panky* is Taylor's fifth Haskell Blevins mystery novel.